NEED ME

Also by Shelli Stevens

TAKE ME

NEED ME

SHELLI STEVENS

APHRODISIA

KENSINGTON PUBLISHING CORP.
http://www.kensingtonbooks.com

APHRODISIA BOOKS are published by

Kensington Publishing Corp.
119 West 40th Street
New York, NY 10018

All Kensington Titles, Imprints, and Distributed Lines are available at special quantity discounts for bulk purchases for sales promotions, premiums, fund-raising, and educational or institutional use.

Special book excerpts or customized printings can also be created to fit specific needs. For details, write or phone the office of the Kensington special sales manager: Kensington Publishing Corp., 119 West 40th Street, New York, NY 10018, attn: Special Sales Department, Phone: 1-800-221-2647.

Aphrodisia and the A logo Reg. U.S. Pat & TM Off.

ISBN-13: 978-0-7582-3529-9
ISBN-10: 0-7582-3529-1

First Kensington Trade Paperback Printing: July 2010

10 9 8 7 6 5 4 3 2 1

Printed in the United States of America

Acknowledgments

I'd like to thank my editor, Peter Senftleben, for his work and advice on this story! Brainstorming with you, Peter, was a blast! And I'd like to thank my agent, Laura Bradford, for her continued support. To Lauren Dane for her wonderful quote. To Nic, Emma, Jackie, and Lacy for our write offs, and NaNo for upping my speed on the completion of this book! Thanks to my friends Jess Granger, Joan Goodman, Danielle Redmond for your thoughts and advice on this book. To my girls at Naughty and Spice: Karen, Lilli, and Amie. To the Romance Divas, to GSRWA and the GSRWA 2009 board, my family and friends, and of course all my readers! I wouldn't be here without you! And thanks to anyone else I may have forgotten to thank (because of course I'll forget someone!).

Acknowledgments

1

"Take me. Now, Lieutenant!"

Brendon slammed his hand against the palm recognition box while deftly undoing the fastenings on the front of his commanding officer's uniform.

The door to the storage unit slid open and he pushed her inside, pulling her breasts free from the uniform just before the door shut behind them.

"Gods," she breathed, reaching down to free him from his trousers. "I've wanted this all day."

He gave a soft laugh and thumbed her nipple, smiling when she cried out. "I'll bet you have, you saucy bitch."

She pumped his cock with her hand. "I could have your ass for talking to me like that, Lieutenant."

Brendon turned her around, slamming her against the shelf as he jerked her pants down to her ankles.

"Actually, ma'am, I do believe I'm going to have *your* ass." He slapped one round cheek. "And you'll like it."

She groaned, pressing back hard against him. "Please, make me come."

He gave a soft laugh and plunged two fingers inside her. Her body clenched around him and she screamed.

"You like that, ma'am? Who's in control now? Who's giving the orders?"

"You are." She groaned. "You are!" Her body clenched around him as she climaxed suddenly.

Brendon spun her around and pushed her to her knees.

The woman's mouth found him, moving hungrily over his cock. He closed his eyes, sliding his fingers through her short hair.

He looked down, watched her in the semidarkness lift her mouth from his cock and the trail of saliva she left.

"Take me, Lieutenant." She stood up and turned around, lifting her bottom toward him. "Hurry, before someone realizes we are gone."

He fingered her again, gathering her cream to smear over her asshole.

When he entered her a second later she didn't even make a faint noise of pain. This woman was obviously used to being fucked in the ass. She gripped the shelf, smashing her body back to meet each of his hard thrusts.

"Yes. Yes!" She screamed, rubbing her own pussy as she brought herself to another climax.

Brendon felt his balls tighten, gripped her shoulder and then let loose. He came hard and fast, emptying himself inside her.

He was still catching his breath when a series of beeps signaled someone had just put their hand against the palm recognition box to open the door.

"Oh gods." He pulled out of her, fumbling to put his cock away.

The door slid open and light blinded them both. His commanding officer spun around, making a pathetic attempt to cover herself with her hands.

Brendon blinked, before his eyes grew accustomed to the light and the two men standing outside.

His stomach dropped and his balls shriveled.

Well, shit.

The five-star general stared at them both and gave a weary sigh. "Lieutenant Marshall. Why am I not surprised? And Colonel Rodgers, I wish I could say the same. I'll need to see you both in my office. Immediately." He cleared his throat. "Or, er, after you have once again attired yourselves."

Brendon tipped back the last of his aliaberry wine and sighed, thrusting a hand through the spiky strands of his short brown hair. "Fucking demoted. I still can't quite believe it."

Ryder, a fellow soldier and friend, glanced over at him and raised an eyebrow.

"Is that so? Might I remind you that you were caught with your pants down, having just screwed your commanding officer in a closet while on duty?"

"No, thank you, my friend. I actually do *not* need reminding." Brendon stood up and walked to the window of the sky lounge they resided in.

Pods whizzed by in the air, while down below the streets bustled with activity. And to think just over two years ago, the future of this planet had been threatened.

He'd fought that day during the surprise assault from the seemingly allied planet Zortou and had lost more than one friend during the bloody battle. Fortunately, Belton had been victorious and the well-being of the planet prevailed.

He turned from the window to look back at Ryder, another soldier who'd fought in the battle. They'd both survived that day, coming out as stronger soldiers because of it. Going in, they'd already been the best of the best.

Which was why it was a real bitch that he'd been demoted over a simple moment of friskiness.

Brendon returned to his chair and sat down, his mouth curled down in a sulk. "The worst part is that it was a rather *bad* fuck."

Ryder let out a muffled laugh, choking on his wine. "Gods help you if Colonel Rodgers heard you say that."

Brendon winced. "Not that she could. She's been reassigned to another unit. Demoted as well."

"Pity."

"Perhaps." He scowled and turned around to face Ryder. "But how undignified is my fate? Who on this planet would want the position of guarding semen? Semen!"

"Actually, 'specimen samples' is the correct term, my friend."

"Call it what you will, it's still the spunk from some soldier's prick."

"What did I miss?"

Brendon kept scowling and watched as Emmett, another of their friends, sat down at the table and poured himself a glass of wine from the pitcher.

"You started without me?" Emmett asked and drank a hefty sip. "Any particular reason?"

Ryder stood and set coins down on the table. "Brendon is a bit upset after being caught screwing his commanding officer and has since been demoted to guarding semen."

"*Specimen samples!*" Brendon corrected and pounded his fist on the table.

"My." Emmett blinked and shook his head. "Apparently I missed a lot today."

"Indeed." Ryder's lips twitched, his expression softening. "I should not stay any longer. My lovely wife is at home in her fifth month of pregnancy and I'm an ass for having neglected her this long."

"Hmm. She encourages you to get out more. But you do

dote on her." Brendon took another sip of wine. "Say hello to the lovely Talia for us."

"Of course." Ryder gave them a casual salute and disappeared from the lounge.

Brendon watched his friend leave with a pang of jealousy. Not that he'd ever acknowledge the emotion. To be jealous of a man who'd resigned his life to be spent with one woman? The very idea nearly made him break out in a rash. Still, there was no denying that Ryder was more content now than anyone could remember him being.

"You know," Emmett began, "perhaps if you tamed your wicked ways, you would not keep finding yourself in trouble."

Brendon turned back to his friend and arched a brow. "Wicked ways?"

"Must I spell it out for you?" Emmett leaned forward and guffawed. "Your weakness for pussy."

Instead of being affronted, Brendon's mouth curved into a slight smile and he shrugged. "I will hardly deny that I have a fondness for the fairer sex, my friend. Nor that they seem to have an equal affection for me."

"Yes. Perhaps it's because you're so damn tall and likely hung like a beast."

Brendon laughed, but didn't rebuke the suggestion.

"Though I am surprised," Emmett continued, his expression bemused, "that your commanding officer would risk everything for a quick tumble."

"Yes, well. I'm not quite sure about her reasoning. Though I was hardly about to protest her advances. The woman has a mouth that could—"

"Please." Emmett raised a hand and winced. "I have no need for the particulars."

"Hmm." Brendon refilled his glass of wine and gave his friend a considering look. "Tell me, have you found yourself a nice little woman to warm your bed?"

"I have not, nor do I need one. My focus is on the advancement of my career."

Brendon chuckled and resisted the urge to call his friend's bluff. Not that he doubted Emmett wanted to rise among the ranks, but the fact that his friend denied needing a woman was complete crap. Every man needed a woman, if even for a few minutes.

He could not resist murmuring, "Of course. Give your right hand my apologies."

Emmett about spit out his wine as he lifted his amused glance to meet Brendon's. "You are trouble, my friend."

"Yes. So I've been told many times." Brendon sighed and shook his head.

And, unfortunately, it had caught up with him. He took another sip of wine and scowled.

Guarding a damn semen lab.

Nika's foot slammed into the collapsible mannequin and it crumpled under the contact. Her heart fluttered against her chest and she spun, ready to take out her next target.

"You are ready."

Nika stilled, the blood pounding through her veins no longer just the result of adrenaline.

She rose from the crouched position she'd fallen into. Turning, she used the back of her hand to wipe the sheen of sweat from her brow.

"Truly?" she asked, hating herself for the tremor in her voice.

The instructor nodded, her gaze unreadable as it swept over Nika from head to toe.

"Rachel will be pleased." The instructor folded her arms across her small chest and nodded. "I have informed her that you will be on your way shortly to meet with her. After you have showered, of course."

Excitement bubbled through her, but Nika gave a slight nod to not let her true reaction show. "Of course."

"I doubt we will meet again, Donika." The instructor dropped her arms and strode past her, lifting one eyebrow. "You've done well. You're perhaps one of my best students. Goddess be with you, for you will need her guidance in your upcoming mission."

The door to the gym slid closed on a hiss, and once again Nika found herself alone. The only break in the silence was her labored breathing from her workout.

I am ready.

The realization swelled her chest with pride as she walked toward the bathing chamber. For two years, she had trained for this position. Had fought to prove herself on a planet of women who doubted her.

Standing in front of the mirror in the bathing chamber, she pulled the loose top from her body and pushed down the pants.

Wincing, she began to unbind her chest. Her breasts tingled as blood rushed through them. The nipples hardened in the cool, climate-controlled room.

Lifting her hands, she cupped herself, massaging her breasts and squeezing feeling back into the soft mounds.

Her breasts were part of the reason they had doubted her for this mission. Her chest was too large and would be hard to disguise during her assignment. All previous envoys had been tall and lean, with little curve in their hips and breasts so small they needed no binding.

Though Nika was tall and lean, her hips and breasts posed a problem. One she had insisted she could overcome by binding her breasts so tightly that she could pass for a man. And by wearing clothes that would almost disguise her hips.

As always, she was the outsider that everyone was skeptical

of. The strange woman who'd arrived on this planet seeking refuge.

Nika sighed and pinched the darkened nipples to the point where it almost hurt, watching the pink flush deepen in the tips. Her lips twisted with disdain even as pleasure shot straight to her pussy.

And here was just another way she would be considered an outsider. The hint of pain could bring her pleasure. Though, fortunately, the women of the planet knew nothing about her sexual enjoyments since she had never taken a lover here.

Releasing her breasts, Nika pulled her hair down from the severe topknot and shook the blond waves around her shoulders.

She'd never actually taken a lover willingly in her entire life. Her only sexual experience lay in her erotic servitude as a Rosabelle back on Zortou.

Her stomach clenched and for a moment the memory of those awful years threatened to send her into an emotional tailspin.

Being forced to serve the two brothers day after day, to clean their living quarters and service them in the bedroom. Or out of it. She'd simply had to service them any time they got a whim to take her.

In the mirror she watched her blue-green eyes cloud with revulsion.

In reality she'd been the same as any droid moving about: robotic in her actions and completely emotionless.

She'd been quick to learn that feeling anything could be nothing but detrimental if she meant to survive. But then there were days she'd questioned whether surviving was even worth it.

Drawing in a slow breath, she closed her eyes. *You are not in that life anymore. You are no longer that woman.* She repeated the mantra until her pulse slowed again.

Opening her eyes she met her gaze in the mirror and saw a confident woman completely in control of her emotions.

She turned and went to turn on the showering unit, preparing to meet with her sponsor.

Nika walked into her sponsor's chambers, pushing aside the familiar burst of nerves. This was nothing new: each time she entered Rachel's office she grew edgy. There was something about the woman that made her uncomfortable. Today was no different.

The doors hissed shut behind her as she entered the room. She lifted her head and strode in with a self-assurance she'd once feigned but now commanded.

Her steps faltered as she spotted her sponsor reclining naked on the couch, one of her many lovers lying between her thighs.

Rachel ran a hand through the younger woman's platinum hair, lifting her hips as the woman's mouth moved over her pussy.

"I apologize," Nika began, thankful her voice was neutral since inside she felt all too uneasy. "I thought you were to be informed of my arrival."

"I was, darling." Rachel gave a lazy smile and lowered her heated gaze to the woman who licked her pussy. "I simply saw no reason not to mix business with pleasure."

Heat spread to Nika's cheeks, but she murmured a calm, "Of course."

Rachel lifted a brow. "Unless you'd like to join us?"

The younger woman lifted her head from between Rachel's legs and licked her lips, looking Nika over with interest.

"Thank you, but no."

The woman laughed softly and, still holding Nika's gaze, lowered her head to flick her tongue over Rachel's clit.

This dance was not unfamiliar to Nika. Rachel had always left the door open into her sensual world and invited Nika to partake in the pleasures that could be explored on the all-female planet.

Nika wasn't the least bit tempted, although the fact often made her feel a bit guilty for residing on Tresden. But the lack of men on the planet was also the very thing that kept her here. It offered her a sense of safety. Of peace.

"Vivecca called me with the news," Rachel murmured. "Congratulations."

Nika drew in a deep breath, and her discomfort eased a bit as satisfaction moved through her. "Thank you, ma'am."

"You're welcome. I must say that I'm pleased. Though I agreed to sponsor you, at times I feared you might not be suitable for this mission." Rachel's gaze moved to Nika's breasts. "But it appears your instructor finds you able."

"Indeed." Nika crossed the room and sat down on a nearby chair, crossing one leg over another. "When will I be sent to Belton?"

Rachel gave a soft laugh and started to answer, then lifted her hand in a gesture to wait for a moment. Her gaze drifted down to the woman between her thighs and her mouth tightened with displeasure.

"Lick me faster, Fiona," she commanded quietly. "If you want to become one of my favorites, you must listen to my instructions."

"Yes, ma'am." The woman resumed her task, her nimble tongue flicking faster over the older woman's clit.

"Now. Where were we?" Rachel paused. "Right. Your mission to Belton. You will want to arrive with enough time to learn the area. Gain the trust of those who know and guard the lab."

"Of course. And I have already been given the necessary material to don my space tourist alias."

"It seems you are well prepared." Rachel's eyes fluttered shut. "One moment . . ."

She gripped the younger woman's hair tighter, rocking her sex against Fiona's mouth. Rachel let out a long groan and her heels dug into the couch.

A moment later her body went slack, and her eyes opened again. She licked her lips and smiled.

"Very well done, Fiona. Please. Come sit beside me now."

Nika averted her gaze as the woman moved up on the couch and settled next to Rachel. She was never comfortable watching Rachel and her women. In a sense, it reminded her of the life she used to live.

Only this time she had a choice, and she had no desire to sexually entertain another person. Be it a woman or man.

Any needs she had she took into her own hands. Literally. Which was actually quite liberating as she'd been denied the right to pleasure herself as a Rosabelle on Zortou.

"Donika?"

Nika pulled her gaze back to Rachel. The older woman watched her with amusement as she cuddled with her newest lover, one hand idly toying with the woman's breast.

"Yes, ma'am."

"You are free to go and pack your things. I have arranged for you to be on the next pod destined to leave the planet by nightfall." Rachel smiled gently. "Though by no means do I expect you to succeed in your mission right away, I will expect you to check in with me."

"Of course."

Nika's heart pounded with excitement, and she swiped her tongue over lips. Finally she had a purpose and a mission. A way to prove that she was so much more than a woman groomed to give pleasure.

And Rachel had believed in her. Had picked her for this mission. Though the older woman had always made it clear she desired Nika in her bed, she'd never forced the issue. She had always left the choice up to her as Nika had trained for her mission.

Nika's voice trembled as she murmured, "Thank you, ma'am."

"You're quite welcome, Donika." Rachel's smile faltered. "You will be missed."

Nika frowned, concerned by the heavy finality in Rachel's last words. "I will return."

"Yes. Of course you shall."

Nika stared at her a moment, her heart thudding. She wasn't sure Rachel believed the words she'd just uttered. Did she truly fear Nika would never return? Not succeed in this mission?

"Be well, Donika," was the way Rachel dismissed her, already turning her attention to the younger woman's body that she now played with.

"Thank you, ma'am."

Still puzzled by Rachel's response, but seeing no point in dwelling upon what it could mean, Nika gave a curt nod and turned, striding out of the room and toward her future.

2

Nika stepped outside the Planetary Customs building and sighed. What a relief it was to have her paperwork approved and to be done with the mandatory detox chamber.

She stretched her legs, her gaze sweeping over the foreign planet she now stood upon.

The area outside the landing zone bustled with people. Men and women strode around what looked to be the market during midday.

What caught her attention the most were the men. There were so many of them.

Wariness slid through her, and ice seemed to seep into her veins. She tried to ignore the unease, which was easier said than done since it had been over two years since she'd last seen a man.

"Welcome to the planet Belton, ma'am. May I take your bags for you?"

She stiffened, turning to face the deep voice that had come from behind her.

A man, almost a boy really, grinned at her as he reached for her luggage. Obviously he was an attendant of some sort.

"Could I summon you a sky taxi? What is your destination?"

If she was to fit in on this planet, then she'd very well better learn to feign at least indifference to the opposite sex.

Forcing a brief smile, she nodded. "Thank you, that would be lovely. I'm seeking accommodations in a local lodge." She paused. "Someplace near the Broughlin military complex as I'm visiting a cousin stationed there."

"Easy enough." He grinned, showing two oversized front teeth and waved down an approaching sky taxi. "I know of a great place over on Union Boulevard."

Some of the tension left her body. It was hard to feel afraid of a male when he seemed so . . . endearing. He certainly was not a threat or violent like most of the men had been on Zortou.

She closed that emotional door before it could fully open again.

"Here you are, ma'am."

She watched as the sky taxi came to a halt next to the platform, hovering in the air. The door to the pod slid open and the young man leaned in and gave instructions to the computer.

He pulled back out and nodded. "There, all set. The pod will take you directly to the lodge. Enjoy your stay on Belton."

"Thank you." She pressed a coin into his hand and gave him a brief smile before climbing into the taxi.

The door slid shut, and the pod lifted into the air, zipping forward and away from the platform.

Her stomach fluttered with a sudden burst of nerves. She was here on Belton. After several hours of intergalactic travel, the length of the day had caught up with her. Her eyes fluttered closed, the thought of a warm bed making her muscles grow lax.

She didn't realize she'd fallen asleep until the taxi came to an abrupt stop and announced their location. Blinking her eyes open, she grabbed her bags and climbed from the pod.

The building in front of her seemed decent enough. It was a couple of stories high and built of steel and wood. There were few businesses around the structure, and it appeared to linger on the edge of a forest. And if her memory served her correctly, the military complex would be not far around the perimeter of the woods.

Adjusting her grip on the bags, she strode into the lodge to see about getting a room.

The woman behind the desk glanced up and smiled. She tossed her blond hair over her shoulder while her blue eyes lit up with curiosity. "Hello. Do you seek a room?"

"I do. Thank you." Nika set her bag down. "I plan to stay for a while, seeing as I am visiting a cousin stationed at Broughlin."

The woman's smile widened. "Well, we can certainly accommodate you. Being winter, we're in the off-season and have plenty of rooms to rent. I'm Molly, the owner of The Crow's Nest."

Owner? Nika managed to hide her surprise that a woman close to the same age as herself owned such a business on a planet full of men.

"Lovely to meet you. I'm Rebecca." The lie about her name came all too easily. And the ID she gave when filling out the paperwork backed up her alias.

"Well, I'm glad to have you here, Rebecca." Molly handed her back the ID and sighed. "It can be quiet this time of year in the lodging department. The restaurant, however, is a different story." She shook her head and rolled her eyes. "Being so close to the compound, we bring in quite a bit of business. Our food is wonderful, and the wine is top class."

"I'll be sure to try it out."

"And please, do not hesitate to come say hello or seek me

out if you need anything." Molly shrugged and gave a light laugh. "Truly, it would give me something to do."

Nika nodded. "Thank you, Molly. I will definitely do so."

As she headed to her room, she vowed the opposite. Though the owner of the lodge seemed quite nice, establishing a friendship would not be wise. The fewer impressions she left of herself on this planet the better.

Two hours later she'd napped and then bathed, removing the travel grime.

Nika stretched before sitting back down on the bed. Her luggage was now unpacked. Well, most of it. The bag that contained anything pertaining to her mission had been stored beneath the bed, locked tight with the keycode.

For a moment she allowed herself to dwell on the reason why she was here. Her mission. How important it was.

Every five years the planet of Tresden sent a "chosen one," a specially trained soldier, to infiltrate the highly guarded specimen lab on Belton.

A smile curved her lips and she fiddled with the edge of the comforter. Though many would find the mission almost a joke, all on her planet knew better. Yes, they were taking semen specimen samples, but they were no ordinary samples.

The samples were highly guarded and rightfully so. They were the specimens of the most powerful warriors on the planet of Belton. A world of genetic possibilities lay dormant in each specimen.

And her home planet had been making use of the taken samples after each mission. Returning home with the specimens, they would genetically manipulate the sperm and impregnate the women on Tresden, creating a race of powerful women to ensure their survival and to build the planet's military. All without the need to breed with men.

Looking around the modest room, she pressed a hand against her stomach just before it let out a soft growl. She needed food.

The lodge's restaurant was on the ground level. She'd passed by it after checking in. It had appeared crowded, filled with soldiers along with civilian guests.

The idea of eating among such a crowd—most seeming to be men—set her stomach rolling. But food was a necessity. And so was getting over her unease with the opposite sex.

Nika took a deep breath and checked her appearance in the mirror. How long had it been since she'd worn a dress? Hmmm. Since back on Zortou.

Pressing the fabric down her body, she straightened her shoulders and tried to reunite herself with the sensation of wearing a gown. Truth be told, it was almost a bit liberating compared to the trousers and top she'd been used to wearing.

Perhaps she should do something with her hair?

Go downstairs and dine. Stop stalling.

Grabbing her metallic clutch off the bed she headed out of her room and toward the restaurant.

"Feel free to head out, Lieutenant."

Brendon stumbled against the wall, blinking away the last of the drowsiness as he looked up from the door he guarded.

Gods, had he almost fallen asleep on duty?

Clearing his throat he nodded at the soldier who'd come to relieve him.

"Slow day?" The other soldier's mouth twitched as he lowered his weapon to lean against the wall.

"Is there ever a day where it's not?"

"Not since I've been here." The man hesitated. "Though they've been warning us things could change any day now."

Brendon bit back a snort and shouldered his weapon. The

most activity at the lab had been the scientists going in and out during their lunch break.

He gave a slight smile. "I guess we shall see. Have a good night."

Stepping outside the heavily secured lab, he found that nightfall was descending upon the city.

It was too early to return to his bedchamber. Perhaps Emmett would meet him for a drink or supper. Pulling out his communications mobile he dialed his friend's number.

A few minutes later he headed to the Crow's Nest, where Emmett and a few other soldiers were supping.

The doors to the hotel slid open on a hiss and he strode inside, winking at the woman behind the desk.

The pretty white-haired girl blushed and looked at him through her lashes, fidgeting with a pen she held in her hand.

Smile widening, Brendon increased his pace and turned toward the restaurant. The roar of voices guided him into the crowded room.

The place was packed with soldiers—men and women, though mostly men. The majority of women in the restaurant appeared to be civilians. But that wasn't such a surprise. The Crow's Nest was notorious for being the local hangout for soldiers, which in turn could really bring in the ladies who loved a man in uniform.

He caught sight of Emmett waving to him from a table by the window. Brendon gave a half wave back and took a step toward them.

"Brendon Marshall. You little devil!" A voice squealed at him from the right.

He turned just in time to catch the chesty redhead who hurled herself into his arms. Her lips smacked against his in a solid kiss, before she pulled back and smiled.

"It has been all too long since I've laid eyes on you, soldier," she said coyly. "I do believe the last time I, er, *saw* you was during that night we spent together after the Harvest Festival."

His lips curved into a smile as he tilted his head and gave her a teasing look. "Did we spend time together at the Harvest Festival?"

The woman—Wendy, was it? Wanda?—gave him a playful slap and giggled. "You know quite well we did." She leaned in close. "And I must admit I wouldn't mind *seeing* you again soon. Say, even later tonight?"

Hmm. The possibility of a quick tumble had merit. "I may be open to the idea. Do you still have my number, sweetheart?"

"On my express-dial." She winked and ran a hand down his chest, licking her lips. "I'll give you a call later."

"Looking forward to it." He flashed her a quick grin and turned away, resuming his course toward the table where Emmett sat.

A glimpse of blue from the corner of his eye made him pause. He turned his head slightly to investigate.

She watched him from the corner of the restaurant, eyes narrowed and an expression of irritation and disgust on her face.

Mmm. Who was this woman?

He slowed his steps, taking a moment to run his gaze over her. Pale blond hair shone soft in the light of the restaurant, falling around her oval face and past her shoulders. Her eye color was indistinguishable, for she sat in shadow.

The blue dress she wore seemed fairly conservative, covering more skin than it showed. But still, it could not hide the soft swell of her breasts. He lowered his gaze farther, but the rest of her body was hidden beneath the table, to his disappointment.

She must have noticed his attention, for her cheeks suddenly grew pink, and her attention shifted back to the plate of food in front of her.

With a soft laugh of genuine amusement, he pulled his gaze

from her reluctantly and continued his course to the table where his friends sat.

"You never cease to amaze me," Emmett quipped the moment he sat down. "Within seconds of walking in that door, you had women practically mauling each other to get to you."

"You jest." Brendon signaled a waiter for a glass of wine. "I had but one woman maul me."

"Yes, the rest backed off once Wanda staked her claim."

Wanda! Ah, he'd have to remember that for later.

Though, when his gaze lifted, it wasn't to seek out Wanda, but the intriguing blonde in the corner. Pleasure slipped through him when he again caught her watching him.

Once more, she jerked her head down and this time he watched her lips move in what was likely a quiet curse.

"So, Marshall. It *semens* to me that you're enjoying your new job?"

The table erupted in loud bursts of laughter.

Brendon turned back to his friends and scowled, accepting the wine the waiter had brought him.

"Yes, laugh all you'd like." He took a sip and shook his head, trying to keep a straight face. "It is by far the noblest of duties, and I imagine you're all quite jealous."

The men laughed harder and Emmett slapped Brendon on the back. "Quite noble, my friend."

"All right, enough." Brendon joined their laughter. "Have you eaten? I'm quite hungry. I worked up a massive appetite guarding the fruit of your loins."

"Well, at least you are in good spirits about it," another man called out and lifted his wine in toast. "And a demotion over the repute of being a ladies' man is hardly something worth sulking over."

Brendon's smile widened. "I'll drink to that."

* * *

The spiced meat that had tasted so amazing, so succulent upon her tongue a moment ago now tasted like dirt.

Nika forced herself to chew the bite of meat in her mouth. She finally swallowed, reaching with unsteady hands to sip her water.

He still watched her. She could feel his eyes on her even now. The man across the room. Tension coiled through her body with awareness. Even without looking up his features were engraved in her mind.

Tall. Quite tall, actually. Lean and muscled. His short—almost shaved—brown hair made her think he must be military, though he wore no uniform.

And his eyes. Such a dark penetrating brown. Though they'd only turned on her for a moment, she'd felt trapped, unable to look away. Time had stopped, and the noise around them had diminished until she heard only the rush of blood through her veins.

And then she'd forced herself to look away, turning her attention back to her supper as her face had heated with embarrassment.

She'd known it had been a bad idea to come down and eat alone. Yet what other choice did she have? Possibly she could have convinced the lodge to send food up to her room, though it was not standard.

And truthfully, she'd been fine until he had come into the restaurant. There was something about him. Something so blatantly sexual, primal and dominating. And she would have noticed it even if women had not been melting at his feet like they were ice on a summer's day.

A high-pitched laugh had her head jerking up again, and her attention was once more drawn to the man's table.

Yet *another* woman had appeared to flirt with him. What a complete scoundrel.

Grinding her teeth together, having had her fill of more than just food, Nika pushed back her chair and stood.

She set coins upon the table and proceeded from the restaurant. Pausing by the stairs, she hesitated. The idea of returning to her room seemed somewhat stifling.

Her gaze darted to the door and the grounds outside. She had not yet explored beyond the lodge. Though it had grown dark, perhaps the nightfall would provide a good cover for her to learn more about the area.

Without further hesitation, she headed out the door. The brisk air stroked her body, and she shivered. Perhaps she ought to go back inside and grab a jacket?

Looking over her shoulder, she thought she saw the man from the restaurant walk past the reception desk.

With a groan, she ducked farther away from the building. Fortunately, he likely wouldn't have seen her in the dark. But surely he hadn't been seeking her out?

Spinning away, Nika set out at a brisk stride. Though the air was cold, it was also refreshing. After having spent most her life forced to remain indoors on Zortou, she would never tire of the liberty of being allowed outside.

She moved along the path that followed the perimeter of the lodge. When the path split and one direction led to the bright lights of the military compound, she made a quick decision to take it.

The wind lifted her hair, sending strands across her face and into her eyes. She thrust them aside and increased her pace. Her flesh broke out in goose bumps, and her teeth began to chatter.

Gods, she was a fool for not grabbing that jacket. Maybe she *was* unfamiliar with this planet, but winter was upon them and she should've known better.

The trail grew darker the farther away she went from the lodge, but the lights of the compound continued to guide her.

Nika looked around the trail at the trees that surrounded her, listening to the sounds of the animals that lingered in the night. What sort of animals roamed this planet?

Unease slid down her spine as something rattled a nearby branch.

It's nothing, Nika. Likely some little animal seeking food. Harmless and—

"You know, it's cold out here."

Nika gasped, raising her fist instinctively to deliver a blow. She caught herself as she recognized the scoundrel from the restaurant. Drawing in a breath, she tried to calm herself.

It certainly wouldn't be good for her cover if she were discovered assaulting a local soldier.

"What are you doing out here?" she asked tersely.

"I could ask you the same thing, ma'am." His voice was deep and smooth, tinged with amusement. "You do realize you're approaching a restricted military compound."

"No, I did not realize, sir," she lied. "I was simply out walking."

"Call me Brendon." He stepped closer and his gaze slid over her, lingering on her nipples that had tightened from the chill. "Can I offer you my coat?"

"Thank you. But, no. I'm not cold."

White teeth flashed in the moons' light as he gave a soft laugh. "Of course you're not. Then might I escort you back to the lodge?"

Really, there was no hope for exploring the compound. Not with him determined to remain with her. Pushing aside her annoyance, she gave a brief nod.

He took her arm and a shocking spark of pleasure slid through her blood. She inhaled sharply, her muscles tightening as she cast him a sidelong look.

What sort of magic did he possess, that the female population would swoon at his feet, and even just the smallest touch against *her* skin could spread tingles of energy?

"Your skin is chilled," he murmured, his fingers tracing circles against her bare elbow. "Are you certain you're not cold?"

A shiver ran through her, but it was not from the cold this time.

"Perhaps you're simply overheated from all the women throwing themselves at you," she taunted lightly, arching a brow.

He laughed again, a low husky sound that quickened her pulse and spread heat low in her belly.

Nika blinked furiously, trying to dispel whatever insanity was threatening. What was the matter with her? Where was the repulsion or anger toward this man? It was a feeling she'd come to experience when a male grew too close.

"You have yet to tell me your name, ma'am."

"Nika." Her eyes widened and she snapped her teeth together.

Now why in the world had she just given him her true name? *Stupid! So stupid, Nika!*

He laughed softly and alarmed her further by lifting her wrist and pressing a soft kiss to the inside. Her steps faltered as her knees weakened.

Though her breath caught, she forced herself to show no outward reaction.

"You intrigue me, Nika. I have been watching you."

"Yes, you have."

He tilted his head back and laughed louder, exposing the solid column of his neck. Her gaze followed the length of it down to his chest covered beneath his shirt. So hard and wide. Very much male, but not at all unappealing.

Her heart tripped. This was madness. Truly it had to be. How was it possible she was attracted to a man? And why *now*, while on her first mission?

Her gaze moved to his lips. So perfectly formed and sensual. And though she'd never craved the touch or caress of another being, she couldn't help but wonder . . . what his mouth would feel like upon hers?

His laughter faded and the thick silence made her jerk her gaze away from his mouth.

She found him watching her once more and she stilled, unable to look away from the intensity of his stare. Hunger flickered in his gaze and the air between them nearly crackled with something so hot and tempting.

"You still feel rather chilled, love," he said softly and reached up to touch her cheek. "Let me warm you. If not with my jacket, then in other ways."

His head descended, blocking out the moons' light. Before she could protest, his mouth covered hers.

She stiffened, waiting for the fear to sink in, for the flashbacks to the men who'd owned her back on Zortou.

It didn't come.

Instead, each soft brush of his mouth across hers sent bubbly heat throughout her body. *How amazing!*

Nika leaned into him, curling her fingers around his shoulders as a slow ache began between her legs.

Brendon slanted his mouth across hers and then his tongue probed the seam of her lips.

Only wanting to follow this thread of pleasure, she slid her arms around his neck and then parted her lips.

Brendon's tongue slid inside, immediately seeking hers to stroke and tease. Her mind spun, and each slick caress upped the fire in her blood.

His hand, which rested on her waist, moved slowly upward and her breath caught as she realized his intent. She should stop him. Now. And yet the idea of ending this sensual moment made everything inside her cringe with disappointment.

She turned her body just enough so that a moment later she felt his palm close over her breast. The world tilted and a moan of pleasure gurgled in her throat.

Brendon lifted his head just slightly from her mouth. "Nice handful you have, love."

She knew she ought to stop this, but it was rather difficult. Never had she felt sexual pleasure from another person. The only pleasure she'd gained had been from her own ministrations.

And now, having tasted the possibility of pleasure—from a strange man, nonetheless!—the temptation was all too great to follow the rainbow and see if the possibility of rapture lay at the other end.

And why shouldn't she explore it? She had the control now. The moment she wanted to stop, she'd stop. She had the control. The idea in itself was a novelty.

He pinched her nipple lightly, rolling it between his fingers.

"Let me pleasure you, Nika," he murmured against her ear, maybe sensing her inner turmoil. "Tell me, do you have a room in the lodge?"

3

Brendon waited for her response, his cock throbbing within his trousers. Gods, he wanted to toss the little minx down in the bushes and lift her dress. Plunge into the hot wet center he knew awaited him

And yet something within him warned him to proceed with caution with her, that she might be a bit skittish.

"I do have a room," she admitted huskily.

"Good." His blood rushed faster and he smiled, slipping his hand down her waist to cup one taut ass cheek. She was soft here, but not entirely. This was a toned woman, someone who apparently enjoyed being athletic.

A thrill of anticipation raced through him.

"Would you like my mouth on you, love? Everywhere?" He whispered the endearment before catching her earlobe between his teeth and tugging. Maybe a little too hard, he realized with regret.

She gasped, and his brows lifted when he felt her nipple grow hard.

Hmmm. Perhaps she liked things a bit harder? Brendon

tightened his fingers around the tip of her breast. Carefully monitoring her reaction, he squeezed harder, twisting slightly until she let out a strangled moan and looped her arms around his neck, burying her face against his shoulder.

Indeed. This one liked her pleasure with a bit of an edge. He slid the hand on her ass over to her hip, and then inward.

He splayed his fingers low across her belly and was rewarded when she arched into him. He caught her earlobe with his teeth again, biting lightly as his tongue flicked over the plump flesh.

Time to check for certain how much the little minx was aroused. He slipped his hand lower to cup the swell of her mound through the gown she wore.

With his middle finger, he pressed against her slit, pushing the fabric and his digit inside her pussy. It was damp and warm.

His breath caught and for a moment his own self-control spun dangerously out of bounds. Gods, he wanted this woman. He wanted her with a suddenness and ferocity that left him a bit stunned.

Who was she? She was no local who lingered in the Crow's Nest trying out her charm. If anything, she appeared to have a disdain for the women and men who'd been flirting so commonly.

And yet here she was, nearly melting in his arms—which should be no surprise, since most women tended to have that reaction with him. But he'd thought she would be different. A challenge, even. And yet here he was, so close to conquering her.

A thrill of triumph swept through him and he gathered the fabric of her dress in his fist, jerking it up her body and over her hips.

He slid both hands around to grab her bare ass, digging his fingers into the soft flesh. His mind spun and before he could stop himself, he was seeking her mouth again.

His lips slammed against hers, tongue thrusting deep to control the kiss. She didn't fight him, but pressed her body harder against his, matching his intensity. Her tongue flicked against his as she rubbed her tits against his chest.

Fuck. He wanted her. Now!

Brendon abandoned one ass cheek to wedge his hand between them, desperate to touch her hot pussy. He pushed aside a piece of her dress that had fallen back down and cupped her smooth mound in his palm.

Heat burned against his hand and the hint of moisture promised as he moved the heel of his palm against her pubic bone.

Nika wrenched her mouth from his, her lips parted. He caught her gaze, saw the wildness in her eyes just before he pushed one finger into her tight little pussy.

The walls of her sheath gripped him and he hissed out a breath, his dick straining against his trousers. So slick and hot. Gods. He would have her. Here on this trail. To hell with the bed.

He added a second finger, fucking her with the two digits. She made the sexiest little panting sounds, her eyes glazed with pleasure as her body rode him. Each time her body jerked on his fingers, her tight nipples grazed against his chest.

Slipping his thumb into the wet folds, he sought her swollen clit. He wanted to watch her come. Wanted to see that thread of control she clung to snap. He found the tiny bud and massaged it, felt it swell under his ministrations.

"Gods." She gasped, her arms still wrapped around his neck and her breath hot against his arm. "Brendon."

"Yes, love. I want you to come for me," he muttered thickly. "I want to feel you come all over my fingers. Come on, Nika. Let go."

Nika let out a strangled groan, and her body clamped around

him, her muscles rigid. A second later the hot cream of her release coated him.

"Oh gods, oh gods, oh gods," she chanted, her fingers tugging at his hair as her body racked through climax.

He kissed her forehead, his own body so fucking taut with the need for release. He thrust his hips against her, pressing his cock against her belly.

Nika's body finally went limp against him as she let out a soft moan.

Now. He could wait no longer. Fumbling with his other hand, he freed his cock and gripped the pulsing length, stroking his thumb over the thick head and the drop of fluid gathered there. He moved his hand to her ass, ready to lift her and plunge deep.

Nika's hands slammed into his chest, pushing him with enough force that he stumbled back a couple of steps.

"If you don't mind"—she licked her lips and gave him a slight smile—"I'd actually like to stop now."

Brendon blinked, his teeth clenching as he assured himself he'd heard her words correctly. She wanted to *stop*?

"You want to stop?" he repeated. The heat moving through his body had less to do with lust now and more to do with anger.

"Mmm hmm." She watched him from beneath her lashes and stepped back, pushing her dress back down her legs. "I've dallied for far too long tonight. I have things to do."

Dallied for too long? Was that what she called letting him finger her hot little pussy?

Annoyance and disbelief warred inside him. Finally he ground out, "What game do you play, Nika?"

"I play no game. You asked me if I had a room and I answered the truth." She gave a light shrug and glanced back toward the lodge. "I certainly did not invite you back to it. Besides, I simply have no desire to continue."

"Bullshit. You have the desire," he growled. "I just had my fingers all over that desire."

She gave a soft laugh. "Yes. You did. And it was quite enjoyable." With one last smile and a considering look she turned and walked away. "Have a good night, Brendon."

Of all the nerve . . . Brendon started to hurry after her and then faltered, curses falling rampant from his tongue.

The little tease! Never since he'd been a young man had a woman done such with him. Bring him so close to release and then play coy. But this went beyond coy! He'd brought her to climax and then the little minx had practically skipped away, leaving him with a rock-hard cock and frustrated enough to put his fist through a wall.

Unfortunately—or fortunately—there were no walls nearby.

Wincing, he tucked his erection gingerly back into his trousers and fastened them again. He scowled and set out back to the lodge. And if Nika had any sense, she'd best be well hidden from him.

Arriving back into the warm building, he was disappointed to discover the mysterious blonde was indeed nowhere in sight.

"Back again?"

He spun, his hopes rising, only to fall again when he saw Wanda leaning against the counter near the reception desk.

She strolled forward and grabbed the front of his shirt. "Been thinking of me, have you?"

A flush rose to his neck as he watched her eyes drop to his still-hardened cock.

"I can help you with your little problem." Her tongue swiped across blood red lips.

Wanda offered the possibility of a quick tumble. To have a guaranteed release. He ran his gaze over her. Large tits, tiny hips. An hour ago she he would have fucked her on the spot.

And yet now . . . now, he wanted nothing to do with her. The only pussy he wanted to bury his cock in had run upstairs to hide.

The realization raised his irritation a notch, and he let out a frustrated groan.

Wanda must have interpreted his response to be encouraging, for she gave a soft laugh and pressed herself closer.

"I bet we could get a room—"

"This lodge does not rent rooms by the hour," Molly's voice rang out firmly. "You'll have to do your fornicating elsewhere, Miss Wanda."

Brendon let out a sharp laugh and stepped back, his amusement rising as Wanda's face turned red enough to match her hair.

Emmett stepped out of the restaurant just then, eyebrows raised as he took in the scene.

"Thank you, Wanda," Brendon said quietly. "But I'll have to pass anyway."

Wanda's eyes rounded, and her mouth flapped. "Well! Your loss, soldier." She spun around and faced the owner of the lodge. "And you. Maybe if you loosened up a bit—perhaps made your own attempt at *fornicating*—you would not be such an uptight bitch."

Emmett stepped forward, his expression incensed. "Now listen, that was quite uncalled for."

"Oh go fuck yourself. Or her; she obviously needs it," Wanda snarled and strode out the door of the lodge.

Brendon winced and strode over to the owner, clasping her hand. "I apologize, Molly."

She forced a smile, but he could tell Wanda's words had hit their mark. Which was sad. The poor girl didn't deserve such a bitter attack.

"Say, Molly, you didn't happen to see a lady pass through

here a few minutes ago?" he heard himself ask before he could fathom whether it was a good idea. "Blonde, blue dress?"

Molly's gaze dropped, and she shook her head. "Sorry, Brendon. I have not."

He sighed and looked away. "Thank you. Perhaps I'll see if she went into the restaurant."

Even as he went into the restaurant to check, he knew. She'd gone, and he was shit out of luck unless he went door to door to the rooms upstairs to find her.

And he knew without a doubt Molly would never allow that. No, he was stuck with a raging hard-on, and a temper just as fierce.

Molly watched Brendon disappear into the restaurant from beneath her lashes and immediately felt guilty for lying.

But Rebecca had asked her to when she'd hurried in through the doorway, calling out a harried, "Please, if anyone asks, you did not see me!" as she passed.

Interesting that Brendon, one of Molly's favorite customers, had been the one she'd been fleeing from.

"Molly?"

She glanced up, forgetting she was not alone. Emmett, another one of her regulars, stood near the desk, his expression drawn tight with concern.

"Are you all right?" He stepped forward and shook his head. "She shouldn't have said what she did. It was downright spiteful."

"Oh." Her cheeks heated with color. So he'd heard that bit, had he? For some reason it made her stomach sink with humiliation. Maybe because there had been truth to Wanda's words. "It's quite all right. I shouldn't have said what I did to her."

"Well, if you ask me, it's no more than she deserves." Emmett scowled and reached out to touch her hand.

A spark of heat tingled through her arm, and she licked her lips in surprise. She stared at where his dark hand covered hers, and a tremble of awareness ran through her body.

Lifting her head she met Emmett's dark brown gaze. Something hot flickered in his eyes, and her stomach flipped.

He did not remove his hand from hers, and the heat from his touch continued to spread through her body. What was this? She'd never noticed Emmett in such a manner before.

Liar. Of course she had. On the days when he would come in with his friends she'd always find her attention drawn unwillingly to him. To the quiet, dark-skinned man with the sexy, husky laugh.

"How is work?" she asked quickly, the words nothing more than to fill the thickening silence.

Amusement flashed in his gaze now. "Work is well. Quite uneventful."

"Which is a good thing, is it not?" she quipped and allowed herself a smile. "Would you wish us another battle like the one we had two years ago?"

His expression sobered, and he shook his head. "Never."

Guilt stabbed, and her smile faltered. "I should not jest about such events. I'm sorry."

"No harm done." He hesitated, his gaze searching hers. "I should rejoin the men for dinner."

A twinge of disappointment twisted inside, but she covered it with a quick nod.

"Yes. I have things that must be done." She paused and added, "Thank you, Emmett, for your kind words."

Surprise registered across his face. "You know my name?"

Her cheeks warmed, but she straightened her spine and tried to shrug it off with a light flirt. Winking, she murmured, "I make it my business to know the names of my customers. Especially my regulars."

She pulled her hand free with regret and gave him another wide smile. "Have a lovely night."

Walking away, for she intended to check on Rebecca, she felt his gaze following her, burning a trail over her body.

Turning into the stairwell, a rush of warmth filled her blood, and once she was out of his view she let out a soft sigh. Leaning against the wall, she closed her eyes and shook her head.

Developing a mild crush on one of customers could not be a good thing. Not since her husband had died three years ago had she felt the stirrings of desire for a man.

Until Emmett.

But there was nothing to be done. There was no indication that he returned her interest. Was there? Well . . . even if there was, running the lodge alone left her little time for a social life, let alone one that involved sex.

Sex. Her mind flickered with the image of Emmett on top of her. His muscled body lay between her thighs as those large hands cupped her breasts . . . Her nipples tightened, and a long-forgotten ache bloomed between her legs.

"You've gone mad, Molly. Absolutely mad," she hissed to herself and hurried up to the second floor to check on her boarder.

Rebecca did not answer the door after her first knock, so she knocked again.

"Rebecca? It's Molly."

She heard the locks release and then the door hissed open. Rebecca stared at her curiously before her gaze slipped beyond her almost with suspicion.

"I am alone," Molly assured her. "May I come in?"

Rebecca hesitated before giving a short nod, stepping back. "Forgive me, Molly. I thought you were . . . someone else."

Molly stepped inside and gave her a sympathetic glance. "Would this someone be a local soldier that towers above most others?"

The other woman's expression turned wary. "Possibly."

Molly glanced around the room, happy to see her guest had settled in already.

"I don't mean to intrude," Molly said quickly. "And I promise not to stay. I simply had to come assure you that you have nothing to fear with Brendon. He's a right decent man."

"Is he, now?" Rebecca looked away and gave a slight nod. "Perhaps a decent man who feels himself entitled to everyone woman on this planet."

"He is a bit of a flirt," Molly conceded, and then her mouth flapped in alarm. Had she misread the situation? "Oh gods, has he done something to you against your will? Are you quite all right?"

Rebecca's expression flickered between amusement and guilt. "I am fine. Truly. It was nothing but a . . . misunderstanding."

Molly studied the other woman closely, watching to see if perhaps she lied and had indeed been subjected to something awful. After a moment she realized the woman spoke the truth. Or something close to it.

No. Whatever had happened outside the lodge may not have been something Rebecca wanted to dwell on, but whatever had happened Brendon had done nothing too awful. Nor could Molly have imagined he would have.

"I know I said as much earlier, but please don't hesitate to come to me if you need anything." Molly turned toward the door and hesitated before leaving. "He did ask about you. When he came into the lodge."

Rebecca blinked and tilted her head. "Did you . . ."

"I told him I had not seen you."

The other woman visibly relaxed and nodded. "Thank you. For everything, Molly."

"You're welcome." She opened the door and slipped out, with a final, "Perhaps we could have lunch tomorrow?"

Rebecca nodded and Molly watched her eyes light up with anticipation before she carefully schooled her expression again.

"Perhaps."

"Sleep well," Molly murmured and slipped from the room.

For some reason she was drawn to her guest. She sensed in the woman a vulnerability beneath that hard exterior. Quite hard, in fact.

Yes, Rebecca wanted the world to perceive her as confident and tough, but Molly could sense her hunger for friendship.

Strolling back down the hall, she wondered what—if anything—Rebecca might have to hide.

The door shut behind Molly, and Nika bit her lip and jammed a hand through her hair.

Gods, she felt ridiculously guilty for deceiving a woman she barely knew. Every time Molly had called her Rebecca, Nika had felt like even more of a fraud.

Which you are, you fool! She turned on her heel and went into the bathing chamber to wash her face.

She was not on this planet to have sex or make friendships, though she'd come damn close to accomplishing both tonight. And she hated to admit it, but the notion of nurturing this budding friendship with Molly held far too much appeal.

She hardened her resolve. It was too much of a risk. And mistakes such as these could cost her the mission. Could even expose her planet as the sponsor behind the past larcenies.

Nika turned on the faucet, her blood chilling at the thought. Never could she be the one to blow the cover on years of illicit missions. In fact, she knew the result if she were to be captured or her identity became at risk of being discovered. Her life would be taken. One black pill, the size of a melon seed, would ensure it.

She ran her palms under the water and then splashed it across her face. Looking up in the mirror, she watched the droplets run down her chin and fall onto the counter.

The moment out on the trail with Brendon flickered through her head and a tremble ran though her. Guilt pricked lightly inside her, but she stomped it out. Obviously, he'd been all too eager to continue with their little moment. But knowing that she *could* stop him—that she had the power—had been such a rush.

And power was everything. If there was one thing she'd learned about being a damn Rosabelle, that was it. Because she'd had none.

Still, it was a silly thing to do. Letting him touch her out in public and achieving the ultimate pleasure. What had possessed her? It was as if she'd gone mad.

She'd orgasmed. Never had a man brought her to orgasm—seeing as her owners had never tried. And the pitiful moments during their rutting had brought her no pleasure. Thank gods the men had lasted no longer than a couple of minutes each.

Her stomach clenched at the memory and she shook her head to dispel it. Why was she reliving such atrocities? Sadly, it happened more than she wished it would.

It had only been two years since Belton had defeated Zortou's surprise attack. Two years since she'd been given her freedom.

And now you seek to steal from the very planet that liberated you, a voice mocked in her head. She thrust aside any feelings of shame. There was no time for it. Surely the planet would not miss a few samples of semen. Granted, it was like the gold standard of the stuff, but still. The bottom line was it was still just some men's spend.

You are a professional. You trained for years for this mission. And you will not blow it. Success is the only *option.*

All soft thoughts and ideas of lovers and friendships vanished from her mind. What remained was only steely determination to complete this mission. Tomorrow she would make her first attempt to discover the details of the lab, perhaps even risk a first raid.

Stripping off her dress, she climbed into bed and attempted to fall asleep.

Gods, how could she have fallen asleep for so long? If she was late with supper they would kill her. Or make her wish they'd killed her.

Donika rushed around the small housing unit, setting the table just so, before returning to the kitchen to check on the meat.

Any minute now the brothers would return from work and demand their food and ask why there was dust upon the teletron.

Opening the door to the oven unit, she cut into one thick slab of meat. Damn, it still needed at least five more minutes.

There was a loud shrill beep and she winced, glancing sharply over her shoulder to where the door to the unit lay.

The two men entered the unit, speaking quietly to each other as they removed their jackets and closed the unit door again.

Then they turned toward the kitchen, their matching gazes on her.

"Where's my food?" Mac asked gruffly, pulling out a chair at the table.

"Almost ready," she said quickly, smoothing her dress down her legs.

"Almost?" Ron repeated, his gaze narrowing as it moved over her. He licked his thick lips and rubbed his belly. "What have you been doing all day?"

Her cheeks filled with color. "I've . . ."

Ron's hand glanced across her cheek and her head snapped to the side with the blow.

"Never mind," he muttered and gripped her shoulder. "How long?"

"Five minutes," she whispered.

"Well, then, for five minutes you can suck my cock." He pushed her to her knees and pulled his short, fat erection free from his pants.

No choice. She never had a choice. Only to please. Wanting this to be over as soon as possible, she took him in her mouth and zoned out while she brought him to climax.

Ten minutes later she set a plate of food in front of the men and then filled up a plate of food for herself. When she went to sit at the table Mac pushed her away.

"You cannot be rewarded for being late with our supper, Donika." He gestured to the corner of the small room.

Swallowing against her humiliation, she went to the corner and sank down to the floor, eating quietly by herself while the men devoured their food.

Gods. Was this truly all there was to life? Every day to live and serve these vile men? No matter how much she tried to please, to prove herself, it was never enough. She was never good enough.

Though her throat tightened with emotion, no tears burned her eyes. Crying brought no results.

"Get up."

She blinked, not realizing Mac had crossed the room to stand in front of her.

Beneath his trousers his erection was obvious. Her stomach sank with dread. Gods, he must have become turned on watching his brother with her moments ago.

And she had not yet finished her meal. Not that it mattered. When they demanded, she gave.

Standing, she set her plate upon the counter and followed Mac into the bedroom. Whereas Ron would take her in any manner and any place in the housing unit, Mac always used a bed.

With a grunt, he pushed her backward and lifted her dress to her hips. And then he was inside her, riding her while she stared at the ceiling of the unit.

It was over a moment later. When he rolled off her he rubbed his belly and sighed.

"Better hurry and clean up the kitchen, girl," he muttered. "Work was a bit hard and Ron and I would like massages."

Of course they did. A hysterical laugh bubbled in her throat. It was like the same day. Over and over and over—

"Oh, and I nearly forgot." Mac paused in the midst of fastening his trousers and leered down at her. "Happy anniversary to us all."

Nika gasped and jerked upright in bed. Her hair hung in damp strands around her head and she shoved them aside, looking wildly around the room to rid herself of the disorientation.

It had been just a memory. Or a nightmare. They were one and the same.

But that was not her life anymore. Thank the gods, that was *not* her life. She'd moved on and now she was the one in control. Of everything. And without control, she was nothing.

With a grim smile, she swung her legs out of bed and prepared for the day.

Nika left the lodge early. Once outside the building she found a local washroom to alter her appearance.

She needed to look the part of an attractive female, even more dressed up than last night—which was a bit difficult, as she hadn't done such since she lived on Zortou.

Today, it was essential that her femininity be pronounced, and that there wouldn't be the slightest reason to connect her appearance with the shapeless disguise she'd wear as a thief.

She wore an amethyst dress that was cut low and had a white tie beneath her breasts. It accented her curves and highlighted her chest.

Her hair she kept down, combed into a long, sleek wave.

She had all the needed IDs and excuses to get onto the base, and once inside she was certain to have an escort to show her around. Today would be easy. She'd be learning the layout.

It was when she went back—tonight, tomorrow night, next week; whenever the time was right to break into the lab. That was when the real challenge would begin.

And when it did, she knew that the likelihood of hand-to-hand combat was high; the possibility that she might even have to kill was just as great.

The idea wasn't something that settled well in her conscience. In fact, it had lingered heavy in her gut since she'd begun her training. But she knew if it came down to it she would do what needed to be done.

An hour later she was in the gates of the compound awaiting an escort.

"Ms. Owens?"

She spun at the sound and smiled to the man who approached her. Her stomach twisted a little at the realization that it was again another man she'd have to spend time with.

"Hello. Colonel Charleson?"

"Indeed." He closed the distance between them and grasped one of her hands in both of his. "Lovely to meet you, ma'am."

"Thank you for being so kind as to show me around the compound."

"Not at all. We're excited to have an ambassador from the city of Glorus."

"And I am just as excited to be here."

His smile widened. "Come. Let us begin the tour."

An hour later, she'd toured a majority of the compound and

encountered many soldiers in the process. The male population had seemed quite intrigued by her presence, likely because she was a woman on base, made to look pretty, and wore no uniform.

Fortunately, she hadn't seen Brendon, which had been her fear all morning. If she were to see him, gods knew what she would do.

Her stomach twisted at the very thought.

"You've seen the entire compound, ma'am," the colonel murmured. "Well, save for our specimen lab. But I can't imagine you'd be interested in such and likely have other things to do."

Nika licked her lips and hesitated. How to reply? She did not want to seem too eager.

"Colonel, I have no plans for lunch and would love the opportunity to spend more time in your presence," she preened. "Perhaps we could tour the lab and have lunch after?"

The older man flushed and nodded. "That would be lovely. Just let me place a call ahead to the lab and let them know of our arrival."

4

"Lieutenant Marshall. I'd like a word with you in my office."

Brendon jerked away from the wall he leaned against and cringed. Shit. He'd just been caught dozing on the job. Again.

"Yes, sir." Following the captain into the office located just around the corner he inwardly let out a tirade of curses.

How had he not realized that the captain had returned from his early lunch?

"Please have a seat." The older man gestured to the steel chair in front of the long metal desk.

"Thank you, sir."

Brendon curled his body onto the tiny chair and waited for the tongue-lashing he was sure would come.

"Lieutenant, I realize being assigned this position must be quite a disappointment to someone who is used to seeing action."

Now how the hell was Brendon supposed to respond to that? Certainly not with honesty.

Fortunately, the captain didn't seem to expect a response, because he leaned back in his chair and sighed. "The truth is, I was excited to hear about your demotion. It gave me the perfect opportunity to request that you be transferred here. I need a man like you."

Excited about his demotion? Brendon tamped down his irritation and waited for the captain to elaborate.

The other man leaned forward, watching him above steepled fingers. "You are exactly what I need for what is about to come upon us."

Brendon sat up straighter, interest piqued. "And what is that, sir?"

"The anniversary. Every five years this lab is attacked by a very skilled thief."

"Sir?"

"They send one person, Lieutenant. One person to infiltrate this lab and steal hundreds of specimens."

Brendon stilled, his head cocking as his brows drew together. "Someone is stealing semen from the lab?"

Captain Teflick sighed and looked down. "This is why I have called you in here. I do not believe you quite grasp the *gravity* of what you are guarding. What is being taken."

"I understand well enough. It is—"

"No, Lieutenant. You don't." He cut off Brendon sharply. "The specimen you guard is not just the cum from some random soldier's dick."

Heat stole up Brendon's neck, because that's exactly what he had always jested about.

"In these specimens lie the possibility of an undefeatable army. Those samples come from royalty. From the greatest soldiers ever to walk the planet." The captain's voice grew louder and he spoke more quickly. "Even from alien men, who have dark, unique sides that we know so little about. The potential of what could be done with such specimens is endless."

Brendon drew in a slow breath, holding the older man's

gaze. Royal specimens. That alone was enough to set his head spinning. Anyone could use the samples to create royal blood and create an heir. And then there were the alien men . . . He'd only heard of the planet where men drank blood. And another where men shifted into animals on occasion. At times he'd believed the planets to be nothing more than mythical nonsense. And yet now here was Captain confirming their validity.

"The anniversary is upon us." The man stood and walked to the small window that looked out over the fenced-in building. "Any day they could send another man to infiltrate this building. And we need our best guarding it." He turned suddenly, his hard gaze landing on Brendon. "And this man will not hesitate to kill you. Or anyone standing in his path."

Brendon's fists tightened in his lap. "How is it that I have never heard of this treachery?"

The captain let out a soft laugh. "Do you think the military wants this known? It would become the joke that you saw it to be, that someone has infiltrated our compound to steal semen." His lips curled in disdain. "No, the military wants this kept quiet—though they are worried enough to have put out the word underground that there is a hefty bounty for the capture of this thief."

A reward? "And what if I capture this person?"

Captain Teflick smiled. "Then you are simply doing your duty, Lieutenant. Your pay stub is your reward."

Quite unfair if you asked him. Brendon made a silent harrumph. And yet, the possibility of danger, of catching this man sent a rush of excitement through him.

"I will not let you down, Captain. If this thief shows on my watch, he will not live to—"

"Oh no, Lieutenant. We want him alive. He'll have to be . . . questioned extensively."

"Of course."

The older man nodded and then sighed. "You are a good soldier, Lieutenant. I know you should be rising in the ranks, instead of being demoted. Though I will say that in this instance your loss was my gain."

Brendon didn't reply. He could not argue with the fact that he'd fucked up superbly by screwing his commanding officer while on duty. Gods. Did Captain Teflick know the reason for his demotion?

The older man smiled again, maybe sensing his thoughts. He started to say something but then the communication mobile rang.

"One moment." The captain lifted the mobile and spoke to the person on the other end. A moment later he disconnected the line.

"That was a call from Colonel Charleson. He is escorting an ambassador from Glorus over for a tour of the lab. Will you see to this for me?"

"Of course."

"Thank you, Lieutenant. That will be all." The captain nodded.

Brendon rushed to stand again, unfurling himself from the cold chair as he saluted the other man.

"Thank you, Captain." He turned sharply and left the room again.

Apparently his job was not quite as lackluster as it seemed. Anticipation jolted through his blood and his mouth curled with the possibility of being the one to take on this thief.

Yes. Things would certainly perk up if that were to happen. Well. One could only hope. For certainly the thief would realize he'd tangled with the wrong soldier. Nobody attempted to steal on his watch. Whether it was money or semen, it mattered not.

When this thief showed up, he'd realize his days of larceny were through.

He resumed his guard, this time with a new outlook. When the call came through that the colonel and ambassador had arrived and waited at the gate, Brendon shouldered his weapon and went to let them in.

A moment later he let out a sputter of disbelief, his feet almost tripping on the solid ground. Nika was the ambassador? His gaze moved over her and his cock immediately twitched in response.

Gods, she looked amazing. If she'd been attractive last night, today she was stunning.

His breath caught for a moment as he watched her approach. His shock turned to triumph and amusement when he watched her eyes widen in shock. Her gaze darted around as if seeking escape.

Well, the little minx would find no escape from this moment they were about to spend together.

"Lieutenant Marshall. Good to see you again, soldier."

"Thank you, Colonel. You as well."

The colonel turned to Nika and smiled. "May I introduce you to Rebecca Owens? She's an ambassador from Glorus."

Rebecca? His gaze jerked sharply back to her, and he noticed she'd stiffened slightly.

"Lieutenant, I hate to do this, but I received a call that there is a problem in sector eight that needs my immediate attention. Would you mind showing Ms. Owens around the lab while I run over there right quick?"

"Not at all." His smile widened and his blood rushed faster through his veins. Alone with her. "I would be honored."

To further his enjoyment of the situation, Nika's—or was it Rebecca's?—mouth flapped open in protest, but she issued no words.

"I apologize, Ms. Owens." The colonel squeezed her hand. "I will return after your tour and we can have lunch together."

"Thank you, Colonel," was the faint reply she eventually muttered.

Brendon waited for the other man to disappear, watching her and feeling very much like a predator who'd cornered his prey. And in a way . . . he just had.

"Would you please follow me inside the lab, *Rebecca*?"

She ground her teeth together and for a moment he was certain she might refuse and turn away. But instead she gave a sharp nod and strode past him.

"So which is it?" he asked, a bit irritated that once again he trailed after her. "Rebecca or Nika?"

"You think I would tell you my real name last night?" she scoffed over her shoulder. "For a moment's indiscretion on a moonlit path?"

"I have no idea, ma'am." He increased his stride until he passed and then moved in front of her. "What I do know is you're quite the little cock tease. Taking your pleasure and then running."

She gave a soft harrumph. "You should learn some manners."

Brendon leaned forward, until his face was just inches from hers. "And you should have at least sucked my dick before you left."

She laughed and shook her head. "Let me guess, Lieutenant. You don't get told "no" often, do you?"

"Let's just say I can't remember the last time it happened," he muttered.

His chest tightened as he stared at her. Gorgeous eyes. He could finally see them up close and in the daylight. Green on the inside with a circle of blue around the outside. Very unique.

"Will you be taking me on this tour?" Her tone remained neutral, yet seemed to taunt. "Or should I seek out the colonel instead?"

Brendon scowled. The colonel had certainly seemed quite fond of her.

"I'll take you, Nika. And you'll enjoy it."

"Rebecca," she corrected him and glanced around. "And stop with the sexual jokes."

"It is no joke," he murmured. "I take quite seriously my intention to bed you. And seeing as you've given me two names, I think perhaps I'll stay with the first you gave me as it suits you better."

"You are quite persistent." She sighed and then stepped around him, continuing her path into the building.

Brendon gave her a second's head start. It offered him a moment to watch her sweet ass while she passed him.

Her body was so enticing. Subtly curved and yet so firm. His fists clenched as he resisted the urge to slap her ass. Move up behind her and nibble on the back of that creamy white neck.

Damn. He would have this woman. It was just a matter of when.

Nika's heart had yet to slow down from when she'd first seen Brendon standing outside the lab.

Oh sweet gods. What were the chances he'd be the one guarding the lab? That she would have to even see him again!

Fortunately he appeared to be working during the daylight hours, and she would not likely encounter him at night.

Just the thought of getting physical with him—and not in a good way like on the trail—sent a wave of trepidation through her. She was tall and fit, but not only was Brendon taller—quite a bit, which was saying a lot—but he was obviously in good shape.

It was not easy to maintain a calm demeanor as she spoke with him. Everything inside her relived their moment on the path last night. Her body hummed with awareness at his close proximity.

Focus, Nika, focus.

Brendon opened the door to the complex by pushing a code, but unfortunately she hadn't been able to see the exact numbers. Still, she had a general idea, and that would be a good start.

She followed him into the lab, her awareness at peak level now. Glancing around, she tried to memorize every last thing she saw before her. If she could get Brendon to slip away for a moment, then she even had a small camera to take pictures.

Somehow she doubted that would happen, though. Brendon seemed to be quite well attached to her ass. Even now as they wandered down the hall, she could feel his gaze moving over her.

He must have been so irritated after last night. Thankfully there was little he could do when they were in a public building.

"So you guard a building full of specimens, Lieutenant?" Nika asked, inserting a bit of derisiveness into her tone. "Semen, is it?"

If she came across as mocking that would certainly be better than appearing too interested.

"Yes. I do."

If she'd hoped to goad him into feeling embarrassed, she'd failed. His hard response held little apology or humiliation.

"Though I am wondering why you'd care to tour the lab."

His question chilled her confidence just a bit, but she forced a casual shrug.

"I'm touring the entire compound. The idea of a specimen lab intrigued me." She glanced through a glass window at the rows of silver refrigeration units. "And whose samples are they, Lieutenant?"

"That information, Nika, is classified." He stepped toward her, backing her up against the wall.

Her pulse jumped just from the proximity of his body to hers. He invaded her space, made every breath she dragged in be filled with the masculine scent of him.

She forced a light laugh. "No need to slap me with the classified bit, Lieutenant. I was simply curious."

"Brendon."

Narrowing her eyes, she said softly, "I will address you by your rank. You are at work, and I am a visitor. To do anything else would hardly be appropriate."

Brendon's hands slammed the wall on either side of her head and he gave a harsh laugh. "Oh, Nika, what I want to do to you right now is hardly appropriate either."

Her heart slammed against her chest, partly from surprise and partly from . . . gods, it could not be excitement.

"You are on *duty*," she scoffed.

He winced and gave a soft laugh. "Yes. You'd think I would learn."

What could he possibly mean by that?

A door slammed and Brendon stepped back from her, his face once again becoming a mask of indifference.

Footsteps sounded before a man rounded the corner.

"Lieutenant Marshall, I'm running out for a good hour," the man stated, coming out of his office. "Don't hesitate to contact me if you need me."

Brendon gave a quick salute. "Yes, sir."

The man gave a warm glance at Nika. "Good day, ma'am."

Off balance by the sudden interruption, she lowered her gaze, falling into a curtsy. "Good day, sir."

Before she could rise, she froze. Oh gods. What had she done? She'd gotten distracted and had fallen back into her habits as a Rosabelle.

Straightening again, she lifted her gaze and felt her stomach sink with apprehension. They knew it. They knew exactly what she had once been.

The older man's gaze turned sympathetic before he nodded, turned, and left.

She swallowed hard and avoided looking at Brendon.

"You were a Rosabelle." It was not a question.

Nika bit the inside of her cheek so hard she was certain it would bleed.

"It's nothing to be ashamed of," he continued softly.

"Don't you dare," she snapped, turning to face him. She knew her gaze spit fire. "You have no idea."

"No, I don't." His gentle gaze searched hers. "But I am not unfamiliar with what your life was like. My good friend is married to a former Rosabelle."

Oh wasn't that just charming? She forced back the sarcastic response. She wasn't surprised. Many Rosabelles—women forced to essentially be whores by the men who owned them—had sought refuge on Belton. Had probably sought immediate companionship with the nearest penis since that was all they knew. But not her. *Never* her.

Gods, and now she'd lost her cool. She needed to keep in control. She could not afford such an emotional outburst again.

"I wish to continue this tour and then leave," she said firmly, not wanting this conversation to continue.

"Did you become an ambassador after the liberation?"

The air locked in her chest, and she struggled to breathe. Damn.

What had she just gotten herself into? Giving him her real name. And outing herself as a former Rosabelle.

How many times would she blunder her way through this mission? And after the extensive training she'd had.

It was Brendon. He rattled her brains and made her thoughts turn to mush.

"We're all alone now. Are you sure you want that tour?" he asked quietly, arching an eyebrow.

"Of course," she replied sharply. "It's the reason I'm here."

"Is it?"

"You speak in riddles, Lieutenant."

"Do I? Perhaps I should speak in actions instead of words."

He held her gaze and her pulse quickened. She dampened her lips at what he could possibly be intending. Would he dare . . . ?

He trailed a hand over her bare collarbone and her nipples tingled, tightening into hard points.

Her knees shook and she bit back a groan. She would not lose control again. She would not—oh gods!

His finger dipped below the bodice of her dress and over the curve of one breast.

Stop him. This is hardly the time or the place. And yet because it *was* so forbidden, it sent a shiver of excitement through her. Dampened the sensitive flesh between her legs.

"You've got tits made for sucking, love." He lowered his head toward her. "And I intend to get a mouthful."

He grasped the neckline of her dress and tugged it downward. Both her breasts spilled over the fabric, bared and vulnerable to his gaze.

"Hell, look at that." He caught one mound in his palm, squeezing the flesh. "So soft and yet that pretty nipple is so hard and red. Just begging to be sucked. Or maybe you prefer biting."

"Please." She licked her lips and glanced around, not sure if she was begging for him to continue or stop.

"I like it when you beg me, love." He lowered his head and nuzzled one breast. "I like it quite a bit. And I intend to hear it more than once before tomorrow morning comes."

He held her gaze and she watched his lips part, saw his tongue slide out before it scraped across her nipple. The wet friction sent pleasure shooting through her entire body, making her muscles shake and moisture gather between her legs.

"So sweet." He licked her again, curling his tongue around the sensitive tip of her breast. "So damn responsive."

"Brendon . . ." His name left her lips on a shaky sigh.

"Yes. Say my name, love." He bit down on the nipple, drawing a ragged gasp of pleasure from her. "And scream my name when my mouth is on your pussy."

She choked at his words, blinking in shock as he went to his knees in front of her. He shoved her dress around her waist and slid one hand in to cup the swell of her sex.

Sparks of pleasure rocked through her as he palmed her and then stroked her with his long, rough fingers.

"Look at how smooth you are," he whispered. "What a hot little pussy you have. Gods, I cannot wait any longer to taste you."

"Wait . . ." She let out a panicked squeak, delving her hands into his hair as she backed up to escape him.

He followed, leaning into her and pressing his face between her legs, nuzzling her hot flesh.

Gods! Her eyes slammed closed and she dragged in a huge breath, trying to stay afloat as pleasure spread throughout her body like wildfire. Never before had she had a mouth on her like this.

Brendon slid his hands up her thighs to cup her ass, pulling her hips closer as he pressed kisses against her mound.

"Open for me, love," he commanded softly. "Move your legs apart. Let me taste you."

Wordlessly, she obeyed, nothing but a slave to pleasure at this point. Her feet moved just inches away from each other, but it must have been enough.

His tongue found the slit of her pussy, firm and abrasive. He slid deep inside and stroked her low and then high.

"Gods!" What a sinful feeling! Her legs shook and she tugged at his hair, holding him to her now. Because the idea of his mouth not on her was unthinkable.

"Mmm. You're so wet, love. And the taste of you: intoxicating." He let out a soft groan and licked her again, this time moving high inside her folds and staying there. His tongue wiggled around until it found her clit.

Nika rose to her tiptoes, her ass clenching against his hands.

"Relax," he murmured against her flesh with a soft laugh, before drawing the little button into his mouth and suckling.

She panted, trying to escape his mouth. Trying to get closer. Anything to help this exquisiteness come to a peak. She needed to regain her senses.

His tongue delved deep into her channel, thrusting in and out in a firm and arousing mimicry of sex.

Nika opened her eyes, watched the metal walls around her spin. She felt her balance in standing precariously at risk.

"Damn. I can't get enough of you," he ground out and licked her harder. He lightly bit the lips of her pussy before moving up to capture her clit again—this time with his teeth.

The pressure was so close to pain that it sent her spiraling over the edge. Her eyes slammed shut to the explosion of lights in her head.

Her body jerked against his mouth and her fingers struggled to grasp the strands of his hair. But the short tendrils slipped through and she fell heavily back against the wall, her chest rising and falling as she fought to catch her breath.

The heat of Brendon's mouth between her legs disappeared and she heard the catch of his trousers coming undone.

Her eyes flickered open just as she felt the thick bulbous head of his cock nudge between her legs.

Oh gods, no! This wouldn't do. He was on duty. How had either of them let it go this far? It could only cause serious trouble for them both if they were to be discovered. And she could not afford to draw any further attention to herself.

"Brendon," she gasped, reaching down to wrap her hands around his cock to halt his progress. "No. Please, we cannot. Not here."

Dismay flickered in his gaze. "Tell me you would not do this to me again."

She licked her lips, almost inclined to have him proceed as she felt the throb of his hot, silky steel length in her hands. He felt sinful. Wonderful. Tempting. So different and forbidden.

But she could not. It risked too much. They both risked too much.

"Meet me later," she said softly, knowing as she spoke she lied. She absolutely could not afford to get caught up in this pleasing madness again. "Tonight at the Crow's Nest."

His eyes glittered with warning. "Not tonight, Nika. Now. There's no one around."

Watching him from beneath her lashes, she gave a soft shake of her head. "I'm sorry, Brendon. But I cannot. I have a reputation to maintain. And might I remind you that you do as well."

She watched his expression morph from disbelief into anger.

He stepped back from her and growled, "I cannot believe this. But then, what else should I have expected after last night?"

He didn't really seem to expect an answer, but when she hesitated, he yelled, "Just go already, damn it! Before I do something we both know we want."

Nika grimaced and sidestepped him, pulling her bodice back over her breasts and smoothing the skirt down over her legs once more. Before she could stay and maybe change her mind, she spun away and fled the lab.

5

The Crow's Nest was quite crowded for a weeknight. Emmett took a sip of his wine and glanced around the room, awaiting the arrival of the rest of his friends. But most of all for Brendon.

He'd spoken to the other man earlier on the communication mobile and had been quite taken aback by his churlish mood. Something was definitely afoot. And by the gods he couldn't wait to find out. It would add a bit of excitement to his own dull day.

He sighed and leaned back in his chair, cupping the glass of wine in his palm. His gaze drifted around the room and landed on the woman talking to a customer in the corner.

She was a delightful little thing, Ms. Molly. All wide blue eyes, luscious curves, and long blond hair. Too bad he had absolutely no interest in getting involved with a woman right now.

She leaned down to retrieve a plate from the table and her dress tightened over her plump round ass. His cock stirred, and he bit back a sigh. Right. No interest whatsoever. His lips twisted sardonically. Shit. Who was he kidding?

"I asked you to stop."

He heard her sharp words, and his ears perked. Setting his glass down on the table he stood, his brows drawing together. He'd taken just a few steps to the table where she stood when he noticed the man at the table reach out to touch her ass.

Fists clenched, Emmett crossed the room and grasped her arm, pulling her back behind him. Molly's eyes widened in surprise, but she made no protest.

"Something I can help you with, sir?" He turned his attention to the table.

"Not so much," the man drawled, his gaze steely beneath a false layer of amusement.

Emmett held his ground, meeting the man's stare with ease. "Maybe next time, be a little quick to respect a lady's wishes when she asks you to stop."

"Maybe you oughta mind your own business, soldier." Something flickered in the man's eyes. For a moment they even seemed to glow red. What the hell? Unease stirred in Emmett's gut and then he knew. This was no man from Belton. He must surely be one of those rumored aliens from Multron. A blood drinker . . .

"Emmett." Molly touched his arm lightly. "It's quite all right. Truly."

Refusing to back down, Emmett gave the man a hard look. "No more trouble. Or we'll see to it you leave and aren't invited back."

The man held his gaze for a moment and then gave a wide, cold smile.

"Well, I don't want any trouble. I promise to be a good little boy from now on."

Molly let out a small groan and spun away, rushing from the room. Emmett watched her go, his mouth curving downward.

Damn. She was obviously more upset than she let on. He

cast one last warning glance at the alien man and headed out after her.

He found her in a small office near the reception desk, dabbing her eyes with a linen cloth.

His stomach clenched with tenderness, and he stopped in the doorway.

"Molly?"

"Please, I am fine. I promise, Emmett," she muttered on a rush.

But she wasn't. Anyone with two eyes could clearly see that.

He stepped inside the office, not waiting to be invited, and pressed the door closed. It hissed shut, locking with a metallic click.

"Come here." He opened his arms and took a step toward her, not sure whether she'd welcome his embrace or think he was crazy for offering it.

To his relief she let out a sniffle and lurched into his arms.

Emmett closed his eyes, wrapping her close against him. It was hard not to notice the light flowery scent she wore, or the curves of her warm body. Or the way her soft breath feathered his chest as she let out little sobs.

"Tell me what happened, sweetheart."

"Nothing, really. I promise. I have just had the most awful day. My laundress has quit. We have run out of yard bird and probably will have none until Friday," she said between sniffles. "And then when I was doing my rounds at the tables that man was awful. He . . . he . . ."

Emmett tightened his arms around her, his gut telling him he wouldn't like what she was going to say.

"What happened?"

"He grabbed me and pulled me to the table, squeezing my bottom." She drew in a shaky breath. "And he said vulgar things about what he could do with a girl like me."

"Fuck." Emmett smoothed an arm down her back and ground his teeth together. "I should go right back out there and tell him what I could do to a guy like him. Namely, smash his face in."

Molly gave a watery laugh. "Please. There is no need. He's just a crass bounty hunter staying at the lodge. A blood drinker. I've dealt with men far worse."

"But you shouldn't have to." He set her back a few inches and lifted her chin with one finger. "You should have droids waiting the tables instead of doing it yourself. Then perhaps this wouldn't have happened."

"Droids have their place," Molly admitted. "But I prefer the personable contact of helping out with my guests. It has proven to be better for business."

His gaze stroked over her face and he bit back a soft sigh before admitting, "Yes, I must say you're quite preferable to a droid."

"Thank you." Her smile was weak.

"Anytime." He leaned down and brushed his lips across hers in a quick, reassuring kiss.

The moment his lips touched hers, though, any thoughts of it being a chaste touch flew out the window. Her lips were soft and cushiony, a warm welcome for his mouth.

She made a soft noise of surprise and her hands came up lightly against his chest. Lifting her head, she looked up at him with those wide blue eyes.

He felt heat work its way up his neck. "Forgive me, Molly."

"No." She shook her head. "Please."

And then she wrapped her arms around his neck, drawing his head down to hers.

Emmett lost any resistance he may have had and covered her mouth again with his own, grasping her hips tight in his hands.

Her lips parted and he slipped his tongue deep to find hers.

She made a soft sigh of delight, her tongue coming forward to rub against his.

He let out a ragged groan, his cock hardening even further, brushing against the soft curve of her belly. His hips arched, grinding against hers, and she let out an answering moan.

Emmett jerked his mouth away and tried to step back. What was he thinking? He was not being rational. Trying to fuck the lodge owner in her office?

"Molly, wait."

"No, please. Emmett. Do not ask me to stop." She reached behind her and unfastened the button on her dress. A moment later it fell from her body and pooled at her feet.

Gods! His mouth filled with saliva as he drank her in. Her body was small and curved, her breasts large and more than a handful. Her hips were wide and soft thighs cushioned a pretty pink pussy.

"Molly," he choked out. "What are—?"

"I have not had a man since my husband passed away, Emmett," she said softly. "And I would very much like it if you would indulge me now, since I have taken an interest in you." Insecurity flashed suddenly in her gaze. "Unless this is something you do not wish."

"Oh gods, Molly." He reached for her again, dragging her naked body hard against his. "I wish. I very much wish. But would you prefer to go elsewhere? Find somewhere more comfortable?"

She gave a light laugh and ran a finger over the top of his uniform. "There is a desk. Surely we could use that. On top. You could bend me over. Or you might sit in the chair and I could—"

He crushed his mouth on hers again, silencing her erotic suggestions. How had he not realized the sweet little owner of this lodge was a little seductress in disguise? And thank gods she'd chosen him.

Reaching between them, he cupped her breast in his hand and felt the nipple that was already tight for him poke his palm. Bend her over the desk, indeed. She had no idea how close he was to doing just that.

Her nimble fingers undid his uniform, peeling the shirt from his shoulders and leaving his upper torso bare.

Emmett reached for his trousers, unfastening them and sliding them down his legs before kicking them free.

Naked flesh melted together. He pressed a leg between hers until her bare sex rode his thigh. The hot moisture there made the breath catch in his lungs.

He caught her ass in his hands and lifted her, moving her over to the steel desk in the corner. As he set her down she let out a squeal.

"Sorry, it's cold." She winced and reached for him again.

Emmett's throat reverberated with a low laugh as he pushed her backward until she reclined on her elbows.

"I will see that you are sufficiently warmed, sweetheart." He smoothed his hands down her body, loving the contrast of his dark skin and her pale flesh.

The pink parts on her especially fascinated him. The nipples were so light in color. He reached to run his thumb over one tip and watched as the flush deepened in the areola. The nipple elongated as if seeking his mouth.

And who was he to deny her? With a chuckle he leaned down and caught one pert tip, drawing it deep past his lips.

Molly cried out, her body writhing on the desk. He cuddled her large breasts in his hands, suckling one nipple while rubbing the other one in a slow rhythm.

Her hand slipped between them, and a second later he felt it wrap around his cock.

He groaned, thrusting against her fingers as he switched his mouth to her other breast.

"Gods, I do want you, Emmett," Molly whispered. "I have needed this more than you could know."

He lifted his head, breathing unevenly. "Do you need *this*?"

Still holding her gaze, he kissed a trail between her breasts and down the slight rise of her belly. Each kiss brought the scent of her musky arousal closer to his mouth.

Her stomach clenched, and he watched her lips part, her eyes darken.

Nuzzling the curls that shielded her pussy, he was pleased to find them already damp. He lowered his gaze to the pink folds between her legs.

Gods. He needed to touch her. Taste her. He parted her flesh with unsteady fingers, exposing the slick shine of her arousal.

His cock twitched, and he let out a strangled groan. Lowering his head, he went in for the first taste.

Musky. Succulent. So good. He buried his tongue inside her, seeking more of her slick desire.

"Yes. Oh gods, yes." She gripped the edge of the desk and her thighs tightened around his head.

Soft. Warm. Cocooning him against the essence of her femininity.

He flicked his tongue up to find the pearl of pleasure he knew would bring her release. Her clit was hot and swollen, just begging for his mouth, and so he took it, suckling it gently to drive her pleasure higher.

"Emmett, oh gods! I'm going to come."

Yes. Come, sweetheart. He couldn't even draw his mouth away from her juicy flesh to murmur the encouraging words, and instead used his tongue to push her release.

A moment later she was there. Her sharp scream made him glad for the steel doors that shielded them from the lodge.

Her thighs gripped his head, squeezing his ears so hard he was certain they would cave inward. Her cream spilled fresh and hot on his tongue, and he lapped it up, riding with her through the orgasm.

She finally went limp, her thighs gradually releasing their grip on his head.

Emmett rose to his feet and gripped his cock. He could wait no longer.

Still weak from her orgasm, Molly stared up at Emmett, who now massaged his cock and eyed her like a starving man.

Gods, she'd finally lost her mind—and didn't it feel wonderful?

"Sit on the chair," she urged him, scooting off the desk. "Let me ride you."

A visible tremble racked his body as he moved around the desk to sit in the mobile chair.

Molly followed him around the desk, licking her lips as she eyed the thick jut of his cock. Gods, he was quite a bit larger than what she was experienced with.

Despite her aggressiveness, which still continued to surprise her, she felt the first stab of apprehension.

Emmett must have seen the sudden worry in her gaze, for he held out his hand and murmured a soft, "Come here, sweetheart."

Molly placed her smaller hand in his and felt that familiar zing of chemistry shoot through her blood.

She moved onto his lap, letting her legs slide on both sides of his hips. His cock pressed hard against her ass and she knew she just had to lift herself up and back a bit.

His hands, so dark and deliciously rough, slid up her stomach to cup her breasts again. Her body turned liquid and she sighed, moving herself just enough to rub the head of his cock against her slit.

Pleasure rocked through her and made her blood hum.

"I want your mouth, Molly," he ordered softly. "Kiss me."

Her heart fluttered, and she licked her lips again, before leaning forward to press her mouth against his in a soft caress.

He took control of the kiss, sliding his tongue deep while his hips lifted just enough to push the head of his dick the slightest bit into her.

She groaned, sparring her tongue with his, and sank down a bit farther. Slowly, inch by inch, she slid his cock into her.

So good. She pulled her mouth away to look down at where they were almost fully joined.

The erotic sight almost undid her. Pink lips spread wide over the thick black staff.

"All the way down, Molly," he muttered, squeezing her breasts. "Come on, girl. Or I'm going to lose all control and to hell with slow."

"So do it," she gasped, rotating her hips over his cock. "Fuck me, Emmett. Please."

He let out a growl and moved his hands to grip her hips. With one lift of his ass, he embedded himself to the hilt.

"Oh!" She cried out and squeezed her eyes shut. *Better to just jump in quick than ease your way in.*

"Damn, sweetheart. You feel incredible," he choked out. His hips began to buck up in a constant rhythm, pushing in and out of her. "Ride me, Molly."

Molly gripped his shoulders and did as instructed, rocking back and forth on his cock, rotating her hips to hit different angles.

Her eyes closed. Gods, it had been too long. She missed this. The fullness of having a man inside her, his rough hands caressing her body, and the absolute ecstasy of his mouth bringing her release.

"Harder, sweetheart." He moved a hand between her legs and rubbed her clit. "I'll make sure you fly with me."

"Yes," she whispered and moved faster on him, pressing herself down harder onto his cock. "Yes!"

His finger wiggled faster on her, and the tightening of a release built quickly in her muscles. She squeezed her inner walls around Emmett's cock and was rewarded with his guttural groan.

The pleasure stacked higher inside her, building and expanding until everything in her head went white and the sensation toppled over the edge.

Her body shook through the climax and her nails dug hard into his shoulders.

He took over, gripping her ass and pounding up inside her until a moment later he cried out and she felt him come warm and thick inside her.

"Oh my." She pressed her head against his shoulder, letting her tongue flick out over his damp salty flesh. "That was quite incredible."

"Mmm." Emmett massaged her ass cheeks, his chin resting on her head. "You have no idea."

Lifting her head she gave him a small, somewhat shy smile. "It's been a while for me."

He met her gaze through hooded eyes. "Would you believe me if I said likewise?"

Surprise jolted through her and her lips parted. Could he be serious?

Emmett let out a soft laugh and touched her cheek. "You needn't look so stunned, sweetheart."

"I just . . . I suppose I am." She shrugged and moved her hands over his chest. He was truly a beautiful man. "I can't understand why."

"I've always put career before women," he admitted.

"Not a bad philosophy. I do the same."

Her reply made her realize exactly what had just happened. And that she was still at work. Gods. Her eyes widened and she fumbled to get off him.

"I should return to work," she muttered. "Someone may realize I'm missing."

"Molly." He caught her hand before she could retrieve her dress. "Thank you."

Her stomach flipped, warmth swirling in her blood and she gave him a wide smile. Oh yes. This soldier could be quite the distraction if she let him be. So it would be best not to let this become more than a one-time event.

"Thank you, Emmett." Before she could stop herself, she leaned forward and pressed another kiss against his mouth. "I shall remember this moment for quite some time, I imagine."

Confusion flickered in his gaze, before he gave her a lazy nod.

"And I as well."

After Emmett had dressed and left the office, she slid the doors shut and leaned against the steel frame.

Pressing a hand against her chest, she tried to pretend her heart wasn't still all aflutter.

She'd had an itch and scratched it. She could go back to life as normal and work on increasing her traffic at the lodge. She was a businesswoman first and foremost.

Yes, life as normal was so much more . . . stable.

6

Brendon downed half his glass of aliaberry wine in one swallow and then slammed the glass back on the table.

What an absolute crap night. His mouth tightened and he glanced around the restaurant for Emmett. Where the hell was his friend?

Gods, he should've gone with his first instinct and just returned to his bedchamber and jerked off.

Even now his cock throbbed with the second denial from Nika. Or was it Rebecca? Who the hell knew at this rate? What he did know was that the little minx had his emotions twisted up into the worst damn knot. And his cock suffered a much harsher fate.

He should not want anything to do with her after what she'd pulled on him. Twice now! And yet he couldn't get her out of his mind. Couldn't forget the image of the blue-green eyes narrowed in passion. Or anger. No matter how she looked at him, it twisted him all up inside.

Damn. A woman had never affected him like this. Where

had he gone so wrong this time? He lifted his glass of wine again and took a smaller sip this time.

"Brendon, my friend," a voice boomed out. "How are you this fine evening?"

He lowered his glass, peering over the rim in dismay as Emmett approached the table positively beaming. What the hell? The man never beamed.

"How am I? I'm complete shit. And I'll not thank you for asking." Brendon narrowed his eyes. "Where have you been? And why do you look as though you've won the galactic lottery?"

"Hmm, perhaps I have in a way." Emmett sat down at the table and poured himself a glass of wine from the pitcher. "I have been . . . about."

"About what?"

Emmett threw his head back and laughed. After a moment he calmed and said quietly, "Indulging in a bit of feminine pleasure, honestly."

"You fucking jest!" Brendon roared.

"No. Not at all."

And by the expanding grin on his friend's face, Brendon knew Emmett spoke the truth. How was it that the man who'd proclaimed to not need a woman could have one on a whim, whereas he, who'd never had trouble getting laid, could not even gain a paltry hand job from his newest interest.

"Gods, I do not believe this," he muttered and drained the rest of his wine. "I'm going to need another glass. Who is she?"

"She is none of your business," Emmett fired back and took a sip of wine. "A gentleman never kisses and tells."

Brendon scowled.

If *he* had been less of a gentleman, he could have been fucking Nika's sweet little pussy right now. He'd known he could have had her. Could have kissed her until her knees weakened again, and then taken her against the wall. Because he knew with every fiber in his being that she would have let him.

And yet he hadn't taken that step. He'd instead walked away with a raging hard-on and a temper that could start a war.

Yes. Being a gentleman was quite overrated.

"Say, Brendon. Have you ever seen that man over there?" Emmett asked suddenly.

Brendon turned to look at the table Emmett gestured to and his gaze narrowed. He recognized one man. The one who stared back at them, his gaze alternating between black and a glowing red.

"Not sure," he murmured. "But possibly trouble."

Emmett scowled and turned his back to the group. "No doubt trouble."

"Something I should know about?"

Emmett seemed to hesitate and then shook his head. "Nothing I couldn't handle. He's a bounty hunter and a blood drinker, I know that much."

Brendon reared back in surprise, equally intrigued to see a legitimate blood drinker and to know that he was a bounty hunter. Likely he was hunting for the bounty Captain Teflick had warned him about.

"Let me know if you need help handling it. I'm certainly a bit bloodthirsty myself tonight."

"And why is that? What has your hide so chapped, my friend?" Emmett gave him a considering look. "Perhaps that woman?"

"Which woman?" he asked sharply.

"The one who had you all twisted last night as well."

"She's a witch," Brendon muttered. "I should simply tumble with the next woman who approaches me and expend my lust elsewhere."

Emmett arched a brow. "So why don't you, my friend?"

Brendon's gaze drifted around the room and landed on a female who sat with her friends. She watched him intently and, once realizing she had his attention, her mouth curved into an enticing smile as she trailed a hand over her cleavage.

"Why don't I, indeed," Brendon murmured and pushed his chair back. "Excuse me."

As he made his approach the woman rose to her feet and met him halfway.

"Hello," she said, her voice accented with a foreign lilt. "I'm Kelsie."

"Brendon." He reached out to touch a strand of her platinum hair. Too dry. So unlike Nika's soft blond—*gods, forget her!* "How would you like to take a walk with me, Kelsie?"

She giggled and nodded, looking at him from beneath heavily painted lashes. "Oh, I would *love* that."

"Splendid." He slid an arm around her waist and she snuggled up right under him.

His nostrils protested her cloying perfume and he turned his head to the left a bit to drag in clean air.

They left the restaurant, and he ground his teeth together, resisting the urge to just tell her never mind.

You've got a cock begging for someone warm, wet, and willing. And you've found her. You've fucked plenty of women. It should not be this difficult.

He slid his hand down her waist, squeezing her fleshy ass and she let out whiny groan. Whiny. Gods.

She slipped another arm around his waist and turned her head to kiss his neck.

"Mmm, you smell so good, Brandon."

"Brendon," he corrected her as her lips brushed the slow pulse in his neck.

Gods, instead of her increasing his arousal, he was quite shocked to realize his cock was actually shriveling.

The door to the lodge opened as they went to step outside. He looked up and his gaze collided with Nika's stunned expression.

Her cheeks flushed red as she took them both in, and for a moment he thought he saw a flicker of anger and hurt in them. And then it was gone, and her gaze was nothing but derisive judgment.

How dare she have the nerve to judge him after what she'd done this afternoon? Lifting an eyebrow, he brushed his lips across his companion's forehead.

And then they passed one another. Brendon and the girl—what was her name?—arrived out into the cool night air, and Nika was back inside the lodge.

He paused, hating himself for turning around, but unable to stop himself. Nika hadn't even looked back at him, though, just strode straight up the stairs, her fists clenched at her sides.

"So where did you want to . . . walk?" the woman asked and then let out another sharp giggle.

Gods, was she intoxicated?

"I don't," he answered briskly, before he realized the words were out. But once they were it just felt so damn right. "I've changed my mind."

She blinked in dismay. "You have?"

"I have. And I apologize."

"Oh." She gave a slow nod and then turned back toward the lodge door. "Well, then, more wine for me. Good evening to you, Brett."

Brendon watched her go without any remorse. Fuck. Nika had screwed him up but good. If he couldn't even bring himself to tumble with a perfectly willing—albeit drunken—woman, he must really be in trouble.

No. Apparently he wouldn't be able to move on to another woman until he had had Nika. And gods knew whether that would ever happen.

Frustration gnawed at his gut and he kicked a rock across the grounds.

Ridiculous. Utterly ridiculous. Muttering with disgust he pondered what the hell he was going to do with his night, since he obviously wouldn't be getting laid.

She was a fool! Nika sealed her door closed and ground her teeth together. And to think she'd actually thought to come back here tonight and apologize to him.

The bastard! Obviously Brendon was not a man used to hearing the word no. He had not even waited a few hours to find another willing woman. And the woman on his arm had seemed all too eager to spread her legs.

Admit it, Nika, you were never anything to him but a convenient object to fuck. Just like you were to your owners on Zortou.

Her stomach twisted with disappointment and self-disgust. She should have known better. Known she could never trust a man.

She needed to complete her mission and get the hell off this planet. Brendon was bad news. He'd been nothing but a distraction that she couldn't afford.

Nika fell to her knees beside the bed and tugged the hidden case out from beneath. Yes. Tonight she would make an attempt to gain the specimen samples.

She knew exactly how she would gain access to the compound, but the lab would be a harder nut to crack—especially seeing as how she'd barely managed to retain anything when Brendon had been working.

What she did recall was the high fence with spiked wire surrounding the lab. She'd observed it carefully, formulating the plan that would get her in.

Certainly it would not be easy, but it could be done.

It was what was inside that would be the challenge. But she loved a good challenge. She had proved herself on Tresden and damn it, she would prove herself here as well.

Tonight she would see just how well trained she was, indeed. Her blood pounded with the thought. She would not fail. Could not.

Pulling out her binding tape, she removed her dress and began the painful process of binding her breasts. It was needed. By the time she was through there wouldn't be a person on this planet who would mistake her for a female.

Nika moved swiftly, reaching around the soldier and slamming the damp cloth over his mouth. He reached up to grab her wrist, but before he could get a good grip, he slumped and hit the floor with a thud.

With gloved hands, Nika squatted down and pressed her face close to his, checking for signs that he breathed evenly. Yes.

Lifting one pant leg, she pulled free a preloaded syringe from the fastening at her thigh. Removing the cap with her teeth she rolled the soldier over and plunged the needle into his buttock.

Depressing the plunger, she injected him with the solution that would keep him unconscious for the next five hours.

She patted her hands down his body until she discovered the rectangular key fastened around the belt of his uniform. Plucking it free, she rose to her feet again and drew in a steadying breath.

That had been almost too easy.

Glancing around the lab, she moved forward with light footsteps. Her attire was loose enough to allow quick, silent movements. Every part of her was covered save for her eyes. And even those had been carefully masked with eye shields that disguised the color of her irises.

She approached the window to the lab itself and swallowed hard. It appeared empty. Fortunately no scientists were at work during the night hours.

This part would be a bit tricky. The key to the inner lab was made to fit in a specific lock. But the lock location was hidden. She'd known that and had hoped to discover the hiding place this afternoon while touring the lab.

But then Brendon had touched her, and she'd become a big mess of confusing emotions and hormones. Gods, she was ridiculous.

The thought of him and that woman in the lodge sent a wave of disappointment through her so sharp it had her throat tightening.

This is not the time, Nika. Get in and get out. If you do this right you could be off the planet within hours.

Lifting her head she ran her gloved hand across the wall of the lab. Looking for something. Unevenness in the panel. A hidden chamber. Anything.

Her finger brushed over a slight ridge, so small she almost missed it. Crouching down, she eyed the panel, pressing on each corner. When she hit the bottom left side the panel hissed inward, spinning around to display the keyhole.

Her pulse quickened and she licked her lips. By the gods, she'd done it. Gripping the key she'd lifted from the guard, she pressed it into the hole.

A series of beeps sounded in the lab, almost jarring in the quiet. And then another whine of noise came, signaling the door to the lab was opening.

She froze, realizing something was off. If the second whine of noise was the lab opening, what had the first beeps been from?

"Yates, where are you?" Footsteps sounded. "It's damn quiet in here."

No! Gods, what was *he* doing here?

Nika rushed to her feet just as Brendon rounded the corner. She only had a moment as his eyes narrowed and he reached for his weapon.

She charged him with a growl and launched into a sidekick, knocking his weapon down before he could activate his electro-mace.

"Son of a bitch," he cursed and crouched down into fighting position. "What did you do to that soldier back there?"

She didn't reply, dared not use her voice in any manner except the guttural roars she made while on the attack.

Brendon lurched forward swinging his fist hard at her head. She ducked and planted her foot in his ribs, sending him stumbling backward.

"Nice move, boy," Brendon taunted, gripping his side. "Did you learn that from your nursery instructor?"

He made fun of her size. Anger sparked in her gut, even as she tried to remind herself it was a good thing that he believed her to be a man.

She wished she could talk with him. Taunt him that he must have the stamina of a teenager to have finished so quickly with that girl to be here now.

But if she gave herself away, then she'd have to kill the asshole. And though the idea certainly held a small amount of appeal, she had no intention of taking a life unless it was absolutely necessary.

"What's the matter, kid," Brendon goaded, circling her. "Can't produce enough spunk of your own, so you have to steal someone else's?"

Oh gods, he had no idea how close he was. Her lips quirked beneath the mask.

Brendon swung at her head again, and when she went to block it he kicked her leg out from under her.

She fell to the ground, rolling to the right when he made an attempt to straddle her and pin her to the ground. From a distance she could pass as a skinny man, but hands on was stretching it.

"If you killed that soldier in the hallway, I *will* kill you." His words were perfectly calm as he advanced upon her again. "To hell with the orders to bring you in alive."

Bring her in alive? Had they been anticipating this mission? A shiver of unease ran down her spine. How come her instructor had not warned her of the possibility? Had Rachel known?

"You're worried now. Aren't you, boy?" Brendon gave a soft laugh and lunged at her. "You should be."

She stepped to the right, spinning into a kick that connected with his back.

He didn't stumble this time, didn't even make a sound of pain. Instead he was ready, bouncing back from the kick and landing one of his own against her ribs.

"Oomph." She stumbled back and grasped her side.

Pain ricocheted through her body, but she ignored it, adrenaline forcing her to remain in fight mode.

"Surrender," Brendon said softly and she saw the regret in his eyes. "I have no wish to hurt you, kid."

Nika could not say the same. She ground her teeth together. Gods, she wished she could grab another syringe and plunge it into him. Knock him out but good. But that would mean baring her leg for him to see, and he would not mistake her for a man after that.

She needed to get out of the lab. Get back to the lodge and recoup. Try for another night. Likely several nights, for she would need to discover a new plan of attack now that they were aware of her presence.

"Surrender. This is your last warning."

She shook her head slowly, knowing she had to fight dirty if she was going to escape.

He came at her again and she slammed her elbow into his face. When he roared in surprise and covered his eyes, she took the moment to jam her foot into his chest and send him flying back against the edge of the doorway.

His head connected with an unhealthy thud and he slumped to the ground.

Her stomach clenched and she swallowed with difficulty. She wanted to go to him, ensure he was not injured too severely. But she didn't have time to feel sympathy for him!

She looked at the lab, wondering if she could get inside and take the samples quickly. But already Brendon stirred on the floor, groaning as he made a move to rise.

Her unease faded. Gods, but the man was thick in the skull.

Nika spun away, fleeing the building and any chance of success.

"I have failed you, Rachel." Nika closed her eyes, her fingers clenching around the communication mobile. "Have failed Tresden."

"You have not failed me, dearest Donika. You have simply encountered your first trial," Rachel said sagely. "We knew this mission would be full of them."

"I know. I had just hoped . . ."

"To have success on your very first attempt? It's not always done, Donika. You put too much pressure upon yourself." Rachel paused. "But I must say it worries me a bit that they have been expecting our presence."

"They have no idea who we are," Nika assured her. "I am certain."

"Very good. Perhaps, though . . . we should use all means

possible to make this happen. To penetrate this lab." Rachel's voice turned thoughtful. "Would it be possible to acquaint yourself with someone who works there? Gain their trust?"

Nika stilled, felt a wave of cold and then hot rush over her as she thought of Brendon.

"I . . . there is someone I've met. He's a guard for the lab." She swallowed hard, wanting to lie but unable to. "He's quite taken with me."

"Donika, this is wonderful. It could be the exact means we need," Rachel said urgently. "You must encourage this soldier's advances. Do whatever it takes to earn his trust."

Whatever it takes. Nika's stomach churned and she sat down on the edge of her bed. "Are you . . . asking me to sleep with him, ma'am?"

"This is the mission you have trained for, Donika," Rachel said softly. "Often the means in which we succeed goes beyond fighting. In the past the chosen one has used seduction as a viable weapon. In fact, one of the injections you should have received before leaving was a form of birth control." She paused. "And surely with your history this seduction should not be a problem."

Nika flinched as if the other woman had slapped her, surprised that she would be so insensitive as to fling such an awful reminder in her face.

They wanted her to bed Brendon. Thought that since she'd been forced to act as a whore on her own planet, she would have no trouble doing the same here on Belton.

"Are you still there, Donika?"

"I am here." She forced the response out calmly.

"Are you unable to complete your mission?"

"No, ma'am. I will complete this mission." She barely hesitated and then added, "I will do whatever needs to be done to ensure the continuation of our kind on Tresden."

Rachel didn't respond for a moment, and Nika wondered if perhaps she was entertaining a woman again.

"I know you will, Donika," Rachel finally said. "If I hadn't believed in you to complete this mission, I wouldn't have sponsored you. It is best you do not contact me again unless absolutely necessary. There is too much risk."

"Yes, ma'am."

"Be well, Donika."

Nika held the communication mobile in her hand long after her sponsor had disconnected the call.

Gods. Would she have chosen this mission if she'd known seduction might be a part of it? Perhaps not.

But to sleep with Brendon . . . The idea sent both a rush of arousal and a wave of unease through her body.

She stood from the bed and rubbed her ribs, wincing at how tender they still were. Thankfully, she guessed them to be just bruised and not cracked.

Walking to the closet in the small room, she searched for another dress. Tonight she would begin a new part of the mission. One she could never have imagined. And one that might risk so much more than her safety.

7

"Your face looks awful, my friend." Emmett shook his head and slid the plate of yard bird wings across the table toward him.

"Thank you for the unwanted reminder." Brendon scowled and touched a hand gingerly to the black swollen area above his eye. Gods, he looked like he'd gone two rounds with a giant. "But it's all right. I think I may have broken a couple of the other man's ribs."

Brendon took one wing, sinking his teeth into the meat. His gaze wandered the room and once again he noticed the blood drinker sitting alone in a corner. Watching him. What an annoying creature.

Scowling at the other man, Brendon turned his attention back to the snack.

He'd almost skipped meeting his friend at the Crow's Nest for dinner. After the day he'd had the idea of going home and sleeping sounded all too enticing.

His morning had been full of meetings and the debriefing

about the incident last night. The entire lab was on high alert. Security would be tighter, more men would be stationed. The chances of someone getting past them again would be slim.

His lips curled in disgust. Talk about a major failure. He'd fucked up and good. Had his ass handed to him by a scrawny little boy.

Which was basically all the description he could give of the perpetrator this afternoon. The damn boy had been covered from head to toe. Even his eyes had been disguised by some damn eye shields that turned his irises black.

"Where is she?" Emmett muttered suddenly, slamming down his drink.

"Where is who?" Brendon grabbed another wing and took another swig of wine, hoping it would cure some of his surliness.

"Molly."

"Molly?" He arched a brow. "The owner of the lodge? I have no idea. Haven't seen her all night. Why do you ask?"

Emmett didn't answer, but his frown deepened.

"Gods!" Brendon sat back in his chair and laughed. "Was it her? Was she the one you—"

"Do *not* say it, my friend. Just close your mouth now."

Brendon laughed and lifted his hand in surrender. "Say no more."

Quite interesting, actually. Never could he have imagined the driven little lodge owner and Emmett becoming bed buddies. But now that the idea had been planted, it made perfect sense. They were both so serious and career focused. Perhaps the perfect couple, indeed.

"There she is," Emmett said suddenly.

"Who? Molly?" Brendon's lips quirked and he sipped another bit of wine.

"No. Your object of lust. Though I don't believe I know her name."

Brendon's fingers clenched around the glass of wine as he lowered it slowly back to the table. His gaze sought hers as she crossed the room.

Damn her. Once again, she looked gorgeous. She wore a thin red gown that clung to every sweet curve on her body. And she never looked away from him as she approached, her gaze confident, almost defiant.

She finally stood in front of him and gave a slight sniff. "A moment of your time so that I might have a word with you, sir."

It wasn't even a request, more of a demand. His irritation with her faded into something akin to amusement. Just who did this woman think she was dealing with?

"I think not," he murmured lazily. "If I give you a moment of my time, there will be no words needed."

Emmett let out a choked laugh next to him, which he quickly converted to a cough.

Her mouth tightened even as he saw the odd mix of heat and wariness in her gaze. "All right."

Brendon froze. "Pardon?"

"If those are your terms then I accept."

Anger flared hot in his belly. What the hell kind of game did she play now? He pushed back his chair and strode forward, grabbing her elbow.

"Take me to your room."

She didn't pull away or tell him to go to hell, simply nodded and turned to lead the way.

Still clutching her arm, he followed her. Confusion and anger warred inside him. If this were another attempt at cock teasing him, then she would have pushed him too far. Because the moment he stepped foot in her room, he had no intention of leaving until he'd thoroughly fucked her.

Watching her ass swish beneath the gown and imagining her supine and submissive had his cock jumping beneath his trousers.

She turned and made her way up the stairs, each step bringing him closer to her room. Before she reached the top of the stairs, he finally broke.

He pulled on her arm, spinning her around. "What game do you play?"

She gave him a slow smile and licked her lips, but her gaze was not so unperturbed. "I play no game."

The hell she didn't. He half suspected to go into her room and find someone there ready to assault him.

His jaw hardened and he exhaled harshly. "Lead on, woman."

Nika spun from him and strode on down the hall. He followed her, wary as she opened the door to her room. She strode in first and then turned, waiting for him to enter.

He entered slowly, one hand on his pocket-sized electro-mace. Glancing around the small quarters, he found it empty. Still suspicious, he closed the door and listened to the electronic lock click.

Then he lifted his head and met her gaze. In her eyes there was desire, but beneath it something else. Maybe even . . . resentment? But that would make no sense. Why would she resent him when she'd been the one to agree to his terms?

"Perhaps you'll tell me what happened to your face," she finally asked, her lips curling upward in amusement. "Was your lady friend last night a bit on the rough side?"

"No lady did this to me." His eyes narrowed at the reminder of what had happened at the lab. "Nor did I bed that woman last night."

He regretted the last admission when her expression slipped from derisive amusement to surprise.

"Why did you bring me here, Nika?"

She lifted one shoulder and pulled a strand of hair forward to wrap around her finger. "Because you requested we meet in my room."

"Yes. So I did." He stalked toward her slowly, waiting to see if she'd retreat. She did not, but held her ground quite solidly.

He caught her chin between his fingers and held her still. Hunger flashed in her gaze, replacing any sign of another emotion that gave him doubt, as she ran her tongue across her lips.

"Twice now you have left my cock in a dire state, love. It won't happen again."

She did not reply, but he saw the muscles in her throat work.

"What have you to say, Nika?"

For a moment she said nothing and then, still holding his gaze, she reached behind her and unfastened her dress. It slipped down her body, catching on one pert tit before pooling onto the floor.

The air hissed from his lips. Gods. It was amazing he didn't come in his trousers.

He let his gaze explore her body. Tall and slender, her breasts were perky, more than a good mouthful. He moved his attention lower, over her toned belly to the smooth lips of her pussy.

His cock pressed hard against his trousers, straining to get out. With a deft hand he freed himself, pulling his cock out and stroking the hard length.

"Gods, I want you. Turn around," he commanded softly. He would fuck her now, before she pulled some silly stunt and tried to run off again. "Lean forward against the bureau."

She swallowed hard, but obeyed, turning away from him. Her palms splayed on the wood surface, her ass pushing out toward him.

"I think we've had enough foreplay over the last two days," he murmured against her ear, pressing himself into the curve of her body. "Don't you agree, love?"

"However you want me, Lieutenant," she agreed in a breathless voice.

Her slim body trembled against him, despite her flirtatious words. She insisted this was no game, yet something felt not quite right.

His cock throbbed against her buttocks, and he ground his teeth together. Why the hell was he overanalyzing? He needed to be inside her. Now.

Brendon slid a hand down her back, his breath catching at how soft her skin was. He moved lower, before sliding a finger between her legs and inside her.

Her pussy was soaked, clenching around him as he added a second finger and worked them in and out of her tight channel. Her body was hot and slick, undeniably prepared for him. She let out a soft moan.

He pulled his fingers from her and placed his hand against her back, urging her to lean forward more against the bureau.

She complied, and he watched her ass rise higher, the swollen lips of her pussy in perfect view now. Gods, she was a sight. All moist and pink. And submissive.

Gripping his cock, Brendon placed the head of his erection between her legs and pushed an inch into her. He stopped for a moment to let the slick cream welcome his cock. To enjoy this second before he took her. Claimed her.

"Tell me no again," he challenged hoarsely. "Tell me you want me to stop."

"I don't want you to stop," she whispered, her voice cracking. "Fuck me, Brendon. Now."

Possessiveness and triumph slammed into him. Her words were all the encouragement he needed. He moved his hands to grip her hips and then, closing his eyes, plunged his cock deep inside her.

Nika let out a high soft cry in the quiet room. He barely heard it. Every part of him went taut with the pleasure of having her tight body surrounding his dick. *Finally*.

So blazing hot and wet. He sank deeper, stretching her, discovering her. Her walls hugged his cock, dragging him to her very core.

"Gods," he whispered when he finally was buried to the hilt. "You are tight, love. And so damn hot."

Her reply was a tiny moan, but no more words.

He drew in a slow breath and slid his hands around to her front, moving up until he covered her breasts with his palms.

Her nipples hardened and she pressed back against him with a soft gasp.

"Yes, Nika." He kissed the back of her neck and slid his cock out of her, before thrusting back deeper. "I think you like me fucking your sweet little pussy. Quite a bit more than you'd like to admit."

She didn't answer, but he could well imagine her biting her lip to keep from responding. It didn't matter. None of it did. Her body did the talking she wouldn't let her mouth do.

He squeezed her tits, remembering she'd liked it a bit harder when they'd been out on the trail.

"Oh!" Her body trembled, her sheath growing creamier around him.

Yes. Indeed, she liked it with an edge. Perhaps this was her game. A wordless, hard fuck against a dresser with someone who was almost a stranger.

And yet she didn't feel like a stranger to him. She felt like someone he'd waited his entire damn life for.

He groaned and thrust harder into her, pinching her nipples and kissing the back of her neck.

"*Please, Brendon.*"

Surprise ripped through him that she'd finally spoken. Or begged.

He abandoned one breast and moved his hand down her belly, stopping just above where their bodies were joined. He worked his middle finger into her damp folds and sought her clit.

The swollen nub throbbed when he touched it. Nika's body clenched around him and she gasped. He pinched the tiny pearl, rubbing it hard and soft, following the pattern of her breathing.

She gasped, her breaths coming out in shallow puffs.

"Yes," she whispered. "Gods, yes!"

"Come for me, Nika. Now," he commanded.

To his amazement, she did, letting out a long moan as she climaxed, her muscles clenching around him. Her release pushed him over the edge. His sac tightened and he growled, joining her in release, emptying himself inside her again and again as her body milked his cock.

He fell heavily against her, his own hands slapping down on the bureau next to hers.

His lips sought the nape of her neck, brushing against the damp flesh.

"Mmm," he murmured, pushing aside her hair. "That was definitely worth the wait."

She stiffened slightly and he winced, realizing how callous that may have sounded.

He slid away from her and placed a hand around her waist, turning her around to face him.

He caught her chin and tilted her head to look at him. Her cheeks were flushed red and in her eyes he saw the remains of her arousal, confidence, and yet a surprising amount of shyness.

His chest tightened with some soft emotion and he stifled it. Instead, he brushed his mouth gently across hers. "Let us shower together, love."

Wordlessly, she gave a small nod and placed her hand in his, following him to the bathing chamber.

* * *

The moons' light slipped through cracks in the steel shades. Nika stared at the sliver of light, unblinking. Brendon's arm thrown over her waist was a stark reminder of what she'd done.

Gods, this was a bit of a mess. Not that she'd slept with him. She'd known she would the moment Rachel had told her to. It was just that she'd enjoyed the sex. More than enjoyed it. She'd begged. Begged!

Her cheeks heated with the memory and she thanked the gods he slept peacefully. His body curved up close behind her.

Sex with her owners had been a forgettable experience. Their touch had been unarousing and any fondling pathetic. When they would penetrate her it would be over in moments, their small penises flaccid almost minutes into the act.

Pleasure had never been a part of her job. And yet tonight, when sleeping with Brendon should have been strictly business, it had been nothing *but* pleasure. The sex had been fast, and hard, and almost ruthless. And yet it had been hot. So wonderfully hot.

For a moment she'd forgotten why she was letting him fuck her, that it was her duty as the chosen one. Her reasons for joining with him had become only to satisfy her thirst for pleasure.

For the first time since she'd accepted this mission, fear built heavily inside her gut. But it wasn't the fear of failure. It was the fear of discovering where this *thing* with Brendon could lead.

Panic bubbled in her throat and she forced herself to take in a slow breath. Sex was never supposed to have been part of the deal. Violence, stealth maneuvers, and quick wits, yes. Sex, not so much.

She closed her eyes and muttered a quick prayer to the gods that she would get through this and not lose part of her heart to the man who lay beside her.

"You must sleep," he murmured suddenly, his voice drowsy.

Licking her lips, she blinked in surprise. "I did not realize I woke you. I apologize."

He gave a soft laugh and moved his hand over her belly. "Don't apologize, love. If you really can't sleep I know a way to entertain you."

8

Heat spread low in Nika's belly and her nipples tightened. The idea had far too much appeal than she cared to admit.

Brendon slid a hand up her belly to cup her breast. A moan gurgled in her throat and her pussy dampened.

His lips gently explored the area between her shoulder and neck, while his finger rolled her nipple.

She arched against him, and his cock jerked against her ass.

"I want you again, Nika," he murmured softly. "Only much more slowly this time."

He slid his hand off her breast and to her rib cage, pulling her onto her back.

Pain shot through her body as his firm touch grazed her bruised ribs. A soft cry escaped her before she could stop it, and she stiffened.

"Nika?" He sat up and looked down at her rib cage, his brows knit with concern. "What is it? Did I hurt you?"

"No, I . . ." Her pulse jumped with fear. She could not afford to raise his suspicion. "Yesterday afternoon I slipped in my room and hit the sill of the window with my side. I have my moments where I can be rather clumsy."

Something flickered in his eyes, as if he were remembering something.

Her unease heightened and she rolled onto her back beneath him, reaching a hand out to run down his chest.

"Did you not say something about entertaining me?" she murmured coyly.

Whatever thought had taken him disappeared as his gaze heated. He looked down at her and his lips curled into a smile.

"Yes, I did."

He lay back down on the bed, propping himself up on one elbow, in a way that displayed his sexy tattoo, which she'd noticed earlier.

"Was I too rough with you last night, love?"

A flush rose through her body and she lowered her gaze, issuing a soft laugh.

"Not at all."

In truth she had loved it. Loved how fast and hard he'd taken her. It had been passion unleashed. Wild and frenzied. And so intoxicating.

"I could not help myself," he said, trailing a finger around the swell of her breast. "I wanted you in a way I'd never wanted a woman. And after our moment on the trail, and in the lab . . . I was so certain you would change your mind."

"That was not kind of me," she agreed, and then confessed, "It was all so new to me. You are my first since Zortou. . . ."

Surprise registered in his expression and then a gleam of possessiveness. He leaned down and kissed the tip of her nipple. "I'm sorry for what you endured in your time as a Rosabelle. I cannot imagine how awful it was."

Heat stirred in her belly from his kiss. She lifted a shoulder in a slight shrug. "I was not beaten as horribly as some were.

My owners were brothers. They shared me and were . . . not good lovers. Or very friendly. But I endured."

"Beaten *as* horribly?" he muttered and then cursed, his gaze hardening in the moons' light. "It is not right for any person to own another. And you should not have had to endure anything."

It felt odd and yet a bit cathartic to discuss this with him. She'd never spoken of her past with anyone. Not even Rachel.

He trailed his finger onto the curve of her breast, circling the areola but ignoring the aching tip.

A tremble racked her body and she sighed. "But we all endure in some way or another. Do we not?"

"Yes. I suppose we do." He lowered his head and a moment later she felt his lips clasp warm and wet over her nipple.

Nika groaned, threading her fingers into his hair as he suckled her. This was madness. A delicious madness that she could not ignore.

Brendon slid one hand down her belly and a moment later his long fingers stroked into the folds of her pussy. Fire sizzled through her veins and she sighed, letting her thighs part farther.

His teeth caught her nipple, tugging hard. Pleasure shot in a direct line from her breast to the ache between her legs where his fingers explored.

He ran his finger from the edge of her entrance and up to her sensitive clit, circling the little bud and stoking the flames in her body.

His tongue flicked the tip of her breast, while his teeth continued a gentle tug.

Nika twisted on the bed, lifting her hips against his seductive touch. Her fingers explored the soft short strands of his hair.

Brendon's finger abandoned her clit and moved back down, pressing at the edge of her entrance. He circled the perimeter with maddening sweeps, until she let out a frustrated groan.

He gave a soft laugh and pressed his finger inside her.

She gasped, pleasure rocketing through her. "Gods, that feels wonderful."

He lifted his head and looked at where his finger moved inside her. "I was about to say the same. Your body welcomes my touch, love."

Yes, it certainly did.

Transferring his mouth to the other breast, he drew the nipple deep and suckled hard, each pull bringing more cream to her pussy.

He added a second finger to penetrate her, moving them in and out of her channel with sure, firm thrusts. The sounds of her wetness filled the room, heightening the erotic moment.

The sensation quickly spiraled, higher and higher, until she was so near to release. He pulled his fingers free to pinch her clit and she plunged over the edge of pleasure.

"Brendon!"

Her body quaked beneath him, her thighs tightening around his hand as he continued to squeeze her clit. She gripped his hair, gasping in air as she rode out the tremors.

A moment later she collapsed against the bed, her body weak from the intense spend.

Brendon released her nipple with a popping sound and gave a murmur of approval.

"I suppose I should clean up my mess now."

Mess? She frowned at him, not sure what he meant—until he slid down her body and buried his face between her legs.

His tongue probed the folds of her pussy, lapping at her cream.

"Yes," he murmured, and flicked his tongue into her again. "Quite the delicious mess."

Mmm. She hadn't thought it possible to become aroused so quickly after her spend, but she was right back on the path of pleasure.

She fell back against the bed, staring at the ceiling of the room and clutching the sheet. Each stroke of his tongue inside her, over her clit, lifted her body onto a sensual wave of ecstasy.

Her fingers clawed at the bedding, and she twisted against his mouth, barely comprehensible pleas spilling from her lips.

"Watch me," he commanded. "Watch my mouth on you."

Nika propped herself on her elbows to watch him and about came on the spot, the sight was so completely arousing.

His broad shoulders pushed her legs wide as his brown head moved between her thighs. His gaze lifted to meet hers just as he pulled his tongue from her, shiny with her juices.

The air became trapped in her throat as she watched him from half-closed eyes.

He smiled and licked his lips, before bringing his finger down to rub her clit again. Holding the folds of her pussy apart, his head dipped and then his tongue flicked over the sensitized nub.

Both of his hands slid to cup her ass and bring her snug against his mouth. Again and again, he licked her clit, before closing his lips around it and suckling.

"I . . . oh gods . . ." Her ass clenched in his large hands and she screamed. "Yes! Brendon!"

Her stomach clenched and her toes curled as she climaxed again. The air left her body on a rush and every color of light flashed in her head.

Brendon kissed the insides of her thighs before sliding back up her body.

"You taste fucking amazing," he murmured against her ear, his palm covering her breast again. "You feel even more amazing surrounding my cock."

His words registered as the head of his cock nudged between her thighs, seeking out her opening.

Bracing his hands on both sides of her body, he lifted himself above her and thrust himself home.

Nika fell back on the bed, her nipples tightening once more. Gods, the way he filled her. And the pressure as he sank deep into her body was exquisite, like nothing she'd ever experienced.

Brendon groaned, sliding farther still until he hit the point inside her where it almost became pain. Gods, she loved it with an edge.

He pulled back out of her, each slide of his cock against her swollen channel creating the most delicious friction. At the entrance to her body he paused and then slid back inside, faster now.

That became their rhythm. Slow out, fast in. Her hips lifted to meet each thrust, bringing him deeper. At one point, he was wedged so tight against her cervix, she was sure he had gotten himself stuck.

He didn't move for a moment, his eyes so tightly closed. "Nika, I must surely be in nirvana."

She squeezed her inner muscles around him and enjoyed watching the spasm of pleasure that swept across his face. She slid her arms around to grip his ass while simultaneously wrapping her legs around his back.

"Fuck me, Brendon. Hard," she whispered. "Make me come from your cock alone."

He growled and pulled out of her, slamming back faster this time. The rhythm of his thrusting grew more chaotic, faster and harder. His sac slapped against her ass, resonating in the room with the sound of their bodies colliding.

Her body jerked on the mattress, pushing higher from the impact of his penetrations.

Her stomach clenched and her muscles gripped his cock. She squeezed him hard. Harder still. Until the pleasure rocked up to her clit and she exploded again.

She screamed, riding the wave of pleasure, her nails digging crescents into his ass while he fucked her relentlessly, pounding into her and likely bruising her inner thighs.

"Nika," he cried out and buried himself to the hilt again.

A moment later she felt him come warm and thick inside her. He fell heavy on top of her, pressing her deep into the mattress with the sheer weight of his body.

And she loved it. Loved the delicious feeling of having his hard, damp body on top of her.

Her hands moved over his back almost to soothe his ragged breaths.

"I think," she murmured, "you may have just worn me out. I might just be able to sleep now."

He gave a soft grunt in response and nuzzled her neck. She closed her eyes with a soft laugh. His cock went flaccid inside her, but still he did not move.

She could feel the fast beating of his heart, knew it must mimic hers pressed beneath him.

Closing her eyes, she knew she'd crossed some invisible line she'd vowed not to. And yet it was a bit hard to care right now.

"Though I hate to say it, I must leave soon." Brendon spoke the words he knew neither wanted to hear.

Sunlight flickered through the cracks in the blinds and he knew it was close to when he was scheduled to be on duty.

Nika lay next to him, her head on his chest. She hadn't spoken, but he knew her to be awake. They'd maybe managed a few hours of sleep after he'd last taken her.

She finally lifted her head from his chest and sighed, looking away.

"Yes, I suppose it's about time."

Brendon's stomach clenched as emotion swept through him. She looked so lovely in the morning. Swollen red lips and sleepy eyes. Blond hair tousled and falling around her naked shoulders . . . His gaze moved lower, over her pert breasts, and then stalled on the darkish bruise on her ribs. He'd been so caught up in the moment last night, he'd failed to take a good look at it.

He frowned at the angry-looking mark. How had she said it had occurred?

Unconsciously, his hand rose to touch the bruise above his own eye.

"It looks terrible," she said softly.

It took him a moment to realize she spoke of *his* bruise.

"Yes, fortunately it shall fade." He grimaced.

"I'm sorry."

He lifted an eyebrow and tugged on a strand of soft hair that curved around her breast.

"No need to apologize, love, it's hardly your fault."

She gave a half smile in response.

"Gods, I wish I had a free morning," he murmured, flicking the strand of her hair over the dark nipple.

"I as well." She smiled and tugged her hair back, sliding off the bed. "But I have much to do today, too."

"Do you?" He slid out of bed and located his uniform. Gods, he would have to shower at the compound. "And what might that be?"

"And wouldn't you like to know?" she murmured coyly. "Will I see you later? Or should I plan on this having been one night of passion?"

Her question knocked the wind from him. He had been so determined to bed her and rid her from his mind, so convinced fucking her once would do the trick. But watching her now, his cock stirred again and he realized how wrong he was.

"Somehow"—he growled and crossed the room—"I think one night with you would never quite be enough."

Cupping the back of her head, he lowered his mouth to hers.

Her lips parted on a sigh and her fingers slid up to grip his shoulders.

His tongue swept deep, finding hers and rubbing softly. When he lifted his head a moment later, her eyes were closed and she leaned into him.

Gods, if his ass wasn't already in enough trouble, he might have considered staying in bed with her and arriving late to duty.

"Go," she scolded, opening her eyes and swatting him playfully on the shoulder. "Find me this evening and we can dine with one another."

"I will want to do far more than dine," he muttered and then dropped another hard kiss upon her lips. "Until this evening, love."

Nika spent a good amount of the morning lounging in bed and watching the teletron. When her stomach began to growl, she finally rose and showered.

She walked downstairs to the restaurant, with surprisingly light steps. She even caught herself humming under her breath. Who would have known one night could affect her like this? Interesting.

She glanced around for an empty table and located one near the window. She'd just settled down when something flung itself across the table from her. Or someone.

Nika reared back, her eyes widening in surprise as she stared at Molly's intense expression.

"Rebecca, please, you must advise me."

Nika frowned, for the quickest second forgetting her alias. Gods. She was a liability right now. She needed to get her head out of the clouds and back to reality.

"Good morning, Molly. What did you need me to advise you on?"

Molly's gaze darted around the room. "I fear I have made a bit of a mistake. I have . . . forgive me if I am taking liberties in speaking so frankly with you. But I have become intimate with a man I probably shouldn't have."

Nika leaned back in her chair. Now didn't this just sound familiar?

"I have very few friends," Molly rushed on. "And I really need a confidante right now. Do you mind terribly?"

"Not at all. Who is this man? And why do you regret it?"

"Oh, I could not *regret* it. It was such a wonderful and—trust me—well-needed moment." Molly sighed and fidgeted with a strand of hair. "But I am not looking for a serious relationship with a man. Not at this time. And I fear Emmett is."

Emmett. That name sounded vaguely familiar.

"Have you told him this?"

"No, I have not spoken with him. I have been quite awful, truthfully, with my avoidance of him." Molly paused and gave her a thoughtful look. "You may know of Emmett. He is the darker man who comes in to dine with Brendon."

"Oh." That was why the name had sounded familiar.

"Speaking of, have you worked things out with him yet? Brendon?" Molly leaned forward. "I have never seen him so intrigued by a woman as he is with you."

Nika's cheeks warmed and the vision of Brendon bending her over the bureau last night filled her head. "Yes. We have . . . worked things out."

"Oh." Molly's eyebrows rose. "Indeed you have. He is a good man. You should give him a chance."

Likely, he was a good man. And Nika was only using him. Guilt stabbed suddenly in her gut and she looked away.

"Molly, might I order some food? I have yet to eat breakfast. And then we should continue our talk."

"Of course!" Molly groaned and rushed to her feet. "Gods, where are my manners? You walked in for food and I attacked you for companionship."

"And I enjoy your companionship. Truly." And it disturbed her more to realize she did not lie.

Molly laughed and winked. "But food along with it would be lovely. Say no more. I'll return with the house special."

After the other woman disappeared, Nika was once again alone at the table. And she realized with dismay that she didn't care for it much. She enjoyed having someone to talk with.

The hairs on the back of her neck prickled, and she lifted her gaze to look across the room.

A thick man in the corner sat hunched over the table, watching her intently.

Nika held his gaze—were his eyes really glowing red?—but it never wavered from her. She finally looked away, a sense of unease heavy in her stomach.

"All right." Molly breezed back in with a plate of food and cup of water. "Yard bird eggs, bread, cheese. I hope it is sufficient."

Nika's stomach growled again, and she gave Molly a grateful smile. "It is more than enough. Thank you."

She lifted a round piece of white cheese and ate a generous bite.

"Tell me more about Emmett," she urged after drinking a sip of water.

Molly's cheeks flushed. "He is very sweet. Truly a very good man. I just . . . have no time for one."

"Yet you had time to bed him?" Nika regretted the words the moment they were out. "I'm sorry, how callous of me. I'm afraid that comes with the companionship. I tend to say what is on my mind."

Molly laughed and shook her head. "No, you are quite right. And yes, I bedded him. But it was not planned. And nor do I regret it." Her expression turned whimsical. "How could I?"

Nika nodded. She understood all too well. Lifting a boiled egg, she broke it in half and stabbed a bite with her eating utensil. "Out of curiosity, why do you have no time for a man?"

"Because I run this lodge alone," Molly said after a sigh. "My husband, before he died, had let it fall into a dismal state. There was no hope for it. I brought it back from sure death. It thrives, except for during the winter. Running this place is my life. And unfortunately, that means I have little time for anything else."

"You certainly seem to have created a miracle, then. For it's quite popular now." Nika leaned forward and grabbed her water again, but her ribs brushed the table and she winced. Reaching down, she rubbed the small area.

"What have you done to yourself?" Molly asked. "Are you hurt?"

Nika bit back a groan, realizing she needed to be more careful. "No, it's just a bruise. I fell the other day."

She glanced around and her gaze once again landed on the man in the corner.

Still he watched her. What was his problem?

"Do you know that man in the corner, Molly?" she asked softly. "No, do not turn around."

Molly's brows rose and she licked her lips. "The one with red eyes?"

"Yes. You do know him, then?"

The other woman's expression darkened. "He is a customer staying at the lodge. A blood drinker from another planet."

"Gods," Nika breathed.

She'd heard of the alien planet whose residents, it was said, drank blood. She somewhat feared it, which she knew was ridiculous. These alien blood drinkers had never caused trouble on planets but their own. So really, she knew she should not worry. And she knew better than to species profile. Especially seeing as she herself came from a background that was a bit controversial.

"I do not like him," Molly confided, leaning forward. "He makes my skin tingle—and not in a good way! Truth be told, he groped me the other day, and fortunately Emmett intervened. That's actually what led up to Emmett and me . . ." She cleared her throat. "Yes, well, you understand I'm sure."

"I do." Nika covered Molly's hand with her own. "And I am sorry the stranger assaulted you. Surely you can remove him from your lodge?"

"It is winter. Already business is slow. I can't afford to remove him." Molly lowered her eyes. "He has been warned by Emmett and will likely try nothing more. Of this I am sure."

Nika cast a worried glance at the man again, noting he still watched them, eyes narrowed. Another chill ran down her spine.

"I hope you are right, Molly."

"Oh, Rebecca, I am so fortunate to have you come to our city at such a time. Truly, I feel at ease calling you a friend in just a short amount of time."

"And I as well." Guilt pricked in Nika's gut, but she forced a smile. Molly knew so little about her, and what she did know was not entirely true.

"When do you leave? To go home to . . . where are you from again?"

"Glorus." The lie spilled all too easily from her lips.

"Right. Now I remember. And you are visiting a cousin stationed at the compound here."

"Yes." Nika pressed the plate away from her, finding her appetite had suddenly diminished. "Tell me, do you intend to speak with Emmett about your situation?"

Molly reached for a piece of cheese from the plate and took a bite. "I'm not sure. Do you think I should?"

"Most likely." Nika murmured and then her eyes widened as she looked beyond Molly. "And perhaps now would be the time, as he's approaching."

"Oh!" Molly pushed back her chair and spun around, but Emmett was already upon them.

"Thank you for breakfast, Molly, please charge it to my room." Nika stood from the table and squeezed her friend's hand quickly in support. "Find me later. I will be out walking."

9

Emmett was momentarily distracted by the thin blonde who scooted past him. So this was the woman who'd kept Brendon until the early hours of the morning.

"I thought you would be on duty," Molly said quietly and turned, walking past him.

"I am not scheduled today." Irritation flickered inside him as he turned and followed after her.

Like an animal chasing a female in heat.

"I see. Well, it must be nice to have a free day. Have you any special plans?"

He caught her arm and turned her, his nostrils flaring. "Yes. To find you and see what is going on in that little head of yours."

Guilt flickered in her eyes before it disappeared and she once again looked calm and unruffled.

"Oh the usual things, I suppose. The finances, how to keep my lodge full, whether I have enough aliaberry wine to last—"

"That is *not* what I meant, and you well know it." Emmett stepped forward until they were just a breath apart.

Molly cast a quick glance over at the receptionist, who watched them curiously.

"In my office, Emmett. Now, if you would."

He didn't even protest that she'd just ordered him around like he was an employee, just strode after her into the room he'd fucked her in the other day.

Even now, his gaze was drawn to the sway of her round hips. The slight bounce of her ass. His cock hardened, and he bit back a groan.

The door hissed shut behind them, and she turned around, irritation clear on her face.

"I have a reputation to maintain," she said firmly. "And I would appreciate it if you would help me keep it upstanding."

"You leave me no choice, Molly. You have avoided me like I bring some sort of plague." He thrust a hand through his hair and glared. "Tell me what the problem is? Do you regret what happened?"

"Yes."

He flinched at having his fears confirmed. And then her face fell and she shook her head.

"Wait. No, I lie to you. I cannot regret what we did," she said softly. "But I regret the situation it has left us in."

His jaw hardened. "And that would be?"

"I'm not sure entirely. But, it is awkward." She hesitated and then blurted, "I cannot have a relationship with you, Emmett."

He blinked, certainly not prepared for that confession. He wasn't entirely certain he wanted a relationship, but then he couldn't be sure he didn't want one either. But if she was squeamish about the idea, he'd certainly slow things down for her.

"You do not want a relationship," he repeated and walked slowly toward her.

She shook her head and licked her lips. "No. I haven't the time for one."

"Nor do I."

Her mouth parted in surprise and she didn't reply for a moment. Then her gaze narrowed suspiciously. "Truthfully?"

"Truthfully."

"Then what do you want from me?"

He just wanted her. He hadn't thought much beyond that.

"Emmett, I must return to work. There are those who would notice that I've brought a man into my office and for how long." Her voice had turned wary and she made to move past him.

"Wait." He caught her wrist, tugging her back toward him. "I cannot say what I want from you. Only that I want you."

Amusement flashed in her gaze and then her lips curved into a wry grin. "Well, at least you are honest."

"Have dinner with me tonight?" When she opened her mouth to protest he touched a finger to her lips. "It is dinner"—and possibly more delicious sex—"not a relationship."

She bit her lip and watched him through narrowed eyes, then gave a sharp nod. "If I can find someone to watch the front desk, then yes. I will dine with you."

"Find someone," he commanded softly. "You will not regret it."

Nika wandered the edge of the compound, exploring more of the trail than she previously had the opportunity to see.

The weather was chilly, and she was glad she'd thought to grab a jacket from her room. She walked for almost an hour before she spotted a lake off in the distance.

Her pulse quickened at the sight and she increased her stride. Each breath of fresh air she drew in was a reminder of how far she'd come.

On Zortou as a Rosabelle, the planet had been so polluted that the citizens had not been allowed outside for more than brief periods at a time. And a Rosabelle had never been given the right to leave her owners' home. Any time outside could damage such a commodity. And that's exactly what she'd been to them.

On Tresden, even though she had every right to explore the planet, she had rarely left her training facility. Perhaps it had been habit. Or maybe it had simply been her drive to succeed in her training that she never took breaks.

But now, while walking outside here on Belton, she regretted that she hadn't made the time.

She reached the lake's edge and removed her sandals, dipping a toe in the water. Frigid indeed. Cool and wet, it sent shivers through her body. It was invigorating, though. Those that might be watching would call her insane to see her wading in the icy water.

A few feet away she spotted a path just beneath the surface, which was almost transparent in appearance. Quite astounding, really: a path that floated beneath the water. Would it truly hold the weight of a human?

She let out a soft laugh and shook her head. She had no desire to find out right now.

Looking over the water, a pang of longing swept through her.

What would it be like in the summer? To swim in the lake? Her mouth twisted. Well, if she knew how to swim. Perhaps that would be something she would learn to do when—

Her stomach clenched and she blinked. Gods, how quickly she forgot. Once this mission was completed, life would not go on as normal. She would gain the samples and send them back to Tresden. After that, depending on how well she completed her mission, her life would change. And at the rate she was going, her life would have to be stripped down and rebuilt.

Already she had left too many clues. She would need to start anew, with a fresh identity. Perhaps even a new face.

"You wish to swim?"

Nika spun around, already on the defensive, one hand raised to deliver a hit.

The man in front of her upped her anxiety, but did not appear to be a threat. At the moment.

She lowered her arm and met the red gaze of the man from the restaurant. He was not a tall man, but larger in girth. Black hair covered his head in patches; he appeared to have lost some. His overall impression was not pleasant.

"No, I do not. Did you follow me, sir?"

"Like you, I took a walk." He smiled and took a step toward her.

His scent was quite rancid. She resisted the urge to wrinkle her nose, but held her ground. He tried to intimidate her. But why?

"Quite a coincidence that we should both end up miles from the lodge, though, is it not?" She saw no reason to be coy.

"I hear you are visiting the city to see a cousin?"

How had he heard that? Her gaze moved over his face, seeking the answers her gut already told her. Because he was a blood drinker. It was quite likely—and gods, she was a fool for not realizing it earlier—that the man had extra sensitive hearing. How much of her conversation had he overheard with Molly?

"I think that is none of your business."

"Actually, it is very much my business." He stepped closer to her, and this time she could not help but step backward.

Her feet brushed the cool water again as unease rushed through her. *Very much his business?*

Do not be intimidated by this filth, Nika. You could kill him in half the time it would take him to count to ten. If he could count that high.

"What brings you to Belton?" she inquired back.

"I hunt."

"You hunt?" She lifted a brow, trying to appear that his answer had not concerned her further.

"Yes," he said softly and pleasure flickered across his face. "I enjoy the hunt. Watching the defeat in those I chase, right before I go in for the . . . kill."

Did he kill humans? Drink their blood? It was what the legend of blood drinkers proclaimed. A wash of cold swept through her and only part of it was due to her feet going numb in the lake.

"Interesting. If you fancy the sport." She stepped to the side and around him, back onto the safety of the shore. "I myself loathe hunting."

"Pity. You should try it, you may change your mind."

"Doubtful," she scoffed and slid her feet into her sandals again. "If you'll excuse me I must return to the lodge."

"I shall walk with you."

"Thank you, but I prefer to walk alone."

"Ah, but it is not safe, ma'am." He turned to follow her. "There are all kinds of evil that lurk, just waiting to pounce on a helpless woman."

"You needn't worry, as I am hardly helpless." She did not add that he was likely the evil lurking.

"Not helpless? And what training do you have?"

Another stab of unease. This man asked far too many questions.

She didn't answer; instead she quickened her pace, hoping that if she ignored him he might disappear.

"What does your cousin do in the military?" He came abreast of her.

"I cannot make it more clear," she finally snapped, turning a hard glare on him. "I have no wish for your company or conversation. Leave me be."

His smile came slow, but in it he exposed two long canine teeth.

I will not be intimidated.

"As you wish." His steps slowed. "Though I'm sure we shall chat again."

"Let's hope not," she muttered and turned away, her steps quite a bit quicker as she fled back to the lodge.

Leo watched her run away and his gaze narrowed. Excitement and lust mingled in his blood.

She was not overtly feminine, her body more toned than with luscious curves. No, her curves were more slight. She was lean and with a lovely face.

Gods, it would be a thrill to fuck her, if he allowed himself the opportunity. He'd been without female companionship since leaving Multron and Bernadette behind—though he had to admit he welcomed the break from his pet human; she'd begun to get on his nerves lately.

He watched as the woman—Rebecca, was it?—disappeared from his vision, and he began to walk again. Could it even be possible? That the man the Planetary Army of Belton put a bounty on was really a woman? A woman who stole specimens and fought and defeated trained soldiers.

Quite interesting. Interesting, indeed.

His gut told him he was on to something. That it was too much of a coincidence that she had a rib injury and one of the soldiers had mentioned inflicting a wound in the same area on the thief.

His lips curved into a smile and he flicked his tongue over one sharp incisor. He hoped it was her. Because if so he would enjoy breaking her. Enjoy her pleas that he not turn her over to the military.

Beneath his trousers his cock stirred, and he resisted the urge to reach down and stroke it. Until he could prove she was the thief and had her in his possession, he could not touch her.

But it mattered not. There were other women willing to let him slake his lust between their legs.

Being a blood drinker apparently aroused as many women as it made fear him. The former was the case with Bernadette, who'd followed him back to Multron after he'd done work on another human planet.

But for now, he needed to satisfy his desires and touching Rebecca was off limits. Too bad that plump little lodge owner had turned him down, though. She would have been a great fuck to pass the time.

He tilted his head as he walked, already envisioning her without the dress. Yes, she'd be quite fun to bed.

Perhaps there was still time to convince her. She might be one that protested until you touched just the right spot on her body, and then she'd be begging like a pooch.

Hmm. The idea had appeal. He quickened his pace, already considering how he'd go about this.

"I thought about you quite a bit today."

Nika's heart tripped as she glanced up at Brendon. "Did you, now?"

"I did." He caught her hand as they walked to a park near the lodge. "There was little else to do. The forensic specialists scoured the lab again for evidence."

Nika stumbled, felt the hairs on the back of her neck lift. "Oh? What happened?"

He hesitated and touched his eye. "Actually, it was how I came by this. There was an attempted break-in at the lab."

She feigned surprise and made a cluck of sympathy. The sympathy was not so much feigned. The wound above his eye truly did look awful. And she'd been responsible for it.

"Did they catch the person?"

"Not yet. Hence the forensic search."

Her throat grew tight.

"Enough about me. What have you done with yourself today?" he asked.

Forcing words out through the tension in her throat, she murmured, "I had breakfast with Molly. Spent an hour working on my report."

"This report—"

"And then the strangest thing happened," she rushed on, knowing he'd been about to ask about her work. And gods, it was nothing but a lie. She couldn't bear to keep lying. "I went for a walk, and I was followed."

Brendon stopped, turning to face her with his expression guarded. "Who followed you?"

"I cannot be certain. All I know is he comes from Multron. I believe him to be a blood drinker."

The air hissed out from between Brendon's teeth. "He *followed* you? Why? Did he harm you?"

"He did not hurt me." She bit her lip. "But he made me quite uncomfortable and said some very off remarks."

"Such as?"

Knowing she could hardly bring up him mentioning her nonexistent cousin, she simply shook her head.

"It doesn't matter. I was just surprised he followed me. You seemed to realize whom I spoke of. Do you know the man?"

"No. I do not know him personally. But I have heard he is a bounty hunter visiting the planet on business."

"A bounty hunter," she repeated, her pulse quickening.

The military would not have put out a bounty on her head, would they?

"You look pale, love. Are you still up for a walk in the park?"

"I am." She pressed a hand to her forehead and forced a smile. "'Tis nothing but a bit of a head cold."

"If you are certain."

"I am."

And she was certain that she needed to keep herself focused. She could not afford to be distracted by fear. Or by passion. And gods, she'd certainly let the latter become a diversion.

Out of the corner of her eye, she glanced at Brendon again. He was nothing more than a means to an end—and she would do best to remember that. If seducing him and being his lover resulted in pleasure, then so be it. But it was still nothing more than part of her job requirement.

Her internal conversation was just the spark she needed to light the fire under her. It reminded her how much was at stake.

She squeezed her hand around Brendon's and brightened her smile. "I am just thrilled to be spending more time with you. Though I must confess, since your admission about the break-in at the lab, I am worried for your safety. Do you work alone?"

He laughed softly and raised her hand to his mouth, brushing his lips across the back of her knuckles.

A tremor of pleasure seared through her blood.

"I used to. But they have raised security since the attempt."

"Have they? So there are more of you working now?"

"Yes. Three soldiers per shift."

Three. That would certainly pose more of a challenge.

"And do you usually work during the day?"

"Most of the time, yes." He hesitated, turning them off the trail and toward an open park. "The night of the attack I had volunteered to cover the shift of a fellow soldier."

"I see." Her mouth tightened. "Quite unfortunate you happened to be there at the time of the attack. I hate that you were hurt."

"Hurt, but fortunately not killed."

She bit her lip, just before she could ask how the other soldier fared. The one who she'd knocked out.

"Were you alone that night? The only person harmed?" she asked instead.

"No. There was another soldier on duty, the man I had come to relieve. The thief had him out cold." Brendon's voice hardened. "For a moment I thought him to be dead."

"How terrible. But he is well now?"

"Yes, though somewhat humiliated to have been taken down so easily."

A swell of amused laughter bubbled in her throat, but she quickly snuffed it out.

She cleared her throat and said lightly, "You know, we never had a complete tour of the lab. If I came in to do another one we could spend more time together while you're working."

"I like the way you think." He grinned and winked at her. "Perhaps tomorrow?"

"Only if you're not too busy."

They stopped in the middle of the open field and she breathed in the cool crisp air. There were not many people about, save for a family that helped a toddler down a sky slide.

Her gaze moved up to the slide high in the air and the lift that would take the child to the top. Her mouth curled into a soft smile as the toddler and mother exited the lift and sat down on the slide. A moment later they sailed down the clear slide, which was not quite invisible, for it shimmered in the fading sunlight.

"It looks fun, does it not?" Brendon asked.

"Indeed. I have to confess that, more so, I'm intrigued to see children. On Zortou, there were none."

"I had forgotten. Your generation was the last to be born on that planet. And among you, only a handful of females," he murmured sympathetically. "Will you be able to have children of your own some day? Or did they . . ."

"Yes, I will be able to if I want to. On Zortou they gave us injections regularly that would keep us from becoming pregnant. Nobody wanted more men on the planet and, once it was discovered that's all that were being birthed, they put an end to it."

The toddler squealed as he reached the end of the long slide and hurried back toward the lift.

"You said you could have children if you want to. Do you?"

Did she want children? She blinked, having not even considered the possibility. "I had not really thought about it. I'm not sure I would be the mothering type."

"I'm not so certain about that." Brendon touched her shoulder, turning her so that she now faced him. His pensive gaze searched hers.

Her cheeks flushed with color and she slid her gaze away from his. She would likely never be a mother, though. To do so would require being intimate with someone. That in itself rarely happened—with this mission being the exception. And as Rachel had informed her, she'd been given the injection to prevent pregnancy.

She watched the child and mother reach the top of the slide again. Something inside her softened, twisted a bit. Being a mother was likely a wonderful thing. . . .

Nika started with dismay, stumbling backward at her own soft thoughts. Gods, what was wrong with her? Thinking about motherhood now? Truly?

"You look quite terrified," Brendon teased, "though I can understand. The idea of being a parent daunts the best of us. Myself included."

"Yes, well. I cannot quite see it ever happening with me," she said tightly.

"Are you on an injection schedule now?" he asked softly. "I did not use any protection."

"I am," she murmured and decided this topic needed to end. Like, two minutes ago.

Turning fully in his arms, she slid her hands over his chest. "Though all this talk about procreating has made me quite excited about the process."

He arched a brow and his gaze settled on her mouth. "Indeed?"

She let her tongue dart out to wet her lips. "Indeed."

"I had thought to invite you onto the slide with me," he murmured. "But perhaps we should indulge in a different form of entertainment?"

Nika let out a burst of laughter. "We are too large for the slide. It's only for children, silly."

"Nonsense." He scoffed and then stepped back, grabbing her hand again. "I make it a habit to ride it at least once a week."

"You jest!" She laughed, but didn't fight him as he tugged her toward the lift.

"Never. We shall enjoy the slide and have a childhood moment. And then once back at the lodge"—he turned and growled against her ear—"we shall enjoy a more adult moment."

Brendon squeezed into the boxed lift with her and she was suddenly forced quite close to him. His hard muscles pressed into the soft curves of her body.

Licking her lips, she confessed, "I am not sure what excites me more."

"Why not both?" He slid his hands past her hips and squeezed her bottom lightly.

Heat spread through her body. Her nipples tightened, pressing against his solid chest.

She let out a soft gasp as the lift rose sharply into the air and she pressed her head against his shoulder. The wind brushed against her cheek the higher they rose.

He moved one hand up to rub her back and pressed a kiss against her forehead.

"Having you this close to me makes me wish we had skipped the slide," he muttered in her ear. "For what I want to do to you right now surely is not appropriate for the eyes of children."

She lifted her head, her eyes dancing with amusement. "The slide will take but a moment and I do so want to experience it. What we do after may take all night."

"Is that a promise, love?"

"Or a threat. How would you feel if I bound you?"

He gave a soft laugh. "And to think I've been thinking of asking you the same thing."

10

Her pulse jumped. She'd been teasing, but the look in his eyes indicated he had not.

The lift jerked to a halt and she swallowed hard.

"Time to go down now."

Go down. The way he said it left no doubt of the double meaning. And at the moment, for the first time in her life, she actually had the desire to take a man's cock in her mouth. Not any man's, but Brendon's. Never with her owners had she enjoyed the chore. Quite the opposite.

"Come, love." His heated gaze ran over hers. "Let us slide and be on our way back to your room,"

Her cheeks reddened and she gave a quick nod, turning and exiting the lift onto the slide.

The sudden realization of how high up they were sent a wave of dizziness through her.

"Gods, we are quite a bit in the air, are we not?" she asked, her voice tight.

How had she not realized her fear of the height would be so great?

"Easy, love. I'm right behind you. Just settle onto your bottom, and I'll slide my legs on either side of yours."

She sat gingerly, gripping the edge of the slide's high walls. Truly, there was no danger of falling off, but still, being able to see under her and over the slide—since it was clear—sent a wave of excitement and terror through her.

Brendon sat down behind her and the slide wobbled slightly, ripping a gasp from her.

"It's all right. It's quite safe." He slid a hand around her waist and urged her to lean back against him.

She did, letting her head rest against the hard curve of his shoulder.

"Ready?"

"No, but I don't suppose I have any choice now."

"Not at all, seeing as the toddler is again on the lift at this very moment."

She bit out a hoarse laugh. Surely if a child could do this, then she could.

"One," he began. "Two."

Before he could say three, he'd pushed them free and they swept downward on the slide at breakneck speed.

Nika shrieked as the ground rushed closer with each passing second. Her hair whipped back from her face and her nails dug into Brendon's legs. The exhilaration and fear combined to make her pulse race and give her a complete feeling of being weightless.

She yelled the whole way down, clutching Brendon until they came to a stop at the bottom.

"Gods!" She laughed and scooted to her feet, pressing a hand against her chest. "That was amazing."

Brendon's face was alight with pleasure and he laughed, glancing back at the slide.

"I haven't a clue the last time I went down that thing."

Nika laughed harder. "You lied! I thought you went down daily."

"Hardly. A grown man visiting the play equipment daily?" He made a face. "How scandalous."

She swatted his chest and he caught her wrist, pulling her close.

"Shall we go down again on the sky slide?" he murmured, sliding his hands down to her waist. "Or are you hoping for another sort of ride?"

The air escaped her lungs on a tiny puff, as moisture gathered heavy between her legs. "Most definitely another sort of ride."

"Wonderful," he growled. "For I am certain I have something for you to ride on, love."

She bit her lip and pressed her body firmly against his. "Promises, promises."

His gaze smoldered just before he lowered his head, covering her mouth with his. He licked at her bottom lip, drawing it between his teeth to nibble on before sliding his tongue inside. She let out a soft sigh and melted into him.

Each stroke of Nika's tongue against his made Brendon's cock just a little bit harder. Gods, he wanted this woman. Watching her carefree and teasing on the slide had just made him realize how much she'd begun to sink her claws into him.

He lifted his head and pressed his forehead against hers.

"Let's head back to your room," he muttered unevenly, rubbing his thumb across her bottom lip. "Before I do something highly inappropriate. Like fuck you on one of the high-speed swings."

She laughed softly and stepped back from him, placing her hand in his again. "Is that considered inappropriate?"

"Naughty minx."

Her laugh deepened. "Let us go. But might I ask why you do not invite me to *your* bedchamber?"

He shook his head, but his fingers tightened around her hand. "I make it a policy to never bring a woman back to my bedchamber."

She opened her mouth to likely ask why not, but then seemed to think better of it.

Good. He hated to admit his reasoning aloud. It wasn't that he couldn't bring a woman back to his bedchamber; he was perfectly entitled. And he knew many of his fellow soldiers did so on a regular basis.

But to do that would be opening himself and his life to speculation. It would leave him vulnerable. Being with a woman at her unit or somewhere else gave him the power. It let him come and go exactly when he wanted. There were no ties. No way a woman could come harass him at his residence if things ended badly.

The walk back to the lodge seemed to take much longer than the walk to the park. Nightfall was descending upon them and the air grew chilly.

Each step they took brushed her hip against his and sent a wave of her sensual perfume beneath his nostrils. He rubbed his thumb across the palm of her hand and was rewarded when she let out a small groan.

When the lights of the lodge came into view the relief was tangible. He resisted the urge to pick her up, to carry her into the lodge and up to her room in true primitive fashion. Something like those fictional caveman films that traded like crazy from the old planet Earth.

The door to the lodge hissed open and they stepped inside hurriedly.

Molly glanced up from the reception desk and her eyes widened in surprise, her hand stopping as it had begun to rise in a wave.

"Good evening, Molly," he hollered, rushing them toward the stairs.

"Hello, Molly."

"Umm . . . good evening, Brendon. Rebecca . . ."

They made their way up the staircase and he cast a sideways glance at Nika. Or was it Rebecca? Likely the latter. The colonel had introduced her as Rebecca as well. Gods, it irked him to know she'd lied to him. She didn't even look like a Rebecca. It was hard to call her such.

"Are you really named Rebecca?" he asked as she opened her room door.

Gods, he hated that he'd even brought himself to ask. Again. Hadn't they had this conversation before?

She slipped inside the door and, with her back to him, answered. Her voice sounded a bit off as she said, "Yes. I apologize for lying the first night. I often give a man a counterfeit name when we meet."

"Often give a man a counterfeit name?" He pressed the button that slid the door shut and his brows drew together. She made it seem as if she picked up men on a regular basis. And yet . . . "You told me I was your first since Zortou?"

He watched her back stiffen and she seemed to be thinking hard before answering.

"Yes. You were the first I slept with. But I have been trying my hand at flirting on occasion."

Is that how she'd mastered the cock teasing? Irritation swept through him.

She turned around and gave him an apologetic smile, closing

the distance between them. "I regret not telling you my real name." Her arms wove around his neck and her lower lip protruded into the most enticing pout. "Can you ever forgive me, Brendon?"

His cock stirred against her belly, and he pressed his hips forward so she would feel the evidence of his arousal.

"I'm certain I can be persuaded."

Arousal flared in her gaze and she licked her lips, lowering her gaze between them.

"I'm certain you can," she murmured and then slid slowly to her knees before him.

The air hissed out from between his teeth as she fumbled with the fastenings on his uniform. Her brows knit together as she struggled for a moment and then her expression turned smug when the fastening came undone.

She parted the fabric with her fingers, sliding them inside. A moment later she wrapped her hand around his cock.

Brendon closed his eyes for a moment, delighting in the feel of her soft fingers stroking his erection free from his pants.

"You have a beautiful penis," she murmured. "I wonder what you will feel like in my mouth. How you will taste?"

"Only one way to find out, love." He opened his eyes again and smiled down at her.

Her expression seemed a bit hesitant as if she fought some demons.

Realization sank in for Brendon. She had likely been forced to do this with her owners.

"Rebecca, if you do not wish to do this, you do not have to."

Though it would nearly kill him *not* to have her mouth on him. Already his cock craved the silky wet suction of her mouth. Of course, he did not admit such.

"I wish to," she said with a soft laugh. "And I do believe it is the least I can do after all I put you through in the first couple of days we met."

"Right you are, woman. Now, then." He cleared his throat. "If you would go about making your amends."

Any tension seemed to leave her body with the quiet laugh she sounded. Then she leaned forward and her tongue flicked over the head of his cock.

Every muscle in Brendon's body went taut with the need to have her continue.

She drew her tongue back into her mouth and closed her eyes, as if savoring the taste of him.

When her eyes opened again they were hot with desire. Her fingers clenched around him and her head dipped again. This time her lips closed around the tip.

Her mouth slid onto his cock, so wet and hot. She moved closer to him, her hands clasping his thighs as she slid him deep toward the back of her throat.

"Gods." He delved his fingers into her hair and held her loosely as she began to move her mouth on him.

She covered her teeth with her lips and drew near the tip of his shaft. Brendon let out a guttural groan. The exquisite pressure sent waves of pleasure through him and his sac tightened.

Her hand slid from his thigh to cup his sac, squeezing lightly as she licked over the length of his cock. Her tongue flicked the head, paying extra attention to the tiny dent on the underside.

"Nika!" He tightened his hands in her hair, vaguely realizing he'd called her by her fake name but not really caring.

She took him in her mouth again, her head bobbing up and down on his cock, sucking him hard each time she reached the head.

Gods. He was going to come. In her pretty little mouth. And heaven help him if he didn't love the idea.

His sac tightened in her hand and he jerked his hips forward, plunging himself deep into her throat and letting out a hoarse cry.

He came hard, everything in his head going bright while he emptied himself in her mouth. She massaged his sac, milking his spend entirely until he was empty and nearly shaking.

She lifted her head and gave a murmur of satisfaction.

Brendon opened his eyes again, taking a moment before his gaze could focus on her, still kneeling at his feet.

Gods, she looked a sight. Still fully dressed and running her tongue over swollen lips.

"Come here," he whispered and caught her hand, pulling her to her feet.

She licked her lips and slid her hands up his arms, squeezing his muscles.

"Take off your dress," he commanded.

Wordlessly, she obeyed, sliding the straps off her arm and unfastening the ribbon that was around her rib cage beneath her breasts.

The dress finally fell free, pooling at her feet. She kicked it to the side and stood nude in front of him. Her alabaster skin glowed in the fading light of the room.

Gods, she was a vision. He reached down and stroked his cock, which had already begun to harden again.

"Recline on the bed."

Nika licked her lips and moved to comply. She climbed onto the mattress and then rolled over onto her back.

Brendon bit back a groan at the erotic sight she made: her long legs slightly parted, the pink lips of her pussy glistening between.

He lifted his gaze higher, over the concave of her stomach to the gentle swell of her breasts. Her nipples, red and firm, made his mouth water.

"Now then, love. I believe you said something about being bound?"

Her breath caught, but she did not protest as he searched her bureau drawers for stockings. He found a pair and pulled them free.

Walking back around the bed, he kept his gaze on her face, watching for any signs of discomfort. But there was only heated anticipation in her eyes.

He caught both her wrists and dragged them above her head. Winding one of the stockings around them, he then secured it to the steel frame at the head of the bed.

She let out a soft moan and tugged at her arms, as if testing to see how well he'd fastened them. There was very little give.

"Lovely," he murmured.

Shedding his uniform, he stepped forward and sat on the edge of the bed and slid one hand up her leg, higher and higher still. He pushed her thighs open and fully exposed her decadent pussy.

The need to taste her was strong. Already he anticipated her cries of pleasure.

He used his fingers to part the folds of her pussy. Hot cream greeted him and he smiled. Yes, she was anxious for him.

Lowering his head, he pressed a kiss against her clit and smiled when she drew in a sharp breath. He kissed it again, nuzzling the hidden nub before flicking his tongue out to tease it.

"Oh." She moaned.

Possessiveness moved through him and he growled, lowering his mouth to her again. His tongue swept lower, pressing into her channel to taste her.

Musky and slick, her cream coated his tongue and he devoured it, eating at her pussy while bringing his thumb up to rub her clit.

Her hips rose against his mouth and the desperate cries he'd been craving started.

"Please," she whispered.

He rubbed her swollen nub faster, pressed his tongue deeper inside her.

Her legs began to slide on the bed, her body twisting beneath him. He laid his free hand across her thighs to hold her still.

Knowing she was close to her peak, he pinched her clit hard and fucked her rapidly with his tongue.

"Brendon!" Her back arched off the bed and she screamed, her thighs clenching around him.

While she climaxed, he slid up her body, pushed her legs apart, and plunged into her still-rippling pussy.

"Gods!" She groaned and tugged at her bound hands, her breasts lifting higher as she squirmed beneath him.

The weight of his body pressed hers deeper into the mattress, until she could no longer wiggle beneath him.

She let out a ragged moan and closed her eyes, seeming to surrender any idea of freeing her hands or having control, and instead wrapped her legs about his waist.

Brendon drew in an uneven breath as he pumped in and out of her sweet pussy. Gods. She was so wet and hot, her body a paradise come to life.

The rhythm of his thrusts stayed steady as he watched the pleasure flicker on her face.

Fuck, he wanted her, for more than just a few nights. He wanted her indefinitely.

He moved harder in her now. Her breasts flattened against him, the nipples scraping his chest.

When he normally would have been tempted to come, he kept going. Their joining was so sweet. So intense. His primal side and the need to claim her everywhere took dominance.

He pulled his cock from between her legs and then grabbed her hip, rolling her onto her belly.

"What—"

"I want your ass," he muttered, running his hands over the firm cheeks of her bottom.

Her hands still restrained above her head, she glanced at him over her shoulder and groaned.

"Yes."

Her fervent reply surprised him, but was a welcome response, as he'd already plunged his fingers inside her to find her cream.

He brought the slick liquid of her arousal back to the rosebud of her ass and pressed it inside, holding her cheeks apart to expose the smaller hole.

After penetrating her for a moment with two fingers, he slid a hand beneath her belly to raise her onto her knees.

With her face and breasts still on the mattress but her ass in the air, that's how he entered her.

Gripping her hips, he slid his cock into the tight channel of her ass. Gods, he hoped she could take him, even as he worried slightly he might hurt her.

"Gods," she gasped. "Yes, Brendon. Take me."

Brendon's nails dug into her hips and he growled, driving himself deep as she screamed in pleasure.

He moved steadily inside her, the tightness and heat of fucking her here was so intense he had to bite the inside of his cheek to hold himself from spending too soon.

His gaze moved over her. Her mouth now parted in a silent

gasp and her eyes were only half open. The combination of the sharp cries she made and her submissive position finally sapped all his control.

With a growl, he plunged harder into her. Faster. Fucking her ass until his balls tightened and his mind became a blur.

Reaching blindly beneath her, he found her clit and squeezed it, sending her tumbling over the edge of pleasure as he finally exploded inside her.

A few minutes later, he pulled his cock from her body and ran a hand down her thighs, which trembled.

"Did I hurt you?" he asked softly and brushed a kiss against her lower back.

"Mmm. Only the good kind of hurt." She gave a soft laugh and rolled over. Tugging at her wrists she arched a brow. "Though I think I'm losing feeling in my hands."

He winced and quickly untied her. "I apologize, love."

"No need. That was incredible." She sat up and caught the back of his head, pulling him forward to nip at his bottom lip. "Only next time, *I'll* tie *you* up."

He gave a soft growl and plundered her mouth in a deeper kiss. When he raised his head he muttered, "You have a deal."

"Do you have to leave tonight?" she asked softly. "You're welcome to slumber in my room."

Stay over in her room. The idea flickered through his head and gained momentum. He'd stayed last night as well. If he made this a habit, Molly might up and charge her for another person.

"I'll stay," he murmured. "But we have not eaten supper."

"It's late. Do we need it?"

He leaned down to kiss one pert nipple. "I do, love. How about I bring us something back?"

She sat up in bed, propping her head up with her elbow. "That sounds lovely."

Brendon sought out his uniform and dressed quickly. "I shall return shortly. Don't miss me too much."

"Impossible not to." She winked and then rolled onto her stomach, waving her ass in his face. "Hurry back."

His blood stirred. Again. "I intend to."

Molly waited in the lobby of the lodge, leaning against the reception desk as she made conversation with the girl who'd arrived to take her place.

Annoyance raced through her veins as she glanced again into the restaurant and out the door to the lodge. Where was he? He'd requested a dinner with her and then refused to show? Of all the nerve!

"So what are your plans for this evening?" the girl asked. "Anything exciting?"

"Apparently not." Her mouth tightened and she headed toward the door. "If anyone asks for me, I have gone for a walk."

"Oh! But I thought . . ."

The girl's words were wiped out as the door hissed open. Molly stepped out into the cool air but welcomed the chill.

What a fool she was. For a moment today she'd thought . . . *what? What did you think? You made it clear you had no time to dally in a relationship. Perhaps he finally took your words to heart.*

She quickened her pace and started on the trail, the air seething out from between her teeth. Still, he could have at least contacted her to let her know this dinner he'd planned would not happen.

Footsteps sounded behind her and she spun around, just as the man lurched forward.

His hand slammed across her mouth, cutting off her cry of fear as he jerked her hard against his rotund body. Red eyes glowed down at her in the darkness of the night and her heart nearly stopped.

Oh gods!

11

"Let's keep it quiet, all right, puss?"

The stink of his hand sent her stomach rolling and Molly thought quickly of how she could possibly get out of this.

"I think there's been a misunderstanding," he murmured and slid one hand down her backside. His fingers dug into her ass cheek and he smiled, baring two fangs.

Her head spun with fear, her body shook.

"I have no wish to hurt you," he said quickly. "Quite the opposite. I think I could bring you much pleasure." His gaze moved down to the swell of her breasts. "If you'd only just let me."

Never! She narrowed her eyes and shook her head.

"Do not say no yet, puss." He released her ass and slid a hand between them to touch her breast. "Does it bring you no pleasure to have my hand upon you?"

It made her want to vomit! She would have shrieked the words had he not been covering her mouth.

"I will treat you well. See that you are content." He lowered his head toward hers. "Let us lift your skirts and have a quick tumble."

He reached for the hem of her dress and then his eyes widened as he was jerked backward and away from her.

The scream that had been trapped escaped past her lips, shrill and terrified.

Brendon slammed his fist into the portly blood drinker, sending him stumbling backward.

"You're gone," he roared. "Get your things and leave this lodge. Now. Before I have you detained for assault, you filth."

Molly wiped the back of her hand across her mouth and took another step back from the two men.

"You cannot evict me," the other man snarled. "I am a paying customer."

Molly lifted her chin. "It matters not. You will leave. Now."

"And I will escort you back and ensure you leave." Brendon's tone dripped ice.

"You will regret this. All of you." The blood drinker let out a snarl and spun away, retreating to the lodge.

"Thank you," she said quietly to Brendon before he could follow the man back inside.

"I'm only sorry I didn't see you sooner." He frowned and placed a light hand on her shoulder. "Are you quite all right, Molly?"

She gave a slight nod, even though she felt as if she might be ill.

"Where is Emmett?" Brendon asked as they walked back toward the lodge.

Her mouth tightened. "I haven't the faintest idea. But the question is a good one."

Brendon glanced at her sharply and grunted.

Once inside the lodge, she looked around nervously, ill at ease that she might see the blood drinker again.

"Molly!"

She turned to the right and saw Emmett exiting the restaurant. His brows drew together as he approached.

"Where have you been? I apologize I was tardy."

"She was being attacked." Brendon stepped toward his friend. "Watch her while I rid the lodge of the filth who attempted the assault."

"*What?*" Emmett stepped forward, his jaw hardening. "It was that blood drinker again, wasn't it? I'm going to kill the son of a bitch."

Molly placed her hand against his chest before he could move past her.

"Emmett, please."

"Stay with her," Brendon agreed. "I'll take care of him."

And then he was gone.

Emmett turned to her, his expression taut with concern. "Oh gods, Molly. I'm so sorry. Did he hurt you?"

She bit her lip and shook her head. She would *not cry* this time. And yet she wanted to. When he pulled her into his arms in the middle of the lobby and soothed a hand down her back, she wanted to.

Turning her head against his chest, she slid her arms around his waist, not giving a damn who would be watching them.

"I was waiting for you to show for dinner," she muttered. "And you didn't arrive, so I took a walk."

"I was detained. Gods, I'm so sorry," he whispered. "I should have called. I'm such an ass."

"You're not an ass. But yes, you should have called." She gave a soft laugh. "I was quite angry with you, actually, or else I might have heard his approach."

Emmett's arms tightened around her. "I want to kill him."

"Bloodshed solves nothing and will only have you detained, silly. You're hardly any good to me locked up."

"He's a fool, Molly. I warned him to stay away. What could he possibly be thinking to try and assault you again?"

"He *is* a fool, for he thought to change my mind."

"I'm sorry I was not with you. I should have been there."

"It is not your fault." She pulled away and stiffened as she spotted Brendon leading the other man down the stairs.

Emmett must have sensed her sudden tension, for he spun and pushed her gently behind him. She gripped his shoulders when he made to stride forward.

"Please, Emmett," she said softly. "Brendon has taken care of it."

The blood drinker's expression was twisted into a mask of fury. When his gaze landed on her his eyes seemed to glow darker red and he bared his fangs.

"Get out," Emmett growled. "And never return, or we won't be as civilized next time."

Brendon gave the man a nudge forward when he would've stopped to argue.

And then they were gone from the lodge and her body went weak with relief.

She sighed and admitted, "I don't like that man. He frightens me, and I usually don't frighten easily."

"He's gone now, and I promise he won't be back." Emmett caught her hand and gave it a reassuring squeeze. "I owe you dinner. It will do you good to have a glass of wine and relax a bit. Would you like to eat here or go off to another restaurant?"

Molly hesitated and glanced into her restaurant. Initially she'd made the decision to have them dine in another locale. That way there would be no reason for gossip. But the thought of leaving the lodge and following that man out into the night sent her stomach into turmoil.

"Here," she said softly. "Let's eat here."

He brushed a kiss across her forehead and led her toward the restaurant.

Gods. She was in trouble.

Nika paced her room inside the lodge and thrust a hand through her hair.

The sun had barely risen, and Brendon had just left for work. Her nerves had been raw since he'd told her what had happened last night between Molly and the blood drinker.

And of the man's parting words. *You will regret this. All of you.* As if him being a bounty hunter and blood drinker had not been enough, now he cast threats to all their safety.

Her blood chilled as she thought again about what he might be hunting for. And of the possibility that the military had put a bounty on her head.

Drawing in a deep breath she moved to the bed and sat down. She needed to make firm her plans. Decide exactly how and when to infiltrate the lab. She would get the samples, send them back to Tresden, and be on her way shortly after.

The memory of last night's intimacy with Brendon heated her blood, made her limbs feel weak again. And then the way he'd helped Molly, had been so protective and strong when dealing with the blood drinker. He truly was a wonderful man. Any woman would be blessed to have him. *And for some reason he seems taken with you.*

Her stomach fluttered and she pressed a hand to her suddenly warm cheek.

She flinched at the realization. She could not afford such tender emotions toward Brendon. Not in the short run and certainly not in the long run.

She forced her mind to switch its course, to focus on her mission and what she'd trained for: breaking into the lab.

The best time to infiltrate the lab might be on a weekend day, when it sounded as if the security might be just a tad bit lax.

Fortunately Brendon did not work weekends, which was a relief. She had no wish to encounter him face to face again. Already she regretted having hurt him once. But she would not attempt another infiltration until she was completely prepared this time.

Climbing off the bed, she knelt down and pulled her case from beneath.

Dialing the code in it made it issue a series of beeps before decompressing and then popping open a moment later.

She reached inside, checking her necessary tools for the mission. Ensured she had enough preloaded syringes and eye shields.

Glancing at the time, she sealed the case once more and pushed it back beneath the bed.

It was time to bathe and prepare for the day. In just a few short hours Brendon would lead her on a tour of the lab again. And this time, she'd be sure not to be distracted.

"How are you today, Molly?"

Nika approached her friend from behind, brows knit with concern. She'd just returned from her tour of the lab and was quite pleased with the results. When she infiltrated the lab this time, she would not leave empty handed.

About to head up to her room, Nika had stopped when she'd spotted Molly alone in the restaurant.

Her arms were folded on a table and her head was lying upon them. The lunch hour had recently ended and the supper rush was still hours off.

Molly let out a sigh and finally lifted her head. "I'm all right, I suppose."

But she wasn't entirely. That much was obvious. Nika pulled out a chair and sat down across from the other woman.

"Did you not sleep well?"

Molly's lips thinned. "No. I did not. I had terrible dreams in my sleep."

"I'm sorry."

"I swear it's as if he has these powers, Rebecca. He invaded my dreams." Molly scrubbed her palms down her cheeks and shook her head, whispering, "He raped me in my dreams."

"Oh Molly, that's awful. Though I'm sure it was simply your fears. He could not possibly control your dreams." But even as Nika spoke she was not quite convinced. He was a blood drinker; who knew what kind of powers these beings had?

The idea that someone could go in and control a person's dreams was unsettling at the least. To use it to visualize a rape was just horrific.

She searched Molly's face, saw how pale she was, how haunted her eyes were, and her gut clenched with sympathy.

"Did Emmett stay with you last night?" she asked softly.

"Yes." Molly nodded. "But not in my bed, just the chair nearby."

"You have no desire to let him in your bed?"

"I have too much desire. But things are complicated." Molly lowered her gaze. "I'm afraid I was rather harsh in my clarifying what I was looking for with him. Specifically, not a relationship."

Nika shrugged and lifted an eyebrow. "So just have sex."

"Rebecca!"

"What?" Nika laughed and pushed her hair behind her shoulder. "There is no shame in taking pleasure when we need it."

Molly flushed, finally some amusement seeping into her eyes. "That is quite true. Emmett seems almost afraid to touch me after the attack." She sighed. "And I think I may have been wrong. The more I try to emotionally distance myself from him, the more I want him in my life. Not just my bed. I'm afraid I care for him quite a bit more than I realized, that maybe a relationship is not such a bad thing."

"No, it is not," Nika agreed mildly, but could not let herself compare Molly's feelings toward Emmett with her own feelings toward Brendon. They seemed quite similar, and that couldn't be.

Her thoughts turned back to being at the lab this morning. There was little doubt she would succeed next time in her attempt. The biggest obstacle would be getting past the guards—three, perhaps two on the weekend.

She would need something more potent and capable than the injections. Something that could take out both men at once. There were items in her case upstairs she had not yet explored. Perhaps there was a way.

Once she discovered it, she'd complete this mission and be on her way back home.

Home. Her stomach clenched and she drew in a slow breath. It seemed odd to think of Tresden as her home. Truly, there was little emotional attachment to the planet she'd resided on for two years.

But it mattered not. She would return shortly. Settle into a life and hopefully find happiness. *Doing what . . . ?* A voice taunted inside her head. *All you've ever known is how to fuck or fight. What will you do when both are no longer your entire purpose in life?*

And leaving Belton meant leaving Brendon. Leaving the one man who'd stirred any form of desire within her body. Not to mention her heart. . . .

"Your thoughts look universes away," Molly teased. "A coin for them?"

Nika blinked and shook her head, pulling herself from her reflections.

"Sorry, I was simply wondering where Brendon was," she lied, and once again her stomach churned, protesting the deception. "We are to have an early dinner after he leaves work."

"He is a good man, is he not?"

Nika barely hesitated. "He is a very good man."

"I have to say, Rebecca, I have not seen him so uninterested in the female population. Well, save for you," she rushed to add. "And that is my point entirely. Ever since your arrival on this planet, he has seemed to only have eyes for you."

Nika flushed. "No, I'm sure he's simply—"

"Besotted. To say the least. Completely." Molly leaned forward and touched her hand. "Do you not think we see how he watches you? Emmett and I have both noticed. The man is smitten."

It could not be possible. Her body felt strangely light at the idea, her pulse fluttery and her cheeks warm. It almost . . . pleased her. A little too much.

"Truly, I do not see how you have time to see your cousin when Brendon monopolizes your company so often."

Her cousin. Her light mood was doused with a sudden realization. Molly thought her to be visiting a cousin, while Brendon believed her to be an ambassador on business. Never when she had begun the lies could she have imagined that Molly and Brendon would be friends.

Obviously they had not compared stories as of yet, but what if they did in the future?

"My cousin is busy as well. We have met for lunch a couple of times," she said briskly and then licked her lips, preparing for another lie. "But did I not mention? I am also an ambassador from Glorus, touring and giving a report back to my city."

Molly's eyes widened in surprise and confusion. "Oh. I had not guessed. Truly, you are a busy woman, my friend."

You have no idea. Nika just offered a slight smile and glanced around the restaurant.

"What will happen when you return to Glorus?" Molly asked quietly. "Do you think you will see Brendon again?"

Her heart clenched and for a moment it was hard to breathe. "I'm not certain what the future holds," she murmured.

But she knew what it didn't hold. And that was Brendon and anything related to Belton. And the realization was far more depressing than she could ever have anticipated.

Finding the time and the tools to infiltrate the lab wasn't as easy as she'd hoped. Two weeks passed by before she knew the time approached.

And despite Rachel's insistence that Nika not contact her as much, she had done so a handful of times, discovering the right combination of herbs and chemicals and timing to render the guards unconscious without killing them.

Rachel had sent the obscure herbs via a messenger a few days ago, and only now was Nika almost ready to attempt another mission.

She sat in her room, memorizing the recipe for the concoction. Soon this would all be over. Soon she would return to life as normal.

Thank gods—for every day she spent on this planet compounded the guilt in her heart. Molly had become a true friend, which was a bit troubling.

And Brendon, gods . . . Even just thinking about him sent

her stomach flipping and her pulse quickening, spread a happiness through her she knew she was not entitled to.

Each night he spent in her bed connected them on a deeper level. And it almost seemed to grow beyond sex, though the sex was still extraordinary. He showed her such tenderness and passion, such things she never could have imagined with a man a month ago.

Tomorrow night, Saturday, she would complete this mission. There was no room for failure now, because she knew on a gut level that if she failed, this time she would not be so lucky as to escape.

And she must escape. Escape this planet . . . and the relationships she'd begun to form with its people.

Brendon left the interior of the lab, having discussed the new safety routine with the scientists on duty, and let the door hiss shut behind him. A series of beeps signaled it was again locked.

"Lieutenant Marshall."

He turned, glanced down the hall to see the approaching captain. Straightening, he saluted the older man.

"Yes, Captain?"

"If I may request your presence in my office. There's been a small development in the break-in."

His blood rushed faster through his veins. Good. He would love to get his hands on the scrawny bastard who had blackened his eye weeks ago.

He followed the captain into his office and sat down in the chair across from him.

"Thank you, Lieutenant." The captain settled himself behind his desk and adjusted a group of files. "The information we have learned is not great in quantity, but great in impact."

Brendon nodded, nearly on the edge of his seat for any information about the man who'd already infiltrated the lab once.

"There was very little evidence left behind. Almost nothing. It took several days of combing the premises to find any hint of DNA."

"But you did?" Brendon said knowingly.

"Barely." The captain leaned back in his chair, his expression pensive. "There are no records of this person on our planet. And, while unfortunate, that is not quite unexpected."

Brendon nodded slowly. "So that eliminates any man from Belton or Zortou, as all incoming citizens of Zortou were required to give a DNA sample."

"Correct. So we can only assume this thief is from another planet."

"Is he human?" Brendon arched a brow. "Is it possible that he comes from the planet Multron? Could he be one of those blood drinkers?"

The captain shook his head slowly and thrust his lower lip out. "No. All evidence points to human. And our thief . . . is a she."

Brendon stilled, his muscles coiling with tension. "It is not possible."

"DNA does not lie," the captain murmured, making Brendon aware he'd spoken the words aloud.

A woman? But how was that even remotely possible?

Heat stole up his neck. "I would have noticed. No woman can fight as such."

The captain laughed softly. "Can they not? I know it must be a wound to your pride to realize a woman bested you."

"That is not it." He lied. It was partially that. "The intruder was built like . . ."

"A teenage boy, you said." The captain paused, letting his meaning sink in. "Or perhaps just a slim woman."

Brendon felt sick. His stomach churned with the memory of how hard they'd fought. Of how he'd nailed the boy—or woman, apparently—in the side with a merciless kick.

Something prickled in the back of his mind, but before he could acknowledge it, the captain was speaking again.

"I have not told all the soldiers on duty of this info, Lieutenant Marshall. And I would prefer not to. I fear many would hesitate to fight a woman, not realizing how skilled of a fighter she is."

The unease increased inside him, but he refused to show it. He had his own misgivings about fighting a woman, but apparently the captain failed to see that in him.

"Why have you told me this?"

The captain splayed his hands on the desk and leaned forward. "Because I want you to be aware, Lieutenant. You are my best soldier by far. You are smart. Quick. Tolerate very little bullshit. The fact that our thief is a woman should matter very little to you."

His words just confirmed Brendon's suspicion that the captain assumed he'd fight a woman without remorse or hesitation. It appeared now he would have no choice.

"Thank you for informing me of these details. I do not take your conferral lightly. Is there any more information I should be aware of?" Brendon asked flatly.

"Sadly, no. That is all we have at this time. But should any more information become available, know that you will be the second to be informed." The captain smiled. "I, of course, will be the first."

"Thank you, sir."

"That is all, Lieutenant. You are dismissed."

Brendon stood and saluted, then turned and left the office.

Well, hell. The thief was a woman. This was just a complication he didn't need. Before, he'd been hoping for another go-around with the boy. But now that the boy was indeed a woman, he wished for the opposite.

He could only pray to the gods that this woman thief struck on somebody else's shift.

12

"So you have not slept with Emmett again?" Nika asked, lifting the tea to her mouth.

Molly sighed and picked up a biscuit, nibbling a bite. "I have not. I sense he is interested again, but . . . he has not outright attempted anything."

Nika rolled her eyes. "So you be the brazen one and attempt on him."

Molly's cheeks flushed. "What if I *am* wrong and he does not want me?"

"You are overthinking this. Of course he wants you."

"But he has kept his distance," Molly said, shaking her head. "Well, after the first few days. He was so very sweet to stay with me after we removed that vile blood drinker from the lodge. He slept in the chair near my bed."

"When did you last see him?"

"Over a week ago. Since we decided I was in no danger." Molly sighed and set down her biscuit. "He has not even come to the restaurant."

Nika took another sip of tea and watched the disappointment flicker in her friend's eyes. "Do you miss him?"

Molly gave a rather large shrug. "Does it matter?"

"Of course." Nika arched an eyebrow and gave a sly grin. "I am certain you must miss him in more ways than one."

A red flush filled Molly's cheeks.

"Ladies," a male voice rang out. "How is your afternoon?"

Nika set down her tea, her pulse quickening. Warmth spread through her body as she spotted Brendon crossing the restaurant floor. Gods, each time she saw him was like being given an injection full of happiness.

"Our afternoon is well," Nika murmured and stood, smoothing her dress down her legs. "And work? Are you finished now?"

His gaze darkened with some hidden emotion and he nodded. "Yes. I am finished for the day." He paused. "Ni—Rebecca, might I have a word with you in private?"

Her throat tightened with sudden anxiety.

"Of course." She followed him out into the lobby, reminding herself there was nothing to fear. "You look troubled. Was all well at work?"

He hesitated, looked away, and then nodded. "Yes. All was well." Clearing his throat, he continued. "Tonight, I was wondering if you would care to have supper with another couple who are friends of mine?"

Relief that it had again been nothing threatening, she gave a slight nod. "I would love to. When shall we leave?"

"Fairly soon, I'm afraid." His gaze softened as he looked at her. "Though you look lovely, so there's no need to change. I missed you today."

She scooted close to him when he slid his arms around her waist.

"I missed you." And it felt good to admit, since it was not a lie. "Will I like your friends?"

"You will. I am quite certain." His gaze clouded over, but then he lowered his head and his mouth brushed hers.

All her thoughts ran together at the soft caress and she swayed against him.

He let out a growl of approval and then lifted his head. "I'm tempted to say forget about supper and take you upstairs."

Nika could almost agree. She licked her lips and smiled. "Well, if you are more inclined . . ."

He groaned and pressed a finger against her mouth. "Do not encourage me. Ryder would have my ass if I didn't bring you to dinner tonight."

"Ah, well, then. There's no hope for it. Shall we go?"

"Yes. Let's head out."

The sky taxi deposited them at a restaurant on the base. Brendon helped her from the taxi and she stood, glancing around as she adjusted the wrap around her body.

Her stomach twisted a bit. Meeting his friends meant there would be two more people who would remember her. Instead of showing her fears, she raised her head and followed Brendon inside.

He seemed to spot his friends right away and lifted a hand to wave. She swallowed hard and smoothed her hands down her dress.

Brendon released her arm to approach a stunningly beautiful pregnant woman. Something stabbed sharp in Nika's gut and she blinked in surprise, completely off balance to realize it was jealousy. Had she ever been jealous in her life?

"Gods, you look lovely, Talia," Brendon told the woman. "The baby's gotten much bigger since I've seen you."

The woman flushed and slapped his shoulder lightly. "You are an incurable flirt, Brendon."

"I am." He grinned and released the woman. "Talia, this is Rebecca Owens, an ambassador from Glorus. Rebecca, this is the wife of my friend Ryder. Speaking of which, where is the rogue?"

"He ran to find me some sparkling water." The woman, Talia, turned her attention to Nika. "Nice to meet . . ."

Talia trailed off, her brows drawing together.

Nika froze, ice sweeping through her veins as she stared at the other woman. Familiarity jolted through her.

"Rebecca you say it was?" Talia leaned forward.

Oh gods. No, it was not possible—it couldn't be—that the glowing woman before her was actually Natalia, formerly the most prestigious Rosabelle on the planet Zortou. She had once been owned by the governing council.

"Wait a moment . . . do we not know each other?" Talia continued, stepping closer.

Brendon turned to Nika, his gaze calm and knowing as he waited for her to respond. Her stomach sank farther, and she knew her fear was realized.

Brendon was aware of her past as a Rosabelle and obviously knew the pregnant woman next to him had also been a Rosabelle.

"I know you," Talia murmured and shook her head, rubbing her belly. "I know I do. Were we not in Rosabelle schooling together back on Zortou?"

Nika's tongue stuck to the roof of her mouth, and she could feel the color leaching from her face.

Of everything she did not want to be reminded of—to be confronted with—this was about number one.

Brendon was at her side in a moment, cupping her elbow. His brows drew together in concern. "Rebecca?"

Instead of his touch being comforting, it sent a spark of anger through her. How dare he? How dare he set up this meeting between her and another Rosabelle without warning her?

"But your name wasn't Rebecca," Talia continued slowly. "No, I believe it was . . . Donika? We were friends, were we not?"

Brendon's grip suddenly tightened around her arm and she winced.

Speak, you fool! Say something!

"Yes, we were friends," she forced out.

Gods, but how many years ago had that been? When they were in school to learn how to please men. How they would giggle in classes about fellatio and coitus. How silly and obscure it had all seemed—until the horror of their reality had been brought to life.

She said numbly, "You look well, Natalia."

The other woman flinched and drew back. "Thank you. But please, I prefer to be called Talia now. I resigned my full name after the liberation. It reminds me of . . ."

"I understand," Nika said quickly, seeing her opening and taking it. "And, yes, I imagine you knew me as Donika. I have since taken a new name as well. Rebecca."

Talia nodded, her blue eyes alight with sympathy and understanding. "It is good to see you again, Do—Rebecca."

"You as well."

But it wasn't. Nika's stomach rolled and she feared she might be sick. Seeing Talia again had brought all the memories and revulsion of their lives to the surface. Peeled back the scab and laid open her wounds for everyone to observe.

"Ah, about time you got here."

The arrival of another male rolled more tension through Nika's body.

"Ryder, I was wondering where you'd disappeared to." Brendon moved to shake his friend's hand. "I just finished introducing Rebecca and Talia."

"Rebecca? Lovely to meet you." Ryder took her palms between both his hands and squeezed lightly. "Let's sit, shall we?"

Nika gave a wan smile and settled down next to Brendon. His hand slid beneath the table to squeeze her knee. She wasn't foolish enough to mistake it as a gesture of comfort; it was more of a warning that he intended to speak with her later.

Her pulse quickened with nerves. He knew now that her given name was Nika. Obviously he was not pleased to discover another lie.

She tried to swallow against a suddenly tight throat. What was wrong with her? It didn't matter if he was not pleased. Pleasing Brendon was not her mission to this planet. Getting the specimen samples and getting out was.

And she kept forgetting that. How often did she find herself relaxing, laughing, going about her day like she was any other citizen of Belton?

But she wasn't. She was an imposter. Someone who would eventually betray them. Her stomach about sank to her toes, but she pushed aside the guilt. She lowered her gaze and hardened her jaw.

Rachel would be disappointed in her. And her trainer. All on Tresden would be shocked and disturbed to realize how emotionally invested she'd become with the people of Belton.

But it wasn't too late. She could still redeem herself . . . would redeem herself.

Yes. She sat up straighter and drew in a slow breath. From now on, she would treat every little part of this mission as a step to her success. She could no longer let her emotions carry her while in bed with Brendon. He was nothing more than a step in her journey. And she'd best remember that.

Right, he means absolutely nothing to you, the voice in her head mocked cruelly.

"Rebecca, I am so pleased to have you join us for supper," Ryder said eventually with a smile, his arm already draped over his wife's shoulders. "I've heard much about you already from Brendon."

"Have you?" She cast a quick glance at Brendon, but relaxed when she saw a flush of embarrassment in his cheeks. "All good, I hope?"

"Most definitely. Just the fact he spoke of you says much. Brendon never speaks of the women in his life."

Brendon cleared his throat. "What shall we sup on tonight? Anyone have any ideas?"

Ryder threw his head back and laughed, while Talia's lips twitched.

Nika bit back a sigh, already mentally exhausted from what was certain to be a long night.

It was rather difficult to enjoy his dinner as much as he wanted to. Brendon took another sip of his wine and snuck a sideways glance at his woman.

His woman. When had his thoughts turned so primal?

Pushing aside his reference to her, he focused on the tension in her face. Clearly, she'd rather be anywhere but here.

Their supper was wrapping up, and he knew within minutes they'd be saying their good-byes. And in reality, he was looking forward to it as much as Nika. He'd be damned if he would call her Rebecca again.

Another lie. Why did she keep doing it? And was she hiding anything else? Something felt off, not quite right with her story and why she was here.

"You look tired, Talia," Nika commented softly.

Brendon's attention shifted back to Ryder and his wife. "Perhaps we should call an end to our evening?"

"It may be for the best," Talia agreed and then yawned. "I just haven't the energy I used to."

"It's the baby." Ryder touched her belly and brushed his lips across her forehead.

Brendon glanced at Nika, curious to see how she'd respond to the tender display. Her expression had grown tight, and the naked longing in her eyes took his breath away.

She must have felt his gaze on her for she turned to look at him. Her cheeks reddened and she blinked the emotion from her gaze, meeting his stare with a once-again blank expression.

"It appears an early night is the consensus," Ryder murmured. "Rebecca, it was lovely to finally meet you."

Talia nodded. "Yes, we must have lunch some time. I'm glad we've had the chance to reconnect."

"And I as well."

"Thank you for inviting us for supper." Brendon stood and shook his friend's hand again. "I will see you tomorrow on the compound."

"Indeed." Ryder nodded and slid an arm around his wife's waist, giving them a final wave. "Good night."

"Shall we catch a sky taxi back to the lodge?" Nika asked quietly. "I find myself quite exhausted as well."

"Are you, now?" Perhaps it was from all the lying. He bit back the extra words and forced a hard smile. He stood from the table. "Then by all means, let's go to bed, Nika."

"I did not say bed," she corrected, standing. "And why have you reverted to calling me Nika?"

"Because it is your name."

Anger flared—and maybe panic?—in her gaze. "It was my name long ago, but no more."

"And yet you gave it to me that first night on the trail."

"My mind was befuddled. Why is a name so important?" Her words became angrier as they left the restaurant together.

"I am not sure. Perhaps you should tell me?"

Her mouth opened and then closed, the tension in her body growing by the moment.

"Please, let's find a taxi and return to the lodge. Arguing solves nothing." She took a deep breath and in the blink of an eye her demeanor changed. She touched his chest through his shirt and smiled up at him through her lashes. "You were right. We should return and go to bed. After all, we get along so much better using our mouths in other ways."

Despite his desire to press the issue, his cock hardened at her invitation. And she knew it, damn her. Why was she so against this discussion?

A little angry with himself, he caught her elbow and hailed a sky taxi that was approaching.

The ride back to the lodge passed in silence, though she kept a hand on his thigh and snuggled close to him, pressing an occasional kiss against the side of his neck.

He enjoyed the caress, but couldn't help but wonder if she was trying to distract him. The question that seemed to be growing in his mind was: from what?

At the lodge Nika slid from the taxi and caught his hand, pulling him after her.

They passed by the reception counter where Molly stood speaking quietly with an employee. They barely noticed as Brendon and Nika slipped by.

But Brendon's attention caught on Molly, and he narrowed his eyes thoughtfully. Molly had grown close to Nika. Well, as close as she would let anyone get to her. Perhaps tomorrow he would try and have a word with the lodge owner.

Yes, that's exactly what he'd do.

Once inside Nika's room, he waited for the door to slide shut and then turned his gaze to her. She'd already removed her clothes and reached for the fastening on his shirt.

He didn't deter her, just watched as she peeled back the fabric and pressed open-mouthed kisses against his nipples. There was something methodical about her actions, almost robotic as she sank to her knees in front of him and freed his cock.

Though when she drew him in her mouth, it hardly felt mechanical.

He buried his hands into her soft hair, holding her against him as she sucked him, watching her through heavy lidded eyes. Her pink lips stretched wide around his shaft, sliding up and down while she cupped his sac in her hand and fondled him. Her tongue flicked over his steely flesh.

His breathing shifted, grew heavier, and his eyes closed. When his sac began to tighten he ground his teeth together, willing his climax to slow.

She pulled her mouth from him, breathlessly. "Lie down on the bed."

Surprise raged through him at the loss of her mouth on his cock, and at her abrupt command.

He moved to the bed and lay down, ready for her to kneel above his mouth so he might feast on her pussy as they'd been doing lately. But she surprised him, instead moving to kneel over his cock and lifting her hair from her face.

Brendon reached for her breasts but she shook her head and leaned backward, out of his reach.

"I need no preliminaries," she said, her tone strangely detached.

"And what if *I* do?" he murmured, raising a brow, but reluctantly folded his hands above his head, waiting to see how far she would take this.

She moved down, sliding him into the slick folds of her sheath and gave a small, yet almost humorless smile. "That is why I took you in my mouth first."

It was all so very strange, her behavior. But he couldn't quite seem to focus on it when the walls of her pussy gripped his cock, sheathing him in hot moisture.

Pleasure roared through his blood, diluted some from what it usually was when he was with her, but still strong enough to render it difficult to think.

She seated herself fully on him and then began to move, rocking back and forth as she braced her hands on his hips.

Brendon watched her. She didn't even seem to need him there, save for the cock she rode. Nika did all the work herself, rotating on him and riding him, milking his cock for all he was worth.

His lids sank lower with pleasure while his fingers clenched behind his head. He lifted his hips, just to take control for a moment, and plunged deeper into her.

She gasped, her cheeks flushing with pleasure as a tremble racked her body, before she bit her lips and the resolution returned to her expression. She moved on him faster, harder. Her hand slipped behind her to cup his sac again, kneading his balls while she rode him.

It was almost like she wanted him to come fast. And damn it, if that was her wish, then she was about to succeed. His sac and cock swelled and he slammed his eyes closed, groaning, just before he climaxed inside her.

Her muscles clenched around him and he heard her gasp. Relief mingled with his pleasure. At least she'd come. He'd begun to wonder if she would even do that.

Nika slid off him when he'd gone slack beneath her and went into the bathing chamber.

She returned a moment later, composed and with her hair fixed atop her head. Anyone looking at her would hardly think she was a woman who'd just ridden a man silly in bed.

"When do you return to Glorus?" he asked quietly.

Nika paused, in the midst of pulling a sleeping gown from one of the drawers of the bureau.

"I'm not quite sure. As early as Monday maybe . . . but I might stay later if needed."

His chest tightened at her words. As early as Monday? That was . . . gods, three days from now. Barely. Glorus was not entirely far, but it would not be as easy to see her.

Would she want to see him, though?

"Brendon, I feel absolutely terrible for bringing this up," she murmured. "But I really must work on my article tonight. I've fallen behind, what with dinner."

His jaw fell and his eyes widened. "Are you . . . are you asking me to leave?"

She turned and gave him a slight smile. "You don't have to, of course. I'll just not be much fun to you, working and all."

Women never asked him to leave after intimacy. It was almost insulting. Especially since he and Nika had been spending so much time together.

He opened his mouth to insist on staying, but then closed it again. His gaze narrowed as he stared at her rib cage. Something pricked in his mind again, warning him this was important, as he stared at the yellowed skin of her nearly gone bruise.

Then it clicked.

There was a rushing in his ears and the room seemed to spin; everything in his line of vision blurred. Until he blinked and once again he was staring at her slightly marred skin around her ribs. The exact same spot where he'd probably kicked the thief at the lab over two weeks ago.

Our thief . . . is a she. The captain's words rang in his head again and again, twisting and destroying everything he thought he knew.

Then the bruise was covered as the green fabric of Nika's nightgown slid down her body.

13

"All right. I will go," he said, surprised to find his voice calm. "Perhaps we can see each other tomorrow?"

"I would love that." She approached him and brushed a kiss across his mouth, cupping his cheek.

He searched her face, trying to envision it covered in black and her blue-green eyes covered with eye shields. It was impossible. Her skin was creamy and smooth, her eyes sparkling, her lips so full and kissable.

But she'd been so interested in the lab. Had asked so many questions . . .

Because she is an ambassador from Glorus.

"I should probably drop by the fitness center tonight, anyway," he said and pulled away from her, retrieving his pants and dressing quickly.

At the door he turned and looked back at her. The green gown hugged her slight curves so beautifully. Her gaze seemed almost resigned and hard. There was little warmth in them with them missing the spark he'd become accustomed to.

A chill moved down his spine and he drew in an unsteady breath. Again she looked almost robotic or . . . what he'd imagine a Rosabelle would have been like. The way she'd fucked him, like she was doing her job and only needed to get him off.

With that thought leaving him a bit nauseated, he turned and left the room.

He moved through the hallway and down the stairs, his head pounding.

This is Nika. You've been bedding her for weeks now. She's worked her way into your heart like nobody else. Made you want no other woman but her.

Once down in the lobby, he was ready to exit the building when he spotted Molly working alone in her office.

Hesitating only a moment, he turned and entered the smaller room.

"Molly?"

She glanced up, surprise and then warmth flickering across her face. "Brendon. How are you this evening?"

"I am . . . well enough." He did not sit, but towered over the desk. Hell, how did he even go about asking this? "Molly, why did Ni—Rebecca tell you she was staying here at the lodge?"

Molly leaned back in her chair, her gaze wary. "Why do you ask? Do you not know?"

"Please, Molly, I know you are her friend. It is just . . . It's quite important you answer."

She hesitated and bit her lip, looking away. "She told me she was an ambassador from Glorus."

A small amount of relief loosened the tension in his muscles. He nodded.

"And that she is visiting a cousin."

The tension whipped back and he blinked in dismay. A cousin?

"Which did she tell you first, Molly?"

"The cousin. What is going on, Brendon? Has she done something wrong?"

His stomach sank and he felt as if he might be ill.

"You've gone positively pale, Brendon." Molly rushed to her feet. "Tell me, what is happening? Did she not tell you about the cousin?"

"Have you seen this cousin?"

Her brows knitted and she looked down at the desk. "Well, no, I have not. I assumed she visits him on the compound."

It was possible. But why would Nika not have mentioned a cousin to him?

"Did she ever give you another name besides Rebecca?"

"Brendon." Molly folded her arms across her chest and rocked back on her heels. Her lower lip jutted out. "I'm done answering any questions. Unless you elaborate on what's going on, it simply wouldn't be prudent."

He nodded and thrust a hand into his hair. "All right, no more questions. Except, have you seen Emmett?"

"No." Her cheeks flushed. "Why would I?"

His mouth curved into a slight smile, and he was almost grateful for the moment of light humor. Did the woman honestly think he wasn't aware of her quick affair with the other man?

"No reason, I suppose. Thank you for your time, Molly." He gave her a quick wink and then turned to leave the office.

As he hailed a sky cab home, though, the lightness once again disappeared. Once more he only had questions. Dark, relentless, stomach-churning questions.

And unfortunately, he knew the angst wouldn't go away until he had the answers to those questions. He only hoped they were the ones he wanted.

* * *

Nika left the lodge early the next morning, her communication mobile clutched in her hand. Fortunately Molly seemed to be occupied elsewhere and was not in the lobby as Nika passed through.

She hadn't the heart to see her friend and have to spill more lies. Gods, she wanted off this planet. Now. Away from people she shouldn't have formed any kind of emotional connection to. And yet she had.

Out in the cold air, she moved along the trail, trying to put some distance between herself and any civilization.

She'd heaved up her stomach contents this morning, nauseated and disgusted with herself for what she had done last night. Without any hesitation and with perfect ease, she'd slipped right back into her role as a Rosabelle.

She had somehow managed to push aside all her emotions and methodically seduce and sleep with Brendon. If it had not been for her small climax at the end—when the pleasure finally pierced through her cold demeanor—she might have convinced herself she was with her owners back on Zortou.

She dialed in the code that would reach Rachel on Tresden. Her sponsor picked up almost immediately.

"Donika, what is the status of the mission?"

"Tonight," Nika rasped. "I'm going tonight. And after I send the items, please ensure a pod is sent to retrieve me shortly after."

"Of course, Donika. You know the procedure. You will notify us the moment the samples are sent up into space. After the rocket has been retrieved by an assigned scout, then we will arrange your pickup, but only *after* you give us your location. The key is to keep a low profile if at all possible after."

If at all possible. That was certainly easier said than done.

"Yes, ma'am," she murmured complacently after swallowing hard.

"You sound quite anxious. Are you worried about your ability to succeed?"

"No. Not at all. It is just . . ."

"Ah. Does your anxiety have to do with the man you've been bedding to gain information?"

She hesitated too long.

"I see. Well, fear not, Donika. Shortly this will be nothing more than a fading memory. You will be back on Tresden where you belong. Your people will revere you and honor your name for years to come."

Where you belong. She'd never felt like she belonged. Not really. This mission was supposed to help her feel more as one with her planet, and instead she'd grown closer to the people of Belton.

"Donika?"

"Yes, ma'am."

"Goddess protect you. You will be in our thoughts tonight on this mission." She paused. "And if we don't hear from you, or if something were to go wrong . . . if you were to be captured—"

"I know what to do."

Her response was automatic. The idea of taking her life with the small black pill sent very little fear through her. It had been engrained in her during training. And she knew the chances of taking it were slim. Not if she did her job right. And she would.

"Farewell, Donika. We shall see you soon."

Their line of communication was disconnected. Nika palmed her mobile and her gaze ran over the land around her, as she drew in a deep breath of fresh air.

Such a beautiful planet, Belton was. Entirely refreshing and peaceful.

Something moved in the trees beyond her and her gaze

jerked toward the noise. Scanning the forest and trail beyond, she saw nothing, but a sense of unease prickled deep.

It was an animal, nothing more.

She turned and hurried back to the lodge. There was much to do before tonight.

Brendon slipped from his post just after lunch, having cleared it with the other guard.

He moved into the administrative office and spotted the woman manning the front desk.

"Gillian, I need a favor," he murmured, flashing her his brightest smile.

"Lieutenant, you know you're not supposed to address me in such a way," the young woman scolded, even as her lips curled. "And what sort of favor are we speaking of?"

"I need information from your computer."

"What information might that be?"

"I need you to confirm the identity of a woman who was recently brought onto the compound."

Gillian stared at him, her lips pursing. "I really shouldn't, Lieutenant."

"But you will?" His smile widened.

She let out a harrumph and turned to her computer. "I will. What is the woman's name?"

"Rebecca Owens."

Gillian nodded, even as her fingers flew across the thin screen.

"Here we are. Rebecca Owens, an ambassador from Glorus."

Brendon leaned forward, eyes narrowing as he stared at the screen. "Hmm. Is there a contact number to speak with someone at the embassy?"

With a nod, Gillian touched a few more buttons on the screen and pulled up the information.

His pulse quickened and he removed his communication mobile from his pocket and dialed in the number.

"Thanks, Gill, I am forever in your debt." He winked and left the office.

"Embassy of Glorus. How may I direct your call?"

"Yes, my name is Lieutenant Brendon Marshall from the Broughlin military complex. I need to confirm one of your ambassadors."

"Certainly, sir," the woman answered smoothly. "And what is the name of this ambassador?"

"Rebecca Owens."

"One moment." There was a pause. "Ms. Owens has been with the embassy for the last two years."

The relief that rushed through him nearly made his legs give out. "I see. Thank you for your time."

He disconnected the call and let out a shaky laugh. Gods, he'd been fearful for absolutely no reason. Nika was exactly who she said she was, and he was a fool to not have believed her. Maybe her past was not ordinary and she was hesitant to open up about some things, but that was just likely because she'd been hurt. It was instinctive.

Thrusting a hand through his hair, he went back to his post. He was anxious to return to the lodge tonight, to hold her in his arms without any suspicion.

Last night, she'd just been thrown off balance. He'd thrust her into a situation where she would have to be confronted with her awful past. Why hadn't he considered the possibility that she would be sickened instead of pleased at seeing another Rosabelle?

No wonder she'd made love to him so clinically last night. She had drawn back into herself.

Guilt pricked in his gut that he'd even dared doubt her. But then, that was his job. It was all part of his training to be suspicious and wary of anyone.

He glanced at the time, already counting the hours left on his shift.

She was not in the restaurant when he entered the lodge later. It had become their routine: she would wait for him there when he finished work.

But as Brendon stood in the doorway, his gaze searching the room, he saw no sign of Nika.

Turning, he went back to the reception desk where Molly was just finishing checking a customer in. Only after the older man had turned and walked away did Brendon approach.

"What now?" Molly asked, her gaze wary. "Have you come to harass me about your lover again?"

His neck flushed with guilt, but he gave a terse shake of his head. "Where is she, Molly?"

She did not answer him, instead turning to input something into the computer.

"Molly?"

"She is upstairs in her room, Brendon, though I cannot say if she will see you or not." She gave him a pointed look. "Or that you deserve to see her."

His voice sharpened. "Does she not want to see me? Has she given you that impression?"

"No. She has not said anything, nor been very visible today. By all means, Brendon, go see her." Her lips curled downward. "It's probably better than avoiding her."

He paused, eyes narrowing. "Has Emmett been avoiding you?"

Molly's head snapped up, her cheeks flushing. "I said no such thing."

"You do not have to. Contact him. I'm certain he misses you."

"That cannot be true. He has not come by the Crow's Nest in quite some time now."

"Hmm. Contact him anyway," he said again and patted her hand. "I'm off to see Nika."

"Nika?" Molly's voice sharpened. "You mean Rebecca?"

"They are one and the same," he called out as he hurried up the stairwell.

At her doorway he paused, listening for any sounds inside. Hearing nothing, he knocked lightly and waited. Silence.

And then footsteps.

"Nika, it's Brendon. Let me in, love."

He heard her footsteps cease on the other side of the door, and then more silence.

"Nika?"

"Yes, one moment," she called quietly.

At least a minute passed before she opened the door to him.

She stood before him, breathing rapidly and dressed in a thin white flowing gown, her face pink. His gaze scanned the room as he tried to discover the source of her being out of breath.

"I was stretching," she explained and pulled her hair down from the knot it was in. "Trying to ease some aches in my muscles."

"Ah." He stepped inside, his gaze sweeping over her body. The faint hint of red nipples poked through the gown. "I believe I have other ways to ease those aches. I'm quite talented with my hands."

Something flickered in her eyes—was it wariness?—before it shifted to something softer, something all too feminine. "Is that so? Perhaps you'd care to demonstrate."

"I'd love to." He stepped inside and pressed the button to seal the door shut once more. "Shed your gown, love, and lay down upon the bed on your stomach."

She slid the thin straps from her shoulders and shimmied out of the thin fabric.

Naked now, her nipples puckered in the air. With an almost shy smile at him, she moved to the bed and scooted onto her stomach.

The bare curve of her spine drew his gaze and he followed it to the soft swell of her firm buttocks.

He crossed the room and sank down on the edge of the bed, flexing fingers that already itched to run over her skin.

Before he gave in to the temptation, he leaned down, smoothing the hair off her shoulder, and pressed a kiss to the nape of her neck.

"I missed you today, love," he murmured.

She didn't answer, but her body softened beneath him.

"And I want to apologize for last night." He set his hands upon her shoulder and began to knead the tension in her muscles. "I was an insensitive lout and did not realize how seeing Talia might make you feel."

She was quiet for too long, and then said, "I imagine you thought I would enjoy seeing an old friend." She paused. "And in truth, I did, I suppose. But it took a while to get past the shock. The memories . . ."

"I'm sorry." He moved his hands down her body, massaging every inch of her back, loving the silky feel of her pale skin. "I would never hurt you. Ever, Nika."

Her body trembled beneath him, and he heard the uneven breath she drew in. A moment later, she rolled over onto her back.

"Make love to me, Brendon," she whispered, her gaze uncommonly vulnerable. "Please."

She was crazy. Insanity had finally taken hold, but Nika didn't give a damn. This was going to be her last night with Brendon and like hell would she turn off her emotions. Not like she did last night, having sex with him as if he meant nothing to her.

Because he did mean something to her. Somehow in the past few weeks, he'd become far too important. He'd taken up residence in her heart, and it hurt too much to imagine evicting him.

She'd deal with the consequences later, when she'd have to find a way to sneak out to complete her mission.

Brendon's gaze heated, moved over her with a soft possessiveness. And then his head lowered and his mouth claimed hers.

One night. Just one more night.

Her arms wrapped around his neck and she parted her lips, letting his tongue inside to caress hers.

They tangled, dancing together in soft touches, before he retreated and nipped at her bottom lip.

Heat spread quickly through her body, from the tips of her fingers to her curling toes. She moved her fingers up the back of his neck, cradling his head against her as their mouths fused together again. His tongue slid against hers in slow, decadent strokes.

He moved his palm between them and placed it over her breast, cuddling her flesh.

Nika arched into his touch, her legs moving against the bed as the ache low in her belly grew. Her nipple hardened against his palm and her body craved the wet heat of his mouth upon it.

She pulled his mouth from hers, urging his head downward to her breast. He groaned and moved willingly, his lips capturing the greedy nipple and sucking it deep into his mouth.

"Oh gods." She arched into him, both hands holding his head against her now.

Brendon's mouth moved to cover her entire nipple, his tongue circling the sensitive tip. After a moment of the sweet torment, he switched his mouth to the other breast.

Her thighs fell open, giving him room to settle between them.

Her legs wrapped just above his waist and she squirmed against him while he nibbled and licked her breasts.

Cream gathered in her pussy, and she clenched her inner muscles, needing to fill the ache inside her.

Brendon seemed to know exactly what she craved, for he released her breast from his mouth and slid farther down her body.

He knelt between her thighs, drawing her legs over his shoulders and cupping her ass.

His mouth dipped and his tongue swept into her slit, sliding from the edge of her channel to her throbbing clit.

"Brendon," she cried out, gripping the quilt on the bed.

He plunged his tongue inside her, sliding deep and tasting all of her.

Her body jerked against him, but he held her firm.

Again his tongue swept over her, but moved low this time. Lower still, pausing to tease the smaller hole between her ass cheeks.

Heat burned her face, and she closed her eyes. Gods, how wicked. How wonderful.

He probed the hole with his tongue, sinking inside, before sliding back out and moving to flick her clit again. Her body clenched and she bit her lip as pleasure spiraled higher inside her.

His tongue circled the bud, faster and harder. And then, when she knew she was about to topple over the edge of pleasure, he bit her clit just enough to break her.

With her body still trembling and lights spinning in her head, he lowered her ass back to the bed but kept her legs held in the air.

His cock pressed against the folds of her pussy and he slid steadily into her, opening her as her body continued to clench through the orgasm.

"Gods, Nika." He gasped, closing her legs and pressing her ankles together.

The position sent him deeper and spread another wave of pleasure through her.

He pumped in and out of her steadily, moving deeper with each smooth stroke, his sac slapping against her ass. His hips rotated, hitting all the extra sweet spots inside her channel.

Her body rocked softly on the bed with each thrust he made inside her.

"Nika," he whispered, his gaze searching hers. The intensity there sent a warmth through her that had little to do with her arousal.

"Brendon," she answered, just his name.

It seemed to be all he needed. He stroked harder into her, his grip on her ankles tightening. Faster. Deeper.

Each slide of his cock against her swollen walls sent stabs of ecstasy through her, built again into that almost frenzied state where she was so entirely close to igniting again.

She closed her eyes and gripped the quilt, hanging on for dear life. When he let out a roar and swiveled his hips just so, he hit that sweet spot inside her again and she went flying.

"Oh gods!" She clenched around him, lifting her hips and gasping as she came again.

Brendon was right with her, letting out a cry as he pressed deep, emptying himself warm and slick inside her.

Nika drew in a ragged breath, her heart slamming wildly against her rib cage. When Brendon pressed a soft kiss against her ankle, she almost melted.

And then he lowered her legs to the bed and slid from her body. The warmth of his seed still within her was an intimate reminder of the intensity of their lovemaking.

Lovemaking. She closed her eyes again as he came to lie beside her. Such romantic terminology she'd thought to never use . . .

Brendon slid his arms around her, pulling her against him.

"Thank you," he whispered and pressed a kiss against her forehead. "Gods, what you do to me. I've never felt this way about another woman, Nika. How fortunate I am that you came into my life, love."

The warmth and peace inside her shriveled as reality took hold. Fortunate? He'd hardly think so come morning.

Tonight, she would betray him.

14

Nika's stomach twisted and bile rose in her throat. She had no choice. This was her mission. The one she'd signed up for. And by the gods, she would complete it. She had to.

The silence in the room hit her suddenly. He was waiting for a response.

She pushed away from him slightly and forced a calm expression onto her face when she lifted her head to look up at him.

"No, Brendon. I am the one who is fortunate to have found you." And at least that much wasn't a lie.

Beyond the information he'd given her about the lab, he'd also shown her what it meant to be touched by someone on a deep level—both physically and emotionally.

But it was time. Time to move forward with her mission and the night ahead of her. First things first, she would need to ensure Brendon slept through the night.

Nika slid out of his grasp completely and swung her legs off the bed. "I am thirsty. Perhaps some wine?"

His lips quirked. "Do you have some?"

"No, but it would be no trouble to run downstairs and ask Molly if she could spare a bit."

"You're not dressed; perhaps I should go instead."

"Neither are you, and it will take me but a moment." To prove her point, she slipped her dress over her head and down her body, then wrinkled her nose. "Whereas you have all sorts of fastenings and ties."

"Ah. I suppose you are right. Well, hurry back, love. I will be lonely without you."

He teased her, she knew, but still her stomach did that little flipping bit.

"I know you shall." She winked and kept a light smile on her face as she slipped into the bathing chamber.

Quickly, she opened her small travel case and pulled out a container that should have held soap. Opening the round case, she plucked out the small bag of herbs. With just a pinch, she'd be able to ensure Brendon slept heavily the rest of the evening, giving her the opportunity to slip out and do what needed to be done.

Hurrying down the stairs, she could feel her heart pounding heavily in her chest. Gods. What she was about to do.

Molly spotted her and a smile widened across her face. "Good evening, Rebecca."

"Good evening. Molly, might I be able to convince you to part with two glasses of wine?" She bit her lip and twisted her hands in front of her, trying to appear embarrassed. "Brendon and I are . . . umm . . ."

"Say no more! How romantic. Give me just a moment." Molly let out a soft giggle and disappeared to the restaurant kitchen.

Nika's chest tightened with brief unhappiness. This could possibly be the last time she saw the other woman. That is, if all went well tonight, and it would.

"Here you are." The other woman breezed back into the lobby, a glass clutched in each hand. "And no charge, these are on me."

Nika took one from her and then on impulse leaned forward to embrace Molly.

"Oh dear, it is nothing really," Molly murmured but hugged her back.

"Thank you." Nika pulled away, knowing she was thanking her for so much more than just the wine. Molly had been a good friend to her.

Drawing in a slow breath, she knew she had to leave and keep it light, or Molly might get suspicious.

"I will see you tomorrow likely," she lied and took the other glass of wine from her.

"Sounds lovely. We can have lunch unless you have plans with your cousin? Or have to work?"

Nika kept her expression neutral, hoping there was no guilt or disappointment in her eyes.

"Lunch would be lovely."

"Rebecca."

Molly stopped her when she would have turned to walk back up the stairs.

"Is everything all right?"

Nika froze at her question.

"Of course. Why would it not be?"

"No reason. I just . . ." Molly hesitated and stepped forward, glancing around them. "Brendon was asking questions about you."

Nika's pulse quickened and she wavered on her feet, as she suddenly grew quite lightheaded. "What kind of questions?"

"I know he would not be pleased with me mentioning this to you." Molly bit her lip and shook her head. "But he wanted to know why you were on the planet. Whether you'd given me a name other than Rebecca."

The room swam, and Nika's fingers nearly crushed the glass. Brendon suspected something. Oh gods. She'd thought she'd covered her tracks well, but apparently not.

"Rebecca? Gods, there *is* something you're hiding, isn't there? Are you in some kind of trouble?"

"No. No, Molly, I promise." The lie tasted bitter on her lips this time. "I'm just startled to find the man I've become so close to has suspicions about me."

Rightfully so. But Molly did not know that.

"I'm sure he's just being prudent. Please, Rebecca, if there is ever anything I can do . . . I'm always here."

"Thank you." Nika nodded, swallowing the sudden lump in her throat. "I should go now."

"I didn't mean to cause any trouble," Molly said softly. "I should have kept my mouth closed."

And thank gods she hadn't. Because now Nika had adequate warning. Nika gave a slight nod and turned and walked back up the stairs. Funny, but Brendon hadn't made love to her like a suspicious man. Quite the opposite, actually.

In the stairway, she paused and pulled the flavorless herbs from the slit she'd sewn in her dress. She emptied a small amount into the glass in her left hand and swirled it around.

Guilt twisted her insides again, but she brushed it aside. It was time to finish this. Now. It was not as if it would kill him, just make him sleep for a bit.

She entered the room again and found him reclining on his back, arms folded above his head and eyes closed. Panic fluttered in her belly that he might've gone back to sleep.

"I missed you."

His soft words, spoken without opening his eyes, relieved her.

Not wanting to appear too eager for him to drink the wine, she set it on the table next to the bed.

"I missed you, too. Your wine, if you'd like."

He propped himself up with one elbow and gave her a slow smile. His gaze ran over her body.

"Why don't you take off that dress again, love? Crawl back into bed with me."

Desire mixed with impatience inside her, causing a frustrating combination. She didn't have time for this—no matter what her body might want. And yet, she couldn't let on that she was in a rush.

She slipped the dress off once more and took a sip of wine, hoping he'd mimic her.

He didn't disappoint. Leaning over to the table, he grabbed his cup of wine and took a small sip. Something flickered in his gaze before he raised the glass toward his nose and sniffed.

Every muscle in her body went rigid. Could he smell it? It should have been odorless. Gods.

"Is it not to your liking?" she murmured and sat on the edge of the bed, taking another sip of her wine.

"This is aliaberry wine?"

"It is, though a late in the season bottle." She paused, hoping he bought her lie. "Perhaps that is the reason it tastes a bit more bitter?"

"Not bitter. Sweeter."

She drew in a slow breath. Gods, she needed to get him to drink it, to stop him from analyzing the taste.

Reaching out, she took the cup from him and sniffed it. Then, knowing it was a risk, she tilted the cup just enough to wet her lips and give the appearance of having drunk it.

She forced a dry swallow and lifted a brow. "Tastes all right to me."

"Hmm." His gaze narrowed on her mouth, but there was

heat in his eyes now. "Perhaps it will taste more decadent upon your lips."

He lowered his head and his tongue lapped up the trace of wine that resided on her mouth.

Tingles of pleasure spread through her as her pulse quickened with excitement.

He'd just given her the perfect solution for getting him to drink the wine. If sex was the way his mind went, then so be it.

Brendon gave a murmur of approval and went to part her mouth with his own, to seek the sweetness of her mouth instead of the wine. Gods, when it came to touching Nika he was insatiable.

But she pushed him back and he gave a growl of protest, until he saw the sparkle of mischief in her eyes.

"Perhaps it will taste more decadent on other areas of my body as well," she murmured and reached for his hand that held the glass.

Her words already sent a vision of sensuality through his mind and his lips curled upward. He allowed her to guide his hand that held the wine back to her body.

She tilted the glass so the red fluid spilled over the edge onto her breasts.

He shifted his gaze downward, watched the wine dribble down the slope of her breast and trail over one hard nipple.

His cock hardened at the sight and he inhaled swiftly, before leaning down to swipe his tongue over the tip to catch the drop of wine.

Nika let out a groan of pleasure and her body arched against him.

With his own desire mounting rapidly, he licked his way up her breast, clearing it of the sticky wine.

"More," he rasped and pushed her onto her back on the bed so she was supine.

* * *

He grabbed the glass of wine and tilted it again, watching the stream of red drizzle over her breasts and down her belly.

Then he was on her again, his mouth caressing each swell and dip he'd anointed. He tasted the combination of sweet wine and her flesh still salty with perspiration from their earlier lovemaking.

His mouth moved lower, dipping into the crater of her navel that held the wine like a chalice. Nika's stomach quivered beneath him and she let out a soft sigh.

He took the wine again and brought the glass just above the swell of her mound. Tilting it, he dribbled a rivulet over her and watched it trickle into the folds of her pussy.

After quickly setting the glass on the table, he moved back between her legs. He lapped up the wine from her smooth mound, following the trail down the apex of her thighs, licking each inner thigh and carefully bathing her as he avoided her sweetest spot. He knew it drove her crazy as her hips lifted toward his mouth and her sighs turned to frantic moans.

Finally, he could deny her nor himself no more. Cupping her ass cheeks, he lifted her toward his mouth and sank his tongue into her creamy slit.

The tart taste of desire mixed with the sweetness of the wine. The result was such a potent elixir he could barely lift his head from between her thighs. So eager he was to taste all of her, drink her until she was dry. And then if that happened, he'd touch her until she was damp again, pour more wine in her.

"Brendon," she cried out, her hands sliding into his hair to cradle his head to her.

His mind spun, heady with the erotic taste and soft warmth of pussy surrounding his tongue. Gods, this woman made him mindless. Made him a prisoner to bringing her pleasure, which in turn gave him so much.

He shifted his mouth to her clit, wanting to bring her to climax. Thinking maybe if she came, he'd be a little clearer in the head as well.

But the longer he stayed buried with his mouth between her legs, the deeper into this thick fog he seemed to go. She was his addiction. The taste of her. The sound of her cries.

Nika's fingers gripped his hair, tugging when she silently asked him to lick faster. He complied, licking and suckling the swollen bud of flesh.

"Oh gods. *Gods!*"

Her bottom clenched in his hands and then she let out a long frantic cry. Her release brought more warm cream to his tongue and he devoured it, pressing a finger inside her to feel the muscles spasm.

She finally went limp beneath him and he lifted his head.

The spinning didn't stop. Gods. He pressed a hand to his forehead and frowned. What was wrong with him?

"Nika?" He mumbled her name and struggled to sit up.

"Brendon?" Her husky tone sharpened and she scooted out from under him. "Are you all right?"

He blinked, his eyelids feeling heavy, the muscles in his body growing lax.

She caught his chin, lifting his head up so he had to look at her. Her gaze scanned his, almost with calculation. Then his vision blurred and he fell back against the pillow.

"Have some more wine," she said quickly and reached for the cup.

"N-no more wine." The words were thick on his tongue and he made a feeble attempt to swipe her hand away as she tipped it against his lips.

It sloshed against his mouth and down his chin.

The wine. Gods. There was something in the wine.

"Nika?" he whispered, trying to hold her gaze, knowing that she would see the realization in his.

Guilt flashed in her eyes, so quickly he wasn't sure it was real, because then it was sympathy as she smoothed a hand over his forehead.

"I'm sorry, Brendon. I have worn you out. Honestly, I am a bit tired, too." She snuggled down beside him, laying her head against his chest. "Let's just sleep for the night. We'll wake up in the morning and feel just fine."

He needed to stay awake . . . needed to . . .

His eyes closed. What the hell had he done?

15

She'd actually done it.

Nika's chest grew so tight she could barely breathe. Tears burned behind her eyes but she blinked them back as she slid away from Brendon's limp body.

She stared down at him for a moment, watched the steady rise and fall of his chest. His lids were now closed over the suspicion that had been in his gaze.

He would never forgive her when he finally awoke. Would she ever forgive herself?

She hardened her resolve and looked away. It didn't matter. Nothing mattered anymore except for completing this mission and getting the hell off this planet.

She stood from the bed and immediately set to her task, pulling the case from beneath the bed and clearing out the bureau.

Once the two cases were packed she glanced around the room and sighed. Brendon still slept deeply. Her gaze swept to the table near the bed and to the half-empty glass of wine.

Unease settled in her gut. He had not drunk the entire contents. Gods knew how long he would be out. Certainly for enough time to complete her mission, but it left little time for dallying.

She grabbed one case and then hurried to the bathing chamber. Easily, she lifted the case and placed it into the sunken tub.

Leaning down, she pressed the code into the hidden panel of the case and quickly stepped backward. She watched, a calm washing over her as the case began to glow red and then quickly melted into itself and the contents inside.

It burned until there was nothing but a film of ash lining the tub. Turning on the water, she rinsed away the rest of the evidence of her stay on Belton.

Once that task was complete, she exited the bathing chamber, knowing she must leave now, for time was moving swiftly.

She headed for the door, her case of supplies for the mission in her hand. Before she could press the button to open the door, she hesitated and glanced back one last time at Brendon.

Her heart twisted, softened, and she swallowed the lump in her throat.

"Gods, I'm a fool," she muttered and dropped her case to the ground.

Hurrying back to him she leaned over the bed and brushed a soft kiss across his mouth.

"I'm sorry, Brendon. If only things could have been different."

With that being the only good-bye she knew they would have, she turned and pressed the release on the door. It hissed open, and she grabbed the case and slipped out, never looking back.

Sneaking past Molly at the front desk was a small challenge. Nika waited on the stairs for the other woman to disappear into the restaurant before rushing across the lobby and out the door of the hotel.

Once outside in the brisk winter air, she tugged her long cloak tighter about her. It wouldn't do if anyone noticed her wearing the same clothes that the thief had been seen in during the first attempt.

The crisp wind pushed back her hood, but fortunately her hair was tucked in a severe knot upon her head. Darkness surrounded her as she made her journey to the compound.

Sounds of the forest cloyed her senses, made every hair lift on her body. She heard all too clearly the scratching of animals among the leaves. Small feet darted across the trail ahead of her, along with the foreboding of something not quite right: an underlying darkness in the night. Of evil.

Her gaze searched the darkness of the trees around her, and she half expected to find somebody watching her. Someone like that awful blood drinker.

You're a fool, simply being paranoid.

Some of the tension eased from her muscles as she grew closer to the lights of the compound and out of the shadows.

She paused and dropped her bags to the ground, removing the cloak from her body. Opening the bag with all her supplies for the mission, she donned the last parts of her disguise. The eye shields and the facial mask—things she could not have left the lodge wearing.

After strapping three syringes to her thigh, she again lowered the loose leg of her pants. She searched the supply case and took out only what she would need for the rest of this journey.

Sealing the case back up and placing the cloak inside, she activated the destroy button and settled it on the ground. She watched it burn itself into ashes, waiting as all the evidence was neatly destroyed and the only things left to identify her were strapped somewhere to her body.

Nika straightened and turned her attention to the compound ahead, drawing in a slow breath. Already in the distance she could see one guard standing out front.

Her lips twisted and she crouched low to the ground, sticking to the scattered shadows as she approached the outer perimeter.

Reaching for the tranquigun, she loaded the chamber with the noxious-tipped dart and took aim. Jerking the activator, she lurched forward.

The guard turned toward her, reaching for his electro-mace but the dart had already found its home in the side of his neck. He reached for it, eyes widening. With fingers still clutched around the dart, he crumpled to the ground in a heap.

Nika glanced around, ready to fight another soldier if needed. But there was no one. Taking a slow breath she strode forward to scale the gate, ready to meet her next challenge inside the compound.

She was quite incredible, really.

Leo stood in the shadows and watched in amazement as Donika easily took out the first guard and then scaled the impressive enclosure surrounding the lab.

From all the overheard conversations, he'd discovered exactly who she was. Not Rebecca, but Donika, a former Rosabelle who'd disappeared after the liberation.

He leaned back against the trunk of a tree and narrowed his eyes. Stroking the hilt of his weapon, he cocked his head and ran his tongue over his sharp left incisor.

Truly, he should go and stop her. Put an end to this now and collect his reward. And usually, that's exactly what he would have done. Though he had to admit that if there was proof of her having stolen the items, it would seal her fate all the more securely. There would be no question that she was indeed their thief.

But there was another temptation for Leo that went beyond the money. The temptation to keep her for a bit. To learn her secrets and perhaps enjoy the pleasures of her body. Why turn her in right away?

No, he would enjoy her a bit first. The blood swelled his cock as the image of fucking her flitted through his mind. She would be a thrill to break. Such a strong woman. One who fought with the strength and wit of a man. Yes. Before he turned her over to Belton, he would enjoy playing with her.

His lips curled into a sneer. He wasn't particularly fond of Belton or its people. Especially after those pitiful humans had removed him from the lodge when they hadn't approved of his attempts at wooing the lodge owner.

Unfortunately, the bounty on Belton required she be caught alive, which was a pity. Already his mouth watered at the impossible vision of sinking his fangs into her pretty white neck, drinking her lifeblood and feeling her weaken beneath him.

Gods, he was starving. There was no way to feast on human blood on this planet. He'd had to settle for animals. To touch a human here would be an immediate death sentence for breaking the unspoken treaty between their planets.

Watching her disappear inside, he gave a soft sigh and looked away.

There was no other solution. He would simply wait for her to leave the lab with the stolen specimens—because it would really be so much more convincing if he was to capture her and be able to provide the stolen goods later.

Knowing he had a bit of time still, he straightened from the tree and went to find something to eat.

The thick hands of sleep tried to hold him under, but Brendon stirred, fighting against the tenacious hold.

Gods, there was something he should be remembering. Something waiting for him when he would open his eyes.

He twisted his head from the pillow and fought to lift his eyelids. It took a moment before they slit just enough to let in the mostly dark room.

Nika's room.

Pushing himself up into a sitting position, which took quite a bit of effort, his eyes grew accustomed to the dimness as he turned his gaze about the room. It was empty. And not just because Nika was gone. It appeared all her stuff was as well.

His heart pounded faster and he flung his legs off the bed, forcing himself to his feet. His head spun and his tongue felt thick in his mouth.

"Nika?" He croaked out her name, knowing it was pointless.

Gone. She was *gone*.

He found the control for the light and turned it. The room filled slowly with a soft light and he blinked, his pupils shrinking in protest.

Why? Why had she left? And where had she gone? Even as the questions pounded in his head, the answer was just behind them, pricking at his awareness and taunting him.

Brendon pulled on his clothing quickly and then left the room. His feet pounded down the hallway and over the staircase, announcing his urgency before he arrived in the lobby.

Molly appeared at the foot of the stairs, her eyes wide.

"Brendon? Are you quite all right?"

"No. Damn it, I am not all right. Where is she, Molly?" He pressed a hand to the back of his head and bit back a groan.

Gods, but it throbbed.

"Rebecca?"

"Sure. Whatever the hell you insist upon calling her."

Molly flinched, folding her arms across her chest. "There is no need to yell."

"Molly, you try my patience."

"And you try mine," she fired back.

Emmett entered the building at that moment, his focus on Molly. But he hesitated when he saw them speaking together.

"Answer the question, Molly." The pain and panic of losing Nika only added to Brendon's urgency and irritation.

"What is this about?" Emmett inquired, coming between them.

Molly started, obviously not having been aware of his presence. Pink filled her cheeks, and she ran her tongue across her mouth.

"You're out late, Emmett."

"Indeed." Emmett's gaze met hers and anyone in the room would have to be blind to not see the heat and frustration in his gaze.

Brendon let out an aggravated growl. The last thing he needed was to sit back and wait while these two figured out their own insecurities.

"Molly." Her name was a warning upon his lips.

She flinched and looked away from Emmett. "I have not seen her since she came down earlier to get the wine."

The wine. His eyes narrowed and the breath hitched in his chest. Anger slammed through him.

"The wine," he said softly and stepped toward her. "Gods, Molly. You were her accomplice? What did you put in it?"

"What?" she yelped and backed up, obviously panicked by the glint in his eyes. "I put nothing in the wine."

"Brendon?" Emmett stepped between them and placed a hand upon his chest to halt his advance. "What is the meaning of this? What do you accuse her of?"

"My fucking wine was drugged!" he roared and turned his glare to Molly. "And you just admitted giving it to her."

Molly's face drained of color, her head moving back and forth. "No. I simply poured from the bottle."

"You make false accusations, my friend." Emmett warned softly, his own gaze narrowing. "Be careful with your words."

"I did nothing, Brendon. I swear," Molly cried from over Emmett's shoulder. "Are you certain the wine was tainted? I cannot imagine that Rebecca—"

"Nika. Her name is Nika. And nobody could have imagined it." He thrust his hand through the air and gestured with his frustration. "She had us all convinced she was a damn seraph. All innocence and sweetness."

"And what has made you change your mind about her?" Emmett asked, lifting a brow.

"Many things," Brendon murmured grimly, "that I ignored for too long. But no more. Gods, if she is who I believe her to be, I can ignore this no longer."

Molly stepped out from behind Emmett, her gaze panicked. "Wait, Brendon. Please do nothing impulsive. Whatever she has done can be undone. She is not a bad person."

Brendon gave a harsh laugh and headed for the exit. "She has indeed fooled us all."

"Brendon . . ."

"Let him do what is needed, Molly," he heard Emmett say quietly.

And then Brendon stepped outside the lodge and the doors hissed shut behind him.

He walked quickly on the trail that led to the compound. With each step he took he pleaded with the gods that she would not be there.

Nika watched the guard crumple to the ground and then hurried forward, stepping over his limp body.

Two down, one to go. She circled around the corner of the lab, the fluorescent lights in the corridor making her squint after having been outside in the darkness of night.

Where was this last guard? Her pulse stayed steady, her training coming to the foreground, and she was able to keep her composure.

"Bastard!"

His loud cry had her spinning, even as a foot slammed into her hips and sent her stumbling backward.

The soldier's eyes were wide with fear and anger as he clutched an electro-mace in his hand.

He rushed her again, clumsy in his fervor to shed blood. Nika thanked her good fortune and crouched low, waiting until he was nearly upon her to bring her own electro-mace up.

She caught him on the side of the head with the spiked club. But instead of depressing the button that would've sent enough electricity through his body to kill him, she counted on the blunt impact to simply knock him out.

He didn't disappoint, but let out a soft groan as he fell back against the wall and slid down unconscious. Already blood seeped from the wound and worry stabbed through her.

Hopefully she hadn't killed him. *Head wounds bleed*, the rational voice inside her head was quick to remind.

He would get help soon. Once she had the specimens, it would only be a matter of time.

Nika drew in a deep breath and approached the soldier to lift the key from him. As she'd suspected, the key was different this time. They had changed the locks.

She approached the hidden panel and unveiled the keyhole. Changed the locks, but they still couldn't keep her out. She felt a perverse sense of pleasure when she slid the key in and watched the door to the inner lab open.

Stepping inside, she was struck by the chill temperature in the room. The soft hum of the lighting added to the urgency of her mission.

She crossed the floor, moving directly toward the freezer unit that held the specimens. It took only a few tries to break the code on the unit.

Nika stepped back at the loud suctioning sound that filled the room. A second later the lid sprang free and rose into the air slowly, icy vapors seeping from the freezer unit.

She waited a moment and then stepped close, peering inside the square container. Her breath caught at the rows of glass cylinder tubes.

By the gods, she had done it. She had actually done it.

Reaching inside, she lifted out the first tiny tube. Her fingers clenched around the slippery glass, which was almost too cold to hold onto.

No time to lose.

She pulled the soft roll of fabric from the belt that was strapped around her waist beneath her outfit. Shaking the fabric into its normal shape as a carrying bag, she set the first sample in.

Then she grabbed another, and another, clenching as many in her hand as she could and filling up the bag.

Her heart pounded, but not with excitement. Why didn't she feel a sense of pride? Of success? Anything besides this growing desolation.

Grabbing one last sample she sealed the bag, knowing she must have taken at least a couple hundred of the tiny tubes.

Now it was time to get out, get to the buried transporter unit and send these guys up into the universe. She'd send word that the mission was accomplished, and the specimens would be picked up. Then she'd send the code for her new location and would be retrieved shortly after.

Exactly as planned.

Nika closed the freezer unit and strode toward the door to the lab. She stepped over the slumped body of one of the soldiers and gave him a quick glance. Reassured by the steady rise and fall of his chest, she continued toward the entrance to the building.

The lights from the outside of the compound could clearly be seen. She increased her stride, eager to escape this building and this planet.

She took another hurried step, the entrance just feet away now.

A shadow stepped into the doorway and snuffed out the light.

Nika stumbled to a halt, her fingers clenching around the bag in her hand as her blood chilled with wariness.

"Release the samples."

Every muscle in her body went soft at the sound of his voice. Her head spun with disbelief. How was it possible? He should've still been asleep.

"Don't make me ask again," he rasped and stepped into the light.

Nika took a step back, uneasy now. To say Brendon was livid would be an understatement. His eyes were narrowed, glittering with rage, his mouth drawn so tightly she could barely remember what a smile had looked like upon it. And his jaw was thrust forward. Hard. A clear indication he was ready to fight.

She drew in a slow breath, her mind rapidly searching for a new plan of attack. A way to get past him. But it wasn't going to be easy. Her throat tightened with the knowledge that they would have to fight again.

He took another step toward her and reached for the weapon on the belt of his uniform.

"Take off your mask." His words were barely a whisper. "Take off your mask, you bitch."

She flinched. So he knew it was she. And the endearment he'd tacked on—though hardly an endearment—had her mouth twitching without amusement.

So this was how it would end for them. Quite possibly one of them would be dead within the next hour.

He lifted his electro-mace and took another step forward.

"You fucked me like the whore you once were, using me the entire time to gain information and entrance into the lab." His nostrils flared. "You played me for a fool. And tonight, you will pay dearly for that."

Her stomach twisted and dropped to her toes, her heart attempting to bounce back from his vicious verbal assault.

He would enjoy killing her, she realized. But only if she didn't kill him first. Though, unlike him, it would bring her no joy to do so.

Survive. Do what you have to, to survive and get these specimens back to Tresden.

The idea of even hurting him again, let alone killing him, made everything go numb inside her with revulsion. Perhaps if she could just disable him for a moment. Take him out of commission without killing him.

She slowly lowered the bag to the floor and bent her knees, crouching low to defend herself from the certain attack.

"Still you do not speak. Do you hope to hide your identity from me?" he taunted, swinging the weapon lightly in his grasp.

Responding to him would only enrage him, erase any doubt he might still have—as unlikely as that might be. But she had to cling to the anonymity, the clothes and eye guards that shielded her identity. Until he pried the mask from her cold, dead face, he would never be completely certain. And she had to use that to her advantage.

"Answer me," he roared and lurched toward her.

Nika sprang up and kicked his wrist, trying to deflect the weapon before it reached her. His arm moved with the blow, but his grip did not loosen.

"Answer me. I will hear your voice!"

She circled him, forcing even breaths in and out of her body, keeping her pulse controlled so she would not make a fatal mistake.

Slipping a hand behind her back and beneath the loose black pants, she reached for the small knife that was strapped to her waist.

Before she could even blink he swung the electro-mace toward her. She saw her death in that moment. Almost welcomed it.

But the mace never connected with her head; he stopped it at the last moment and instead swung his booted foot beneath the back of her legs, knocking her off her feet.

She fell to the floor, the knife clattering a few feet away.

Why had he not killed her?

With no time to process more than that thought, Nika rolled and tried to grab the knife, but he was already upon her.

He straddled her with his knees, forcing her back against the cool floor. With ruthless hands he grabbed her wrists and pinned them above her head.

"Deny it now," he dared, his glittering gaze sweeping over her body. "Do you think that I do not know the body I have so thoroughly enjoyed these past weeks?"

Heat slid through her body, and Nika dragged in a ragged breath, appalled and humiliated to realize she was responding to him in this situation. Against the binding of her breasts, her nipples tightened, and her pussy slickened.

Gods, she was betrayed by her own body. It welcomed the weight of him atop her. Craved him, in passion or fury.

Above her she watched the conflicting emotions in his eyes. The rage, the desire, the betrayal.

He had not connected the hit with the electro-mace. He had instead pulled his punches . . . and likely he expected her to do the same.

That would be his downfall.

Nika let out a soft, throaty moan, just to knock him off guard. It worked. He blinked, loosened his hold on her wrists and that was the only opening she needed.

Lifting her knee, she drove it between his legs.

Brendon choked on a gasp, his eyes widened with pain and shock, before he rolled off her.

She was up in an instant, grabbing the bag of specimens and bolting out the door.

No time. There was no time. Her feet slapped against the earth and the breath dragged from her lungs as she charged into the trees. There was no time for regrets. No time for fear.

He would not be down for long. She had but a fraction of a lead on him.

She found the site of the buried transporter unit and dug at it furiously, tearing through the earth until she'd uncovered the unit. She emptied the vials into the chamber with amazingly steady fingers and sealed it.

Her mind barely registered the sounds of someone rushing through the forest after her.

She slammed her thumb against the ignition lever and the transporter whined to life. Next she initiated the beacon that would notify Tresden that the unit was being sent.

Stepping back, she watched it tremble on the ground before shooting straight up into the air in a blur of motion. Higher and higher, until it was nothing but a faint dot in the atmosphere. And then it was gone.

It was done. Her mission was accomplished.

Her shoulders sagged with relief, her muscles lax as her legs threatened to give out. Brendon slammed into her a second later.

Strong arms surrounded her, cushioning her fall against the earth when she could have easily broken bones.

"You sent it," he growled, his fingers tearing her mask from her face. His gaze sought hers, his expression tortured and furious. "*Damn* you! How could you do this?"

The relief faded, swiftly replaced with panic. Panic and a growing desolation as realization kicked in. Her identity was blown, and she'd been captured.

Her options were gone. There was only one choice left for her. One she'd prepared for and hoped to never have to use.

Nika welcomed the comforting emotional numbness that slid through her as he rolled her onto her back. She refused to let him restrain her arm, instead slipped her hand into the belt around her waist to find the tiny pouch. Pinching her fingers around the small black pill inside, she pulled it free.

Her time had officially run out.

16

Brendon struggled to hold her down, bitterness and disbelief making his attempts not quite as steady.

Until he'd jerked the mask from her face, he'd held onto the tiniest bit of hope that maybe he was wrong. Perhaps it could have been someone else. Anybody but Nika.

But there was no denying the familiar face staring up at him. He knew the full lips, though he'd never seen them flattened into an emotionless line.

He'd failed tonight. Nika had just sent the specimens up into orbit, and gods knew whomever she was working for would receive them before Belton's military could have a chance to retrieve them.

But she would answer to Belton. Tell them everything the minute he turned her over. *And then she will serve the rest of her life in penitentiary.* His breath caught, and he blinked away the sharp stab of misery that thought sent through him.

Beneath him she struggled, pulling her wrist from his grasp again as she attempted to escape.

"There is no hope for you," he said harshly, attempting to curl his fingers around her slight wrist. "Surrender."

Her hand slid free from him again, swinging upward. He jerked his head back, certain that she would hit him. But her fist did not move toward his face; instead, her own.

And then he saw it. The small, shiny black capsule squeezed between fingers that she moved toward her mouth.

The anger rushed from his body and was replaced by freezing terror. Every muscle in his body went taut, almost debilitating him. And then he snapped.

"No!" He let his weight fall heavily upon her body and managed to grasp her wrist, attempting to pull her fingers back from her lips. "The *hell* you will kill yourself!"

His fingers clenched around her wrist, squeezing until he was sure the bones would crack. It would be regrettable but a small concern if it saved her from taking her life.

She didn't budge for a moment, and he squeezed harder. Her lips finally parted as a cry of pain escaped them, and then her fingers opened, dropping the capsule. It fell straight down and his heart nearly stopped as it fell against her lower lip, but then it slid down her chin and fell harmlessly to the ground beside her.

"Kill me," her voice cracked with emotion. "Do not let me live."

The sound of her first words—hearing her familiar husky voice—sent a shudder of emotion through his body. He closed his eyes briefly as he pinned her hands above her head.

She wanted him to *kill* her. Was begging him to snuff out the life that he'd grown so attached to.

Impossible. His jaw clenched and his throat tightened with conflicting emotions. Even now he struggled with the idea of just turning her over to his superiors, for obviously that would be worse than death.

"You cannot let me live," she choked out, staring at him through those hideous eye shields that turned her eyes into nothing more than black holes. "Kill me, Brendon. If you have any mercy, *kill* me. It will be better this way."

The anger returned then, starting low in his belly and slicing through his blood.

He shook his head slowly and transferred her wrists into one hand. With his free hand, he moved down her rib cage, searching for what he knew was hidden somewhere on her person.

"Why do you even hesitate?" She bucked beneath him, twisting her body. Her lips curled into a derisive smile that he knew was meant to taunt him. "Are you too afraid to hurt a woman?"

He discovered what he sought strapped to her thigh and his lips curled into a grim smile.

She inhaled swiftly. "What are you doing?"

Slipping his hand into the loose waistband of her pants, he plucked free the syringe.

"No," Nika whispered, her head shaking. Then again, more vehemently, "No!"

"Yes." Before he could second-guess his intentions, he flipped her onto her stomach and tugged down her pants.

Her pale buttock gleamed in the moons' light, but there was only the faintest hint of desire in his blood as he plunged the needle into the curved flesh.

"Please. No." Nika groaned, attempting to crawl away as he depressed the plunger and injected her with whatever was in the syringe—though he was almost certain what it contained.

Her body shuddered and then she stilled beneath him, obviously realizing she'd lost any chance at escaping.

"They will be relentless," she whispered. "They will break me."

"No, Nika." He recapped the syringe and leaned down to kiss the soft spot just below her ear. "*I* will break you."

He rolled her over again and then lifted her into his arms. She was almost a dead weight now as the substance slid through her blood. Her eyes were wide with horror and frustration, her lips trembling.

"Brendon." His name left her lips on a breathy whisper, and then her eyes rolled to the back of her head.

He tried to ignore the ache of regret and sympathy in his chest, and instead adjusted her unconscious body in his grasp.

Glancing sharply around the area, he strode off into the woods, certain he'd lost his mind. To even be contemplating this he had to be.

And yet there was really no other choice.

Leo watched in dismay as the soldier carried Donika off into the forest. He let out a hiss of annoyance and dug his nails into his palms.

Well, this certainly changed things.

He'd been ready to step out of the shadows and snatch her up himself, and then he'd heard *him* thrashing after her.

Hmm. He hadn't foreseen this coming, although he probably should have.

Quite annoying.

For a moment he considered going after them both and simply taking out the soldier. But that would just leave a messy cleanup and arouse suspicions.

No. He would have to find another way and soon.

He followed them at a good distance, watching with interest where the soldier—Brendon, was it?—would take her.

A few minutes later, he had his answer. The door he'd assumed to have shut on his plan to snag the former Rosabelle for a bounty had once again opened.

* * *

Molly let the door to Rebecca's room at the lodge slide shut and her brows furrowed, the sense of unease in her stomach increasing.

All her things were gone. It was as if the woman had never been here.

She moved back down the stairs to the lobby and pushed a hand through her hair.

It was early in the morning and fortunately the lodge was quiet. The restaurant had served one customer earlier who had eaten a bite and then checked out.

Ever since the confrontation last night with Brendon her nerves had been wound up in knots of anxiety. Emmett had encouraged her not to dwell upon it before he'd left shortly after. He had not even tried to talk or touch her. But then she'd been much too distressed in regard to Rebecca—or Nika, as Brendon had adamantly insisted her name was.

The door to the lodge slid open and she glanced up to see who entered. Surprise and warmth slid through as Emmett strode inside.

His dark gaze moved over her, guarded yet with a bit of hunger in it.

Her body responded, her nipples tightened and the ache blossomed between her thighs. But she couldn't afford to indulge in such pleasures right now. No. Right now she wanted answers.

"Did you even sleep?" he asked softly. "You look tired."

"I slept," she murmured and folded her arms across her breasts, hoping to hide her body's reaction.

He arched a brow and stepped into the lobby. "Though not well, I'd wager."

"No. Not well. I could not sleep when my mind continued to worry about Rebe—Nika."

Emmett's gaze became shuttered—unreadable—as it slid from hers.

"I came by for some breakfast. What is your special this morning?"

Molly's pulse quickened and her lips parted with suspicion. There was something he was not telling her. She knew it in her gut.

"Have you heard what happened to her?"

Emmett turned to stare at her for a moment, his jaw hardening, before he looked away again. Then, instead of replying, he strode past her toward the restaurant.

"Emmett!" She growled in frustration and spun on her heel, chasing after him.

She caught his arm before he could enter the restaurant, attempting to spin him around. His body was like a rock, refusing to budge. Finally she heaved a sigh and walked around to stand in front of him.

Hands planted on her hips she glared up at him.

"Tell me what you know."

"It's confidential."

"How can you say such a thing? She is my customer and friend. And now she is missing."

"I gave my word not to say anything, Molly."

She drew in a ragged breath, anger causing her face to flush with heat.

"All right," she finally said and stepped past him again, moving toward her office. "Then I suppose I must place a call with the local police and inform them of a missing person."

He caught her around the waist before she'd taken three steps, jerking her body back against his rigid one.

"I cannot let you do that, sweetheart." His words feathered hot against her ear. His palm moved over her stomach. "Which I'm sure you understand."

Tingles rushed through her nerve endings. He was touching her again. Finally! But, gods, now was not the moment. She closed her eyes, attempting to stay focused on the topic at hand.

"No, I do not understand." She covered his hand with her own and attempted to remove it from where it made soft strokes, but he did not waver.

The ache between her thighs grew and she closed her eyes, leaning back against him despite her will not to give in.

"I cannot think when you do that," she muttered.

He gave a husky laugh as he lips brushed the back of her neck. "That was somewhat my intention."

He walked them into her office and sealed the door shut. She bit her lip but did not protest.

"I thought you did not want to touch me anymore," she confessed softly.

"Gods, are you serious? How could you *ever* think that?" he muttered thickly. Still behind her, his hand cupped her breast through her dress. "I did not want to press you for sex after your assault. I'm not a complete ass."

Her nipple tightened and she sighed pleasure. "Emmett . . ."

"I've missed you, Molly. Gods, how I've missed you," he said fervently. He slid his hands down to her thighs and dragged her dress upward.

Her mind spun and her heart pounded twice as hard. She was losing focus, completely forgetting that she'd been trying to get information from him about Nika.

"Wait, Emmett," she pleaded, tilting her head back so his lips could find the curve of her neck. "You must give me at least a morsel of information about her, something to appease my concerns that she is not in danger."

"I gave my word to keep silent, sweetheart." He gathered her dress above her waist and then his hand was between her thighs, his fingers teasing over the slick folds of her pussy. "But perhaps . . . I might be willing to give you a morsel, if you were willing to give me a morsel?"

Molly gave an exasperated laugh even as her knees went weak from his ministrations.

"That's blackmail."

He sank a finger into her heat and she almost purred with pleasure.

"Indeed it is and I will not deny using it."

"Emmett." Her nails dug into his forearms and she closed her eyes, biting her lip. "I haven't the time. The lodge—"

"Is completely empty right now. And if you prefer we could make it quite fast."

"You are so wicked," she whispered, but let out a sharp cry when he flicked her clit with his finger.

"Is that a yes, then?"

"Do you give me your word that you will tell me after?"

He gave a soft laugh and caught her earlobe between his teeth, flicking it with his tongue. Then he murmured, "I give you my word."

Holding out seemed so self punishing anyway. She truly missed this with him, had been craving his touch for the past weeks.

"All right," she finally whispered. "Please, Emmett."

"You've been driving me mad." He groaned against her ear and then spun her around. "Perhaps quick is a better idea."

"Undoubtedly." Molly freed his cock from his trousers and caressed his dark shaft in her hand.

Emmett backed her up against the door and then lifted her leg, hooking it around his waist. A moment later his cock prodded the damp folds between her legs.

His mouth crushed down on hers at the same moment he plunged deeply into her.

Molly clutched his shoulders, groaning and curling her tongue around his as he moved inside her. Each stroke stretched her and filled her with a growing urgency and pleasure.

He lifted his head and looked down to where they were joined. His expression tightened and he let out a soft growl.

"No more denying we want this, Molly."

She closed her eyes and gasped when his fingers dug into her ass cheek, pressing him deeper inside.

"Molly?"

"No more," she agreed breathlessly and lifted her mouth for his to take again.

He didn't ignore her request and captured her lips, plundering her mouth with his tongue while his cock did the same to her pussy.

His finger found her clit in a hard rub and the pleasure inside her jumped up another level. Her head spun and she gripped his shoulders now so she wouldn't crumple in a boneless heap.

He increased the pace of his thrusts, moving harder and deeper. When she heard the low rumble in his chest and his movements grew erratic, she knew he was as close as she.

Emptying her mind and focusing only on the sensation, she let herself fly. The climax ripped through her, hurling her beyond the peak of reason.

Emmett gasped. "Gods, Molly. You have stolen my heart."

He came a moment later, crushing her lips with his as he emptied himself inside of her.

You have stolen my heart. His words resounded in her head, mirroring her own thoughts as her body continued to tremble with her release. Her inner muscles clenched around him, milking him, dragging her under that intoxicating wave of ecstasy.

Her mind settled not long after. She struggled to drag in a steady breath as he slid from her body and lowered her leg back to the floor.

Molly pulled her dress back down and gave him a small smile. "Did you speak the truth?"

"You know I did," he replied, making no attempt to pretend he knew not what she spoke of as he pushed a curl off her cheek. "You have my heart, Molly. And I only hope that some day you might give me yours."

Her pulse quickened and pleasure warmed her blood, tingeing her cheeks pink as she lowered her gaze.

Trying to be flippant, she murmured, "Well, as you know I had no intention of becoming serious with any man, Emmett. And yet you've managed to flip my most carefully laid plans. No matter what my intentions *were*, somehow you've ended up with my heart as well."

Emmett gave a soft laugh and caught her hand, placing it across his chest to where she could feel the rapid beat of his heart.

"And make no doubt, sweetheart, I shall cherish it."

She gave a delicate sniff, even as her smiled widened. "Indeed, I should hope so."

Their gazes held for a moment, softened, before she finally dragged her focus away and cleared her throat.

"We should get back out front," she murmured.

He nodded and stepped away from her, pushing his cock back into his trousers once more.

She ran her gaze over him, so warm inside and her heart still racing from their moment and somewhat surprising declarations.

And then she remembered. Gods. How could she have almost forgotten? Stepping forward, she wrapped her arms around his waist and pressed a kiss to his neck.

"But before we go, oh keeper of my heart, you did give me your word."

"My word?" he murmured, his hands smoothing a path up and down her spine.

"Nika?"

"Ah. Yes, so I did." He sighed and pulled away. With a gentle hand, he lifted her chin so she looked at him. "Brendon has her and has promised that she will not be harmed."

Molly blinked, her lips parting in dismay. "Pardon? Not be harmed? What is happening? Why would she be harmed?"

"That is all I can tell you at this time. I'm sorry, sweetheart."

"All you can tell me? But you gave me your word!"

"To share a morsel." Emmett gave a slow grin and shrugged. "I apologize, Molly, if it is not as juicy a bit as you would have liked. But it is all Brendon instructed me to share with you."

"Instructed you?" she sputtered and stepped back from his arms. "You mean Brendon *told* you to pass on this information? And yet you made me . . ." Her cheeks filled with color and she gave a growl of frustration. "Why, you little—"

"Did you not just enjoy what we did?" He lifted an eyebrow is amusement and reached for her again, but she quickly avoided him. "Besides, I simply offered a bit of incentive."

She folded her arms across her breasts and glared. "Is that what you would call it? Well, Emmett, I cannot say I'm quite happy with you right now—no matter the state of my heart. You have essentially answered none of my questions."

"You know that she is well."

"From the mouth of the man who looked as if he would like to have killed Nika last night!" She shook her head. "Brendon's word that she will not be harmed is simply not enough."

Emmett's brows drew together in a scowl and his light demeanor vanished. "It will have to be, Molly. This is not your concern."

"You cannot say what is or is not my concern."

"She was nothing but a customer passing through."

"She became a friend."

"And that was your blunder."

"Oh! I cannot believe I am hearing this," she scoffed and moved to step past him, but he caught her elbow and swung her around.

"Molly, please do not force your nose into business where it doesn't belong."

"That is just it, Emmett. There is something amiss with my friend and you and Brendon give me only the barest of details. How am I supposed to just sit by and trust that all is well with her?"

"Do you trust *me*?"

She hesitated, her chin jutting with frustration. "You know that I do."

"Then it should be enough."

Tugging her arm free, she moved to the door and shook her head. "I'm sorry, Emmett. But it is not."

17

Was she dead?

No. There would be no pain after death.

Nika's brows furrowed, but she did not open her eyes. In truth, she was a bit terrified that the pounding in her head would only multiply if she let her lids flutter open.

She moved her hand to touch her head but was stopped by the hard metal that surrounded it.

Her eyes snapped open, panic locking the air in her throat. The room was dim, making it hard to see much more than shadows. She twisted on the mattress—it appeared she was on a bed—and tugged at her wrists, which were restrained above her head in some form of a shackle.

"You have awoken."

The muscles in her body coiled at his cold words. Lifting her head up an inch, she scanned the room, trying to figure out where he lingered.

Brendon sat furled in a chair near the corner—he was just a large shadow, really. She could not see his face and was somewhat thankful.

The reminder came swiftly that she was alive and what her circumstances were. Her stomach revolted and more dizziness assailed her.

Laying her head back down, she closed her eyes.

Surely this was the interrogation room and someone would be in shortly to begin the horrific proceedings. How long would she hold out under their torture? Certainly she could not allow herself to give any information about Tresden.

Her intent had been to die rather than face captivity. And yet she'd succumbed to being taken alive. So she would still likely die, only now at the hands of the planet's military. Her lips twitched in a humorless smile. Unfortunately, it would not be quite as painless a death.

"When will they come?" she inquired flatly.

"When will who come?"

She heard Brendon unfurl himself from the chair and then footsteps approached the bed.

"My interrogators." She opened her eyes and found him standing above her.

Her pulse quickened and something in her heart softened a bit. With regret. With tenderness. Why did it have to end like this? She should never have had to see him in this situation. He should never have known who she was. Whether by her own escape back to Tresden or through her death. *This moment should not be.*

"Have you not yet realized, Nika?" Brendon took another step forward, and his face—rigid and expressionless—was suddenly lit by the faint glow of the early morning sunlight that poured in through the metal blinds. "*I* am your interrogator."

Her throat tightened and she gave the tiniest shake of her head. "No. It would not be allowed. . . . It is a conflict of interest. . . . I do not believe you."

"Do you not?" He arched a brow and extended a hand toward her.

Nika flinched, but his touch was nothing but gentle as it descended upon her cheek.

"What planet do you represent, Nika? For I am certain that you are no ambassador from Glorus."

A chill slid down her spine as she forced her breathing to remain even. He did not lie about being the one to question her. Which would make this process entirely too difficult.

She did not answer him, but held his gaze without wavering.

"Perhaps that one is a bit complex to answer. Maybe I'll start with an easier question?" he murmured and moved his fingers lightly down her jawline. "Was fucking me part of your job requirement?"

Inwardly she flinched, but on the outside she let a slight smile curve her lips. Perhaps if she goaded him into losing control he would end this. Would snap and simply throttle her. Or at the very least find someone else to take over with the interview.

"Answer the question." His voice came out more harshly.

Wetting her lips with her tongue, she lifted her shoulders in an attempt at a shrug. "Why reply to a question you already know the answer to?"

The rage she expected to come did not materialize. Instead his own lips curled upward. She moved her gaze to his eyes and saw that there was no humor there.

His fingers tightened around her chin. "I suppose a trained Rosabelle would be hard pressed to forget her training."

"Indeed, it came in useful." The words almost made her sick.

He waited a beat before answering. "Undeniably. I must applaud your oral skills in particular."

So it was a game to him, she realized. He played along, likely seeing who would break first in their barbed words. By the gods, it would not be her.

"I'm surprised my oral skills would stand out among the many women who have had your cock in their mouths." She pulled her chin from his grasp. "Surely they all blur together."

"Ah, but they don't, Nika. There is something so decadent about a Rosabelle. The talent you have in knowing just how to please a man. The training—"

"I am a trained *fighter* now!" she snarled, feeling her composure slipping. He knew just how to needle her.

"Yes. You are. And not half bad at that. You fight almost as well as you fuck." He gave a soft laugh. "Almost."

The anger in her belly exploded. She jerked at her wrists, letting out a growl of anger. The metal cuffs bit into her skin but she hardly felt it.

"Would you like a rematch?" she challenged. "Remove these bindings and we will see who is the better fighter."

"No, I do not think that would be wise."

She snorted and looked away from him. "Yes, it would not do to have both of your eyes blackened."

"Nor to have your ribs nearly broken again," he muttered, and he could not hide the emotion and disgust in his voice. His fingers trailed over her rib cage. "What kind of woman fights like a man? What drove you, Nika? What if I had killed you?"

"Impossible."

"Actually, quite possible."

She ground her teeth together and turned her gaze from him again. There was no point in continuing this discussion, though a part of her wished he would remove her restraints so she could indeed prove her point that she could bring him to his knees.

"Why do you need the specimens anyway, Nika?"

She closed her mouth tightly and turned her head to the side to look away from him.

"Do you sell it on a black market?"

Shutting her eyes, she tried to tune him out.

"Would you tell me that there was no pleasure for you while in my bed?"

Her eyes snapped back open to meet his considering stare, and she could feel the heat flooding her face.

"Ah, good. You will not deny the answer to that."

No, she wouldn't. But it didn't stop her from answering peevishly, "*You* were in *my* bed."

"Yes. So I was." He leaned down until his face was just a breath away from hers. "And now you're in mine."

What? Confusion swept through her. Her gaze slid away, moving around the room. Surely he jested. Although, it did seem smaller than any interrogation room she could have imagined. And the fact that she was chained to a bed had seemed a bit extraordinary. She had just assumed they meant to use sexual torture to extract information.

But what if he spoke the truth?

"I do not understand," she said, her voice low. "Where am I?"

"I thought I just told you."

"The military would not allow you to keep a prisoner in your chamber."

His hand moved from her rib cage down to her belly, tracing slow circles. "No. They certainly would not."

His words sank in. The blood slid from her face and she struggled to breathe. Her lips tried to form a response but no words would emerge. He had not turned her over to the military. And that would mean . . . She swallowed hard.

His mouth curved into a slight smile.

"You did not inform your superiors of me?" she inquired, a bit numbly.

Brendon did not reply, just held her gaze while his expression remained unreadable.

Her mind whirled rapidly, trying to comprehend why he

would have done such a thing. What his intentions could possibly be to have taken her back to his chamber instead of following orders.

"*Why*?" she choked out.

"I will turn you over." His gaze slid over her body and, despite the calculating desire she saw there, a tremor rocked through her. "Eventually. When I do hand you over, I would like it to be with all their questions already answered, so no interrogation will be necessary."

"And then I will be sentenced to death."

His hand stilled in its stimulating caress over her belly and his gaze shifted to hers.

"Is that not what you wanted?"

Her chin lifted. "Yes. That is what I wanted."

Brendon's calm exterior vanished into a snarl. "Stop this belligerent prattle. Now who is the fool? Do you really wish to die?"

"What I wish is no longer important."

"Martyring yourself, are you?" He barked a humorless laugh.

"And what about you?" Anger stewed in her now and she shook her head. "Do you not realize the trouble this could place you in? Having taken me? Hidden me? Do you not see the risks you take with your career?"

"You should not be worrying about me, Nika. If you had any sense you would fear for yourself and the days to come," he said fiercely. His palm slid to her waist, toying with the fabric that covered her. "As we just established, the military does not know that I have captured you. Nobody knows where you are right now except me."

Heat slid through her body and she drew in an unsteady breath. "Molly will suspect you."

"Emmett will handle her." He pushed the fabric of her shirt upward, exposing her stomach to the cool air in his chamber. "And I will handle you."

"You will not *touch* me."

"I already am touching you. Are you really in such a state of denial, Nika?" He reached into his pocket and pulled out a silver object. After depressing a button on it, a small knife slid out. "I can do whatever the hell I want to you. And nobody will even know to try and stop me."

A whisper of unease ran through her as she eyed the glittering blade. Even knowing it was useless, she tugged at her wrists and tried to writhe away from him.

Brendon lowered the blade to the high neckline of her shirt and the tip just brushed the exposed skin of her throat. Nika froze, barely breathing and all too conscious of the sharp point that threatened to pierce through her skin if she moved even an inch.

Her gaze scoured his face in search of some hint of his intentions. It was only when he lifted his focus from her neck to look at her that she could see it: the fury that lay simmering just below the composed exterior.

"Yes, Nika, you are completely at my mercy."

She held his gaze, even as a mix of hot and cold rushed through her.

Perhaps facing the military of Belton would have been preferable.

It was quite amazing, really, Brendon mused. That he could hold a knife so close to her throat and still there was not even a trace of fear in those beautiful blue-green eyes.

He'd removed her eye shields once he'd brought her back to his chamber, unable to spend one more moment staring into her black gaze.

The anger that had been stewing in his gut since last night still remained predominant. But as he'd sat into the early hours of the morning watching her sleep, he'd been incensed to discover the desire he'd thought surely to be dead still smoldered.

Even now, with her staring defiantly up at him, and after everything she'd done to deceive him, he was surprised to find he wanted her again.

But it wasn't the soft, almost romantic urge to bed her like he'd had previously. No. This was primal to his core. Angry. Uninhibited.

He wanted to shove her thighs wide and plunge into her wet heat. Fuck her until she was screaming his name and begging for forgiveness, telling him why she'd done it. Why she'd lied. Why she'd pretended to care for him. . . .

He let out a soft growl and his grip tightened on the knife. Her eyes closed and he knew for a moment she thought he would pierce her skin with the blade.

His control snapped.

Gripping the edge of her top, he slashed the knife through it. The fabric fell to the sides, but still clung to her body as her arms were bound above her head.

Nika let out a shaky gasp and turned her head to the side, the relief in her obvious by her now-lax muscles.

"Completely at my mercy," he muttered again thickly.

"You do not want to do this, Brendon."

"On the contrary, *love*." He mocked the once-used endearment. "I very much want to do this."

His gaze lowered to her concave stomach and her bound breasts. "Amazing, really. That I could have ever mistaken you for a man."

Her tone was hard as she said, "You mistook me for a boy."

"So I did." He carefully—so as not to cut her—worked the

knife up beneath the band wound tightly around her breasts. "I obviously did not pay close enough attention."

Nika let out the tiniest whimper of alarm before she bit her lip, her body completely still.

Lifting the knife against the fabric to distance the blade from her skin, Brendon gave a deft flick of his wrist and sliced through the top of the band; then made a few more slashes until he'd cut the fabric off of her.

Her breasts popped free uninjured. Round and swollen. The tips were angry and red from being restrained.

She issued a barely audible groan that sounded like a mix of arousal and despair.

Brendon's cock jerked against his trousers and he forced in a slow, calming breath. Turning the knife, he used the flat side to drag gently over one nipple. It puckered against the metal. The reddened tip of her breast seemed to reach and stroke the silver surface of the blade.

"Did you have no conscience while you betrayed me?" he asked, keeping his tone matter-of-fact.

She groaned. "I could not afford to have a conscience, Brendon."

He paused. Her response was not quite what he'd expected. "Maybe you could not afford it, but did you anyway? You have not answered my question."

"And I *will* not. Let me say it again, you will receive no answers from me."

Brendon's lips curled downward as frustration and emptiness settled in his belly.

"No. I very well may not. But there is something else I will receive from you." He pulled the knife away from her breast and hurled it to the floor where it clattered loudly. "The submission of your mind and body."

Her eyes widened as he reached for the waist of her pants.

"Brendon, please," she begged, tugging at her wrists. "This solves nothing."

Her pleas came too late as he'd already tugged the fabric off her body and tossed it to the ground.

Her body lay naked now and exposed almost crudely to his censuring gaze.

His hand curled around one thigh and he pushed her legs apart. Surprise slid through him as he observed the shimmering of arousal between the folds of her pussy.

She wanted him. Restrained to his bed and being questioned, surely knowing her life hung in his hands—she wanted him. A wave of possessiveness and pleasure rushed through him. But it was mixed with bitterness.

"If it had been Emmett guarding the lab, would you have fucked him?"

"If he had wanted me, then yes," she admitted after a moment, and her lower lip trembled. "But it would not have affected me the way it did when I was with you."

Brendon stared at her, her words causing his blood to pound a bit harder with hope. *You fool. Again you would let her manipulate your mind?*

He leaned back, pulling his hand from her thigh and scowling.

"Lies," he rasped. "You spout nothing but lies from those luscious, poisoned lips!"

Her mouth tightened, but she did not deny it.

Moving off the bed, Brendon stood and lifted his jacket from the chair in the nearby corner.

He could not stay for one more moment. If he stayed he'd just be proving to both of them that he could not resist her. And he could. By the gods he could—and he would! He could not fall under whatever magic she'd seduced him with for the past weeks.

"Are you leaving me?" Her voice rose, a note of surprise in it.

"I will return."

She did not reply and he was thankful for it. Not that he'd expected her to beg him to stay. Or release her. No, she was above that. What she had begged for was her death.

With disgust, his grip tightened on his jacket and he pressed the button to open the door of his bedchamber. It let out a series of beeps and then slid open.

Without a backward glance, he left the chamber and Nika, restrained to his bed.

18

He moved through the hallways, debating where to go, what to do. He only knew he could not return to his bedchamber or he'd lose what little self-control he still maintained.

After leaving the housing units, he opened his communication mobile and dialed. Emmett answered immediately, though Brendon could hear the sound of people in the background.

"Damn, my friend," Emmett swore. "Where are you? Everyone has been asking."

"Taking care of . . . business."

"And how is *business*?" Emmett asked, his voice lowering now as he obviously tried to keep their conversation quiet.

"A thorn in my side right now," Brendon growled. "Where are you?"

"At the lodge."

"I'll be right there." He disconnected the line before Emmett could reply.

It would do him good to put some distance between him and Nika right now.

Guilt pricked lightly inside him—that he was leaving her

alone and chained to his bed—but he snuffed it out. Compared to the possible alternatives, she actually had it quite good.

He reached the lodge a short while later and entered the familiar building. The noise from the restaurant greeted him and he followed the sound to seek out his friend.

A quick glance at the reception desk proved that Molly was not working right now. He forced a smile at the young attendant on duty and then passed her to slip into the restaurant.

His gaze scanned the room, seeking Emmett.

"Shit," he muttered and slowed his pace.

Emmett was not alone, but was joined by quite the group of people. Brendon had suspected that Molly might be at his side, but not the others. Also at the table were Ryder and Talia, and Ryder's little sister Krystal and her husband, Dillon.

Gods, he could not face such a large group at this moment. His social skills were about on par with a rabid beast.

Before he could turn to leave again, Ryder spotted him. He stood and grinned, jerking his hand to beckon him over.

"Hell," Brendon muttered and thrust a hand through his hair.

Talia followed her husband's gaze and her eyes widened with delight. She stood slowly, hand on her pregnant belly as she grinned at Brendon.

Seeing no hope for it, he let out a frustrated breath and resumed his walk to the table.

"Brendon!" Talia cried and opened her arms for an embrace. "I have been hoping you would come by. But where is Doni—er, I meant Rebecca. I forget that she uses a different name now. I would so love to see her again!"

Brendon slid his arms around her in a quick embrace and met Emmett's rueful glance over her shoulder.

"I haven't the faintest," he lied briskly, and patted her back, pulling away. To change the subject, he turned on his heel and smiled down at Dillon and Krystal. "Well, look at the pair of you. I have not seen you both in likely a year. I see you're still all aglow from your marriage."

Krystal gave a soft laugh and glanced shyly up at her husband. "Indeed. Almost two years now."

"Come now," Dillon spoke. "Where is this girl? Ryder has not ceased to speak of her and how besotted you are. I'm curious to see the woman who has finally tamed the untamable heart."

His untamable heart clenched with pain at the mention of Nika, but he was careful to hold a sardonic smile on his expression.

"Ah, now, you are all far too presumptuous," he murmured with a shake of his head, and decided to simply live up to his former image. "You know I shall never be content to settle with one woman."

"You lie!" Talia gasped and narrowed her eyes, placing her hands on her widening hips. "I am not presumptuous. Anyone with a pair of working eyes could see that you're completely enamored. Now, where *is* she, Brendon?"

"Yes." Molly spoke for the first time. "Where is she?"

Brendon's gaze narrowed and swept to her, not liking her biting tone.

Her eyes were hard, her lips drawn tight as she watched him shrewdly.

Brendan swept his gaze up to Emmett, who shook his head and sighed.

"I cannot say where Nika is," Brendon said finally. Which was somewhat the truth. "But I imagine she is off somewhere, lounging and relaxing. Perhaps on a tropical planet?"

The lounging part was not quite a lie. Why, right now she lounged in his bed.

"A tropical planet?" Krystal asked. "Did she have plans to travel?"

"But isn't she an ambassador from Glorus?" Talia quizzed.

"Hmm." Molly shook her head and leaned forward on the table, placing her chin on her steepled fingers. "Are you quite sure you don't know where she is, Brendon?

"Yes. Quite." His tone hardened, and he shot Emmett a glance that clearly said *control your woman*.

Emmett gave a slight nod and his hand lowered beneath the table. Molly turned to look at him and their gazes locked. He gave a tiny shake of his head and her mouth tightened.

Finally she looked away and her cheeks turned pink. Standing, she muttered, "If you will all excuse me for a moment, I should check on the kitchen staff and see if they are handling the excess business well enough."

"Have a seat, Brendon." Krystal gestured to an empty chair next to her. "We've plenty of wine. And honestly, my friend, you look as if you could use a glass."

Brendon gave a soft laugh, though he wasn't all that amused. He seated himself in the chair beside her and accepted the glass Dillon handed him.

Taking a sip, he relaxed a bit, partly because Molly had left and taken her condemning gaze with her.

He scowled and took another drink of wine. He had nothing to feel guilty about. Not a damn thing.

Emmett leaned over to him and cleared his throat. His voice was low as he murmured, "The military is not happy with the breach of the lab and stolen specimens."

The other two couples spoke among themselves, giving Brendon a moment to have this quiet conversation with Emmett.

"No. I don't imagine they would be," Brendon muttered.

He'd made a highly risky move in confiding in Emmett about who Nika truly was. But he knew his friend would keep the secret well—even though, if discovered, both of their careers could be over and they could even potentially be brought up on treason charges.

"Have you garnered any information from her?" Emmett asked.

Brendon scowled and gave a tiny shake of his head. "Not really."

Except for her confession that she would have slept with Emmett if it had been required. Brendon could barely look at his friend with the memory of her words. His insides clenched and the wine he'd drunk tasted like acid in his belly.

"How long do you intend to keep her?" Emmett queried. "Before you turn her over to the military, which, might I add, is going to be quite tricky without arousing suspicion."

"Yes. I'm aware of how complex this situation is." Or to put it plainly, the complete fucking mess he'd created. Brendon pinched the bridge of his nose with his forefinger and thumb and bit back a harsh sigh.

He knew he should have turned Nika over the minute he'd captured her. But everything within him had protested that he hold off. At least for a bit.

"Molly knows very little," Emmett added firmly. "Only that you have her and that she is being treated well."

Brendon grunted.

It was a bit more than he'd prefer Molly know. But he knew how determined the lodge owner could be when she set her mind to it.

"I will ensure she stays out of trouble," Emmett assured him.

Brendon gave a curt nod. "I know you will and thank you."

"She is still in your bedchamber?"

"Yes. Restrained to the bed."

Emmett gave a soft laugh. "You are a kinky fool, my friend."

"Hardly. I've not touched her since I brought her there." Well, just a bit. But he hadn't followed through.

"Is that so?" Emmett's brows rose. "You have far more restraint than I would have, my friend. If I learned my woman was guilty of such . . ." He shook his head. "Punishment in flesh would be only the beginning."

Brendon's hand tightened on the glass and he forced a slow breath in. But it didn't stop the images of Nika secured to his bed from filling his mind. Naked. Aroused. Surprised that he would leave her.

His eyes drifted closed.

He was trying so hard to prove to himself that he didn't need her. Could control his physical response to her. But why? Before the week was out he'd be turning her over to the military. Why not seek his own revenge while he still had her? Use her body as she had used his.

His cock jerked inside his trousers and his blood heated.

Emmett was right. He would not deny himself the pleasure of her body. And this time, that is all it would be. Sex. Making use of her as if she were just some whore on the street. There needn't be any emotions while he fucked her. Hell, it had never been a problem with the women he'd bedded in the past. It would not be such a trial to revert to his former ways.

And why shouldn't he? She had used him. Betrayed him. Feigned something so close to love. He'd almost convinced himself that he deeply cared for her. And then she'd robbed his planet blind.

The anger burned hot in his gut, mingling with his desire for her. It was a toxic combination, but not one he intended to deny.

Pushing back his chair, he set his glass back upon the table with steady hands and a renewed purpose.

"Brendon? Are you leaving so soon?" Talia asked, obviously disappointed.

"I am. I apologize, everyone." He held Emmett's gaze for a

moment and a cold smile slid over his mouth. "But I have just realized I have business that needs to be dealt with."

Nika twisted her wrists in the metal clamps, knowing there was very little chance at freeing herself. Another minute passed before she gave up and let her arms go slack again.

"Gods. Why do I even bother?" she muttered.

Closing her eyes, another tremble slid over her naked body. It was only partly due to the chill in the air.

Even though it had to have been at least an hour since Brendon had left, she still remained suspended in that painfully intense state of arousal. And yet he'd walked away from her—perfectly calm and composed—like she was some slice of meat at the market that he'd decided to pass up.

She'd grown so used to seeing his gaze upon her full of amusement and desire, that—*gods*—it hurt to see it otherwise. To see that look of disgust now. He hated her. Felt betrayed. Which was completely justified, but it did not ease the ache in her heart. Nor the guilt. And the complete helplessness of the situation she was now in.

And what did you expect? That he would still want to bed you? That he would forget all else but the passion between you both?

Closing her eyes, she refused the threat of tears and the sting of pain in her heart as foolish and naive.

For a trained soldier, she certainly had her weakness. And unfortunately that weakness now kept her a prisoner in his room.

There was a series of beeps from the door and she went rigid on the bed. Her heart thundered in her chest as she lifted her head to see who would enter. Though, really, she had little doubt.

The door slid open and Brendon strode through. Impossibly tall, he filled the room as he made his way toward her. His strides were hard. Angry. And when he leaned over the bed and grabbed her chin in his hand, she could see the determination and arousal in his eyes.

"First I am going to fuck you," he said, quite calmly. "And then you *will* tell me everything."

She'd never fainted in her life, but right about now she felt close. Her head spun, leaving her lightheaded and weak. Her mouth went dry as his gaze ran possessively over her.

Fear shivered down her spine. Yes, she wanted him. But not like this.

Her nipples stiffened and she swallowed hard, unable to tear her gaze from his or even attempt to deny his statement.

Seeming satisfied by her acquiescence, Brendon released her chin and stepped back from her. His mouth curved into a grim smile as he reached for the fastening of his trousers.

She watched him pull his cock free. He was already long and hard, as if he'd been thinking about doing this for the past hour.

He came to kneel on the bed in front of her and pushed her legs wide.

Nika drew in a sharp breath. Even if she could have resisted him, she wouldn't have. This moment was as much a part of her destiny as having been chosen to come to this planet.

She closed her eyes, torn between wanting him and hating what he was about to do. She could not stare into the eyes of the man who now hated her. It was different now. Ugly. And she knew once he did this—took her this way—everything would change.

Remaining perfectly still, she waited. Waited for him to plunge himself into her without any preliminaries.

When it didn't come, confusion swept through her and she opened her eyes again.

He watched her now, his gaze both furious and tormented.

Something crumbled inside her and tears pricked at her eyes. "Brendon . . . I'm so sorry."

"No." His voice broke with emotion and anguish flashed across his face. "*No*, Nika. It is far too late for apologies."

His entire body went rigid and she felt him move forward between her thighs. His cock nudged her entrance.

Her throat tightened and a tear crept to the corner of her eye.

Brendon's fingers dug into her hips and, as she watched, his expression melted into something else. Something so vulnerable and helpless . . . something so foreign on the face of a soldier.

"I loathe you, Nika," he muttered brokenly, even as his grip on her hips loosened. "I hate what you've done to me and to the military. But especially to me."

She blinked and the tear slid down her cheek, but there were more to take its place.

The wall that she'd built up inside her came crashing down in an avalanche of emotions. All the fears, sorrows, and injustices in her life raged to the surface. And the guilt: gut-wrenching guilt and regret for what she'd done to Brendon.

She was not strong and invincible. She didn't have any control. What a joke that was. Whether it was her owners on Zortou or the people who'd picked her for this mission, she'd always been just a pawn in someone's game.

"Gods, Nika." Brendon's cock slid away from her and he fell forward, cupping her hips gentler now. His cheek settled on her stomach and he let out a ragged sigh.

The silent tears flowed freely now. When she tried to drag in a breath her whole body shuddered and she let out a choked sob.

Brendon lifted his head and stared at her. Some of the anguish was gone after his confession. His gaze was almost pensive and entirely too calm.

He crawled forward until he knelt next to her shoulders. Her pulse quickened and she tried to blink away some of the tears, willing herself to salvage what little pride she had left.

Reaching past her, he fumbled with the metal shackles that circled her wrists. A moment later there was a beep and the metal retracted.

She blinked in surprise, hesitantly pulling her hands down from above her head as she sat up.

Brendon slid his arms around her and pulled her into the circle of his arms, and then urged her damp face against his shoulder.

Nika wrapped her arms around his waist and let out another shuddering breath. Relief and warmth seeped through her to be in his arms once more.

He stroked a hand down her back and buried his face against her hair. "I need you, Nika. But I will not force you. Please, do not deny me."

"You know I will not," she whispered.

He pushed her away slightly, and then his mouth moved firmly over hers. His hand delved into her hair, holding her head still while his tongue thrust past her lips to capture hers.

She let out a small groan and wrapped her arms around his neck, opening her mouth and undeniably her heart to him.

He eased her back down onto the mattress, his body following to fall heavily upon hers.

Not breaking the demanding kiss, he palmed one of her breasts, grinding the nipple into the center of his hand.

Heat speared through her and she wove her fingers into his hair, letting her thighs fall open so he could move between them.

He groaned and tore his mouth from hers, kissing her jawline and then moving down the curve of her throat. His tongue flicked over the fast-beating pulse there, before his lips closed over her flesh and he sucked hard.

Fire raced through her blood and Nika twisted on the bed, her legs curling around his waist and drawing him tightly against her.

He moved lower, capturing her wrists and pinning them to the side. She did not mind this restraint. It was so much more intimate and sensual.

His mouth closed over one aching nipple. Not gently, but nor did she want him to be. He used his teeth to scrape over the sensitive tip, before he curled his lips around it and suckled to the point where it reached that wonderful brink of pain.

Her heart pounded in her chest. So full of pleasure and . . . She feared the other emotion.

Lifting his head, he said raggedly, "I need you. Now."

"Yes." She pulled her wrists free to cup his face, pulling his head up to hers again. "Yes, Brendon."

He moved up her body, settling himself firmly between her thighs. His cock nudged the swollen folds of her pussy and as his mouth took hers, he sank slowly into her.

She locked her ankles around his waist and closed her eyes, heady in the sensation of him filling her so completely.

When he'd sunk to the hilt, their bodies were flush against each other. She could feel his heart pounding against her breast.

He let out a slow groan, beginning the slow drag of his cock back out of her and then pressing back in, more quickly this time.

The muscles of his back clenched beneath her fingers as he pumped in and out of her in a gradually increasing rhythm. Each slide of his flesh against hers sent more pleasure rolling through her, taking her higher to ecstasy's peak.

He pounded harder into her now as he sought his own release, so forcefully she knew she'd have bruises between her thighs.

Her nails pierced through the skin on his back. Her head spun and she struggled to stay afloat. So lightheaded. Almost as if she were floating above her body.

His cock brushed just the right spot inside her and it was over.

"Brendon!" She arched her back, tears again flooding her eyes as the pleasure finally crested.

"Nika," he choked out, and then buried himself to the hilt inside her.

They both gasped for air, clinging to each other as the climax rocked them simultaneously.

It could have been minutes later—or maybe an hour, even—when he finally became a dead weight upon her.

"Paradise," he muttered raggedly. "You're a forbidden paradise I have no right to indulge in."

Nika's lashes swept down to cover her eyes as her heart clenched at his words. But he spoke the truth and they both knew it.

The heaviness spread from her heart throughout her body. She was so tired. Emotionally and physically.

"Nika . . . whatever am I going to do with you?" he muttered thickly.

And Brendon appeared to only want to speak of things that would cause them more distress. So be it. She owed him at least that much.

"You will do what needs to be done. You will turn me over to your superiors."

He exhaled loudly and propped himself up above her, shaking his head. "How? How can I possibly do that to you, Nika?"

"Because you have no choice." She cupped his cheek and

gave a small sad smile. "You are first and foremost a soldier. We both are. And I *am* guilty."

"Yes, you are. Which does not bear well for your future imprisonment with the military," he muttered and then narrowed his eyes. "I could always release you."

"You could," she agreed with a slight dip of her head, not even allowing a bit of hope to enter her heart. "But what if it were discovered? It's treason, Brendon. Your own life hangs in the balance as well."

"Gods!" He swore and ran his thumb over her bottom lip. "What a mess this is, Nika. And still, you will not tell me where you hail from?"

She stared at him for a moment and then shook her head. "It is best that I do not."

"Nika—"

"Please, Brendon. I am exhausted. Let us sleep. Our problems will still exist in the morning."

He stared at her for a moment and then gave a terse nod. Sliding completely off her, he moved to her side and then pulled her into the curve of his arms.

She did not protest, but welcomed the embrace, knowing it could likely be their last.

But this was her fate. And no matter how much she may regret it now, she'd chosen it.

19

Molly sat at the table, her hands clenched in her lap as she watched the men wind down with their dinner and conversation.

Dillon and Krystal had left a short while ago, but Emmett and Ryder continued to converse.

She wanted this night over and done with. There were plans to be formulated. . . .

"Ouch!" She yelped as something slammed into her shin and she lifted her gaze across the table.

Talia gave her a slight smile and then jerked her head toward the kitchen.

"What?" Molly mouthed.

Talia rolled her eyes and then stood, rubbing her belly. "Molly, will you help me find some juice? I need to settle the babe."

"Juice," Molly repeated, sliding her chair back to stand. "Of course, but no need for you to come, dear. I can bring it—"

"No, really, I need to stretch my legs. I fear I have sat too long." Talia gave her another pointed look.

"Oh. Right!" Molly nodded and cursed herself for being so slow to realize the other woman wanted to speak with her.

She led Talia into the kitchen and went to the refrigeration unit.

"Please, do not bother." Talia stopped her, placing a hand upon her shoulder. "I simply must speak with you."

"All right. What about?" Molly shut the unit door and folded her arms across her chest.

She did not know Talia very well, only from the occasional times she'd visited the restaurant with Ryder and now from tonight when they'd had a chance to talk on a more personal level.

"About Rebecca. Or whom I know as Donika."

The air seethed out from between Molly's lips and she nodded. "Yes. Nika."

"I believe Emmett and Brendon to be hiding something." Talia said, rubbing her belly again. "And in truth I am worried about Do—Nika. You may not know, but as myself, she was a Rosabelle."

Molly reared back, not attempting to hide her shock. "No, I was unaware."

"Yes. She does not trust easily. We had dinner the other night and I could sense it. Not even will she trust me, though there was a time when we were close friends." A flicker of sadness crossed Talia's face before she shook her head. "I fear she is in trouble. Do you have any information?"

Molly hesitated, torn about how much she could say and how little she really knew herself. But as she stared at Talia, she realized that this woman might be able to help her.

Emmett had made it quite clear that he would not tolerate any interference and he would be keeping Molly on high surveillance, which meant sneaking around him to find Nika could be quite difficult.

But nobody would be watching Talia. . . .

"What I do know is not much," Molly began carefully and held Talia's concerned gaze. "But I will gladly pass on to you my information. And I'll do so in hopes that you might be able to help me assist Nika."

Talia's jaw tightened and she gave a nod, causing her red hair to swing forward over her shoulder. "Of course. I will do whatever I can."

"Thank you." Molly gave a small nod and then told her everything she knew.

Brendon jerked upright in bed and blinked, trying to rid himself of the thick fog of sleep that slowed his mind.

What time was it? How long had he slept?

Nika.

His gaze swung to the left side of the bed, but it was empty. The thud of his heart increased with sudden panic.

A noise came from the bathing chamber and he let out a sigh of relief, thrusting a hand through his hair.

Gods, he'd slept well. Too well.

He watched the door to the bathing chamber warily. With Nika's training, it would have been all too easy for her to have knocked him out—hell, even killed him—in an effort to escape.

And yet she hadn't. Which meant they still needed to face the same issues this morning that they'd fallen asleep thinking about.

His stomach clenched and he let out a heavy sigh, swinging his legs off the mattress to climb out of bed. He almost wished she *had* tried to run this morning.

He checked the time and winced. Just under an hour before he was to report for duty.

At the sound of a beeping, he tensed, knowing the bathing chamber door was sliding open even though his back was to it.

"Brendon," she murmured with surprise. "I hope I did not wake you."

"Not at all." He turned, willing himself to be strong. But the moment his gaze fell upon her his resolve cracked.

It seemed she'd bathed this morning. Her hair lay wet against her dewy skin and a towel had been wrapped around her lithe, naked body.

"I have . . . no clothes." Her cheeks almost hinted at a blush as she gave a slight smile.

He gave a slow nod. "Right. I apologize for having ruined your top. Though your pants may still be in order."

"Perhaps I might borrow something from your closet?" She cleared her throat. "Or no, that might indicate that you were helping me."

Brendon strode forward, unable to stop himself and slid his hand around the back of her neck.

"I am not taking you into my superiors yet."

Frustration and pain flickered across her face. "Brendon—"

"First I would like to consider my options—because there must be some," he muttered almost to himself. He didn't expect her to have a solution by any means. "There must."

"Brendon." She slid her palms up to cup his face and gave a sad little sigh. "You delay the inevitable. They will discover who I am. And then you will be held accountable as well."

He shook his head, refusing to give up so easily. But the panic was there under the surface of his calm persona he displayed to her.

Gods. If he gave her over, that was it. The end of any form of her life worth living. But if he didn't . . . it could mean the end of his.

"I must report for duty," he said finally. "I will think over our options while there."

She lowered her hand from his jaw and gave a slight nod. "I

am in your hands now. It, of course, is your decision. Will you leave me locked in your room throughout the day?"

"Yes." He stepped away from her and moved into the bathing chamber to the showering unit. "Give me a moment."

He cleansed himself quickly in the shower and returned minutes later with a towel around his waist. As he donned his uniform, he watched Nika sitting cross-legged on his bed, plucking at the fabric of the quilt.

"No one will enter the room," he assured her. "These are private bedding units and only a handful of soldiers have the codes to everyone's quarters. But they would not enter unless ordered to by their superiors."

"All right."

"Feel free to watch the teletron while I am out. Or perhaps if you can find a book upon my shelf . . . though I am not much of a reader."

"Nor am I." She gave a slight smile. "Do you not worry that I will try and escape while you are on duty?"

"No." He was not surprised by her question, as she seemed merely curious. "I am able to set another form of lock from the outside."

"I see."

He finished dressing and crossed the room to her. "But you would not flee."

"How do you know?" She arched a brow.

"Because you could have killed me last night and escaped just as easily."

Her lips quirked, but her gaze drifted away. "I cannot kill you, Brendon. We both know that by now."

Leaning across the bed, he caught her chin and turned her back to face him.

"Yes, and thank gods for that. It puts us upon an equal playing field," he murmured.

Then his lips brushed across hers—once. Twice—before he jerked his head up with a groan and moved away from her. If he stayed any longer he'd be tempted to call in sick for duty.

"Behave while I am out, Nika."

"I can hardly get into any trouble lounging about your room," she drawled and lay back upon the pillow. "Until later, Brendon. And truly . . . I hope by then you'll have realized there really is no choice."

"There's always a choice." Brendon's jaw clenched as he turned and went out the door to his chamber. "Always."

"I must head out," Emmett said as he dressed in his uniform.

He looked in the mirror to where Molly lay sprawled out on the bed, a book in her hand. The pale pink nightgown she wore showed more skin than it covered. Gods, she was a sight. So tempting. Always so tempting. Even after he'd tumbled with her more than once throughout the night.

She did not glance up at his words, but her brows drew together. "I thought you had the day off?"

"Initially, yes. But it appears I must go in after all." He did not add that Brendon had requested a meeting with him for later this morning.

"I trust you not to do anything foolish, Molly," he warned, fastening his trousers and never removing his gaze from her in the mirror.

"Really, Emmett. I have a lodge to run. I haven't the time for getting into trouble."

"Ah. You remember that and we shall be just fine."

Molly set her book down with an exasperated sigh. "Oh gods, will you cease already?"

He turned from the mirror and moved to her, sitting on the edge of the bed. Reaching out, he settled his hands over her waist and lifted her onto his lap.

"I know you're upset about Nika, sweetheart." He nuzzled her neck and slid a hand up to cup the curve of one full breast. The nipple instantly hardened in his hand. "And I would not put it past you to try something foolish."

Her full mouth curved into a pout and her shoulders lifted with a sigh. "Ah, yes, well, as you said, Brendon has her in his custody and she is well. I suppose I must trust you."

"That is quite a change from the other day." He strummed her nipple with his thumb and she made a mewl of pleasure. Gods, he loved how responsive she was as she squirmed on his lap. With a growl, he added, "But I must say I enjoy you docile and agreeable."

She gasped and slapped at his chest. "Docile and agreeable! You big brute. I'll show—"

Emmett laughed and captured her wrist, placing a kiss to the inside and her pulse fluttered beneath his lips. "I only tease you, Molly."

"Indeed." She sniffed and pouted. Turning her body, she pressed her breast fully into his palm. "You're certain you have to leave so soon?"

"I do," he said, though his cock was damn near begging him to stay. "Save that thought for later, though, and I promise it shall be worth it."

Molly sighed. "Well, you had best be off, then. I shall likely indulge in a bath before heading downstairs to relieve the night shift from the reception desk."

"That sounds like a splendid plan." He gave her another squeeze, enjoying her curves on his lap all too much, before setting her back down. "Shall we meet for supper later?"

"Of course," she said, but her gaze had slipped away as she picked up her book once more.

"Until then," he murmured and headed for the door.

All too quickly, his thoughts slipped from the seductive woman he loved to the situation he was about to deal with.

Damn, he could not wait to get an update from Brendon about Nika. What a bloody mess that was.

Molly waited for the door to close and then dove off the bed, scrambling to find her communication mobile. Gods! She had not thought to have such a break in her luck so quickly.

She pressed in Talia's number and waited for the other woman to answer. It did not take long.

"Tell me you have good news?" Talia asked hopefully.

"I do indeed. Emmett has slipped out for the day. I am free!" Molly climbed out of bed, already searching for clothing. "Can you do it today?"

"I can, but I am not so certain about Dane and Thomas. Let me get ahold of them and call you back. All right?"

Molly knew Dane to be Talia's former assistant on Zortou, and Thomas his lover. Thomas served as a soldier of Belton now and was in just the right position to possibly gain access to Brendon's bedchamber.

"Of course. Thank you, Talia."

"No, thank you." Talia paused. "Molly, we must help her. I know the life she has lived. The pain that will never quite leave her heart. I am more than committed to seeing her free—no matter what injustice Brendon and Emmett believe her to be guilty of."

"I agree. Call me after you talk to your friends."

"Of course. Good-bye for now."

After Molly disconnected the call, she rushed in to grab a quick shower. She was just leaving the bathing chamber when her communication mobile came to life.

"Yes?" she answered breathily.

"Dane and Thomas are in," Talia said quickly, her tone alive with excitement. "Can you meet me near the south end of the compound in half an hour?"

"I can and will. You are a blessing, Talia."

"Stop, I am doing what needs to be done—though I know the men will be furious at our interference."

"Quite certainly. But it cannot be helped."

"No, it cannot," Talia agreed. "I will see you shortly."

Leo stood halfway across the compound, watching the entrance to the housing units that the solider had left not even an hour ago.

Interesting. He'd wager that Donika was safely hidden within the soldier's room. Or perhaps . . . not so safely.

His mouth curled into a smile and he flicked his tongue over his left fang. Mmm. What he wouldn't give for just a taste of the little bitch.

This could be his opening. He'd simply have to find a way inside the soldier's bedchamber, which might be trickier than it appeared.

Then again, he'd had no trouble getting onto the base itself.

With a grim smile, he began a slow approach to the housing units.

20

Nika turned off the teletron and paced the chamber with a sigh. She folded her arms across her breasts, wincing as they ached slightly. Perhaps Brendon had been a little too rough in his loving last night, though when she thought upon it she only remembered the pleasure of his mouth and teeth upon her breasts.

She fidgeted with the cuff of the shirt she wore, glad she'd thought to sneak it from Brendon's drawer. It kept her warm without inhibiting her movement, falling just past her thighs.

A bit hungry, she eyed the small refrigeration unit in the corner of the room. Brendon had told her she was free to have any food in there, but so far she hadn't partaken of any.

She'd been nauseous all morning. She knew it to be from the stress. And unfortunately the idea of food just made her sicker.

And gods, the isolation was awful. It was such a stark reminder of the life she'd lived while on Zortou—even Tresden, somewhat. She hadn't really enjoyed her freedom until she'd come to Belton.

A quick glance at the time showed she still had hours until Brendon would return.

Her stomach rolled and she exhaled a shuddering breath. Though she was excited for his return—any reason to see him again—she did not look forward to the news he would bring. She was all too aware that with each passing moment she grew closer to a life that would not be worth living.

A series of beeps came from the door and she spun, her brows rising in dismay. Had he returned so early?

The door hissed open and pleasure spread through her.

"You've returned?" she murmured.

"I have a short lunch break." He strode across the room and gathered her in his arms, burying his nose against her hair. "Gods, I've missed you, love."

"You've been gone but a few hours." She gave a slight laugh, and slid her arms around his waist, pressing her face against his shoulder and inhaling the comforting scent of him.

"Have you come to any decision?" she asked finally, seeing no point in tiptoeing around their situation.

His chest swelled against her. "I have decided to meet with my superiors and beg for leniency. Perhaps we can retrieve the specimen—"

"It's not possible. They've already retrieved them. . . . By now they assume me dead, Brendon. They would not come forward with the samples."

"Who are you working for?" he demanded, pushing away from her. "I must know, Nika."

"Bren—"

"I swear on my life it will not leave this room. I keep this inside my head only. But I must know."

She stared at him, saw the frustration and pain there. Little by little her resolve crumbled. The secret she'd vowed to take to the grave suddenly did not seem quite so important to hide from Brendon.

"But if you know . . . your own military could try and take the information from you," she said softly.

"I would not break."

"And yet I thought the same about myself." She gave him a wry smile and then let out a quiet sigh. "I come from the planet Tresden. I've lived there for two years since the liberation."

"Tresden." His brows drew together and he gave a sharp shake of his head. "I've not heard of it."

"It is relatively small. Unknown. Peaceful, though. Only women reside on the planet. By choice, of course. It's became a haven for them of sorts."

"Hmm." He stared at her for a moment and tilted his head, understanding dawning in his gaze. "Do they steal the specimens to procreate?"

"Yes. To continue their race. But not any specimens will do. They want strong babies. The best of genetics. To raise a perfect army in case they were to be discovered and attacked."

"That is ludicrous."

"Perhaps," she agreed. "But it is their way."

Funny how she'd come to thinking of the people of Tresden as "them" instead of "us." And now, having been away from the planet for a bit, she could see just how ludicrous the mission might seem to an outsider. In truth . . . it probably was.

Her eyes closed and she had a sudden urge to curl up in the fetal position and sob. Damn it all. What was wrong with her? She wasn't this weak.

"I wish I had never taken this mission," she finally whispered aloud, feeling at peace to finally be able to make the admission. "If I could undo what I have done I would. We are now locked in this web of lies and—" She choked on the rest of her words, tears creeping out of the corners of her eyes.

"Nika, love. Do not cry," Brendon muttered raggedly, and once again she was in his arms, his hands sweeping down her back to comfort her. "We shall find a way out of this."

"How? There *is* no way, Brendon. None."

"Nonsense. Emmett and I have been discussing possibilities all morning."

"Have you? Such as?"

"No more for now." He set her aside and went to retrieve the small bag he'd dropped by the door. "I have brought you food."

"Oh." She took the small round bread he placed in her hand.

Her stomach growled at the smell of yeast and sugar, but she wondered if it would stay put once in her belly.

"Thank you, Brendon."

They sat on the bed, eating in silence. Finally a half hour had passed and Brendon rose with regret on his face.

"I wish I could stay longer."

"You must go," she agreed, and caught his hand, giving it a soft squeeze.

"Yes. But I will return before you realize it." He slid his hands around her waist and lifted her to her knees on the mattress.

Her mouth tilted up to meet his when his head dipped. He kissed her slowly and thoroughly, tasting and exploring her like it was their first time.

By the time he lifted his head, her legs were shaking and her heart had softened.

She stared into his eyes and her entire world tilted. Without a doubt, she had fallen hopelessly in love with this man. The realization ripped the breath from her body and made every muscle in her body weaken.

Gods, this could not bode well for her. For either of them. A panicked whimper escaped.

"I will see you through this," Brendon whispered, kissing her forehead once more. "This is not the end."

The fear ripped through her again, but not for herself this time: at how much he was willing to sacrifice for her. *I love him*.

"I won't let you do it, Brendon," she said thickly. "I will not let you destroy yourself to save me."

His body tensed against her before he sighed. "It is not your decision to make."

She pressed her palm against his cheek, the tiny graze of his stubble pricking into her soft flesh reminding her how real this moment was.

"Do not be a fool. Promise me."

"I can promise nothing," he muttered and pulled away from her.

A moment later he was gone from his chamber.

The minutes ticked by and she was once again shrouded in solitude, with only her distressing thoughts to keep her company.

Finally she slipped into a light slumber once more.

The beeps at the door jerked her from her drowsy state and she climbed off the bed.

Had he returned *again*?

But as the door slid open her jaw flapped in disbelief, unable to help being overwhelmed as Molly and Talia strode into the room followed by two unknown men.

Molly rushed forward and threw her arms about Nika. "Oh thank gods you are well. I was so worried."

"Molly? What is the meaning of this? Why are you all here?"

"We've come to free you," Talia said calmly from behind Molly.

"Free me," Nika repeated uneasily. "But why?"

"Why?" Molly's eyes grew round. "Nika, you cannot be serious. Because you are being falsely imprisoned—"

"But I am not." Nika stepped back with a groan and shook her head. "Truly, you all should not have come here. I am guilty of what they say."

"But we *are* here," the darker of the men said with an exasperated sigh and gestured to the other man. "And Thomas has risked quite a bit by abusing his privileges from the military. So please, none of this 'I'll stay behind' stuff."

Nika glanced at the other man, a uniformed soldier who stood quietly but confidently near the door.

Gods. When would it end? Now there were more people who were risking their necks for her.

"I do not understand," Nika's voice cracked. "Why would any of you do this for me? You do not know me. I am nothing to you. And I am *not* a good person."

"I do not quite believe that." Talia stepped forward, her blue eyes gentle and without judgment. "I may not know you now, Nika. But I know the girl you used to be. The girl we both once were. I know the pain you have endured. The scars on your heart as well as your body. Because I have them, too. And perhaps it led you to make poor choices in the life you lead now, but it is not too late to change. It is never too late."

Nika's throat burned with the effort to hold back tears. She ground her teeth together. She would not cry again.

"You are wrong. It is already too late."

"Talia." The darker man cleared his throat.

Talia turned. "Yes, Dane?"

"Thomas and I will take leave now. You know you can call our mobile if you need farther assistance. But, really, I would much rather we be clear of here as soon as possible."

Thomas shook his head. "I do not mind staying—"

"No." Talia interrupted and lifted a hand. "Dane is right. We are grateful for what you have done, but now you must go. It is too much of a risk."

Thomas gave a slight nod, though he did not look satisfied. "All right. We will leave. Good luck to you, Nika. And please do not hesitate to call us again if you need us."

Dane took Thomas's arm and they left the room together.

Nika watched them go, relieved that at least they were putting themselves farther away from being discovered. She could not let any of these people be punished for her mistake.

The nausea swelled inside her again and she clutched her stomach.

"Excuse me," Nika muttered, pushing past the two women and stumbling into the bathing chamber, where she heaved up what little food contents were in her stomach from lunch.

When she returned, her head was light and she was again fatigued.

"Thank you, Talia. Molly." Nika's head moved slowly back and forth in a negative gesture. "But I cannot allow this risk. I will not be leaving this chamber until Brendon turns me over to the military."

"Do not be a fool!" Molly hissed and stepped forward, grasping her hands. "I know not entirely what has occurred, but there are whispers running about and I have a fairly good idea. You should run while you still have time."

"You do not realize what you ask. I cannot do that to Brendon!" Nika protested, tugging her hands away and crossing the room to the refrigeration unit.

"You would not be doing it *to* Brendon, you would be doing it *for* him," Talia said softly. "And for the babe you carry."

Nika froze, in the midst of pouring herself a glass of water. "What did you say?"

"You are with child, are you not?" Talia asked.

"I assumed," Molly inserted quickly. "The past week while at the lodge you showed many symptoms. . . ."

"No." Nika's heart pounded furiously in her chest at the possibility, even as she knew it couldn't be true. "It is impossible. I was given an injection before I came to Belton."

Talia's brows rose. "The same injections we were given on Zortou?"

"I imagine."

Molly cleared her throat. "What if—"

"It is not possible," Nika repeated, a bit more forcefully this time as she shook her head.

"All right. Perhaps you are not with child," Talia said carefully. "But if by some chance you were and you stayed and became a prisoner of Belton . . . then when the babe is born they would discover the paternity soon enough."

"And would that not point further guilt at Brendon?" Molly inserted. "Put him in further trouble?"

"They would know Brendon was not involved in my mission," Nika said firmly. "That he was just another victim."

Nika pressed a hand to her head, willing it to stop spinning. It was an impossibility. Being pregnant. But what if they were right and by some chance . . . A dark thought flickered through her mind, causing her heart to pinch and her mouth to dry out.

No . . . Rachel would never have done that to you.

"Can you be sure?" Talia prodded, softly.

"It's irrelevant. I am not with child!" Nika yelled, slicing an unsteady hand through the air.

Molly and Talia exchanged meaningful looks and then gave a slight nod.

"All right," Talia agreed gently. "But, regardless, time is running out, Nika. We must leave now."

"I'm afraid time has already run out, ladies."

The raspy voice came from the doorway and they all spun to see. Nika's gaze narrowed as the unidentifiable cloaked man strode briskly into the room.

"Though I must thank you—or your friends who've gone now—for gaining me entrance into this bedchamber. It proved to be quite the challenge for me."

"Oh gods." Molly stumbled backward, just as the man lurched at her.

There was a sickening crunch as something connected with the back of her head and then Molly crumpled to the floor.

No! Nika let out a roar of rage, even as fear also slipped through her. She clenched her fists, turning her attention from where Molly lay motionless on the floor.

She stepped forward, placing herself between the man and Talia.

Maybe she hadn't been able to foresee the attack on Molly, but the devil of a man would not lay one hand on Talia or her baby.

"Who are you?" Talia croaked in alarm. "What do you want?"

It was hard to gather his expression from his shadowed face, but Nika could hear the amusement in his tone as he murmured, "Not you, lovely."

Time to take this bastard out of commission. Nika leapt at him, hoping to catch him off balance as he went for Talia. But he obviously expected that.

Before she could blink—or even get within feet of him—he'd pulled some form of club from his cloak and swung it at her.

It slammed into her rib cage, knocking the air from her body and her to the ground. Pain radiated through her, beyond the slight bruise she'd had when Brendon had kicked her ribs.

She attempted to crawl to her knees, gasping in a silent

breath. From the corner of her eye she watched the man turn and stride toward Talia.

"Please, no!" Talia cried out. "Do not hurt my baby."

"Stop!" Nika ground out, fear for her childhood friend raging through her as she tried to crawl forward.

The man blocked her vision as he grabbed Talia. There was no sickening crunch as there'd been with Molly. But a moment later he lowered Talia's limp body to the floor.

"I will kill you for this," Nika muttered, barely able to pull herself to her feet. "Perhaps not today. But—"

"Save the dramatics." He gripped her hair, tugging her head back.

There was a small sting on the side of her neck, and then the darkness rushed up to meet her.

21

Brendon paced the laboratory, watching the door to the captain's office and feeling another pang of regret that the soldier inside was likely being questioned again to the point of exhaustion.

The soldier knew nothing, had been knocked out before he could take down Nika . . . which was a good thing.

Brendon could answer any question the captain chose to hurl at him and would probably have felt inclined to. But he was not the one being questioned—because he had not been on duty. Though he had shown up that night anyway because he'd realized the truth. He had known Nika would be there.

"You're free to leave, Marshall."

He turned at the voice and gave a slight nod to the soldier who'd come to release him from duty.

"Thank you."

"Hey, Marshall," the man called out as he moved past him. "There are two soldiers outside who seem a bit anxious to see you."

"Is that so?" His gut clenched. Gods, had he been found out?

Straightening his spine, he took the last few steps that would put him outside the building.

Relief swept through him as he spotted Ryder and Emmett standing near the fence.

"Ah, it is just you two." His mouth curved into a slight grin as he approached the men. "Is something amiss? I thought we were to meet at the lodge."

Ryder stepped forward, gaze troubled. "We have been unable to locate Talia and Molly all day. They are not at the lodge or my house, and neither has answered their communication mobile."

Brendon frowned and glanced at Emmett. "Is this true? When did you last see Molly?"

"This morning. Before we met earlier." Emmett shook his head and glanced away. "She has been quite determined to see Nika released from your care. I fear she may be planning something and may have convinced Talia to help."

"That's preposterous. Don't they know I will not hurt her? I am trying to *help* her." Brendon scowled and thrust his hands into the pockets of his trousers.

"They are convinced she is being held against her will," Emmett murmured. "As she should be. The woman is—"

"Enough." Brendon held up his hand and glanced around. "We must censor our words. There are ears everywhere."

Ryder nodded as they all began to move away from the building and off the base.

"We will search for the women, but I am not too worried, for there is little they can do," Brendan said slowly. "Nika is locked safely in my room and they do not have the code to enter."

"Not exactly true," Ryder muttered. "Talia's former servant and his lover might be involved now."

Brendon cast him a sharp glance. "I am not following you."

"This lover is a soldier and, if I recall rightly, has access to the codes for each housing unit."

"By the gods, I hope you jest."

"I wish he did." Emmett sighed.

Foreboding stirred Brendon's gut and he drew in a slow breath, trying to push aside the unease.

"Perhaps we should check upon Nika in my bedchamber," Brendon muttered. "Sooner than later."

Arriving back at his room, Brendon let out a sigh of relief to find the door still shut and locked.

He gave his friends what he hoped to be an encouraging glance as he typed in the code to open the door. In a moment they would all see that Nika was still safely imprisoned—though that still would not answer the question of where Talia and Molly were.

A series of beeps sounded as the code was accepted and then the door hissed open.

Brendon strode in briskly, his gaze scanning the room.

It took only a moment to realize his friends' fears had not been unfounded.

His vision blurred as the realization sunk in. He clenched his hands into fists as the bitter taste of acid filled his mouth. "Gods. What have they done?"

"I will throttle Molly for this," Emmett seethed.

"Talia is just as much the fool," Ryder agreed, his shoulders so rigid with anger Brendon knew his friend was barely restraining it. "To risk so much while pregnant with our child."

"They cannot have left so long ago," Brendon said, shaking his head and pacing the room. "I came back and lunched with Nika. There was no indication that she had plans to escape. No sign that—"

He stilled, trailing off and staring at the door to the bathing chamber. Something had sounded in there, like a wounded animal or such. The door was closed and yet a light shone from beneath.

"What is it?" Emmett asked, stepping toward him.

Brendon lifted a hand, indicating for silence as he approached the door. Another long groan sounded.

"Is that even human?" Emmett muttered in alarm, following close behind.

With one hand on his electro-mace, Brendon reached for the handle of the door to the bathing chamber.

He slid the door open with a deft twist—then froze. Ice slid through his blood at the sight before him.

"Gods!" Ryder did not have the same stunned reaction as he thrust past Brendon to get to his still wife.

Emmett was right on his heels, reaching to help Molly, who was awake but groggy, to her feet.

"What has happened?" Brendon rasped, stepping aside to let Ryder carry Talia to the bed.

"She lives," Ryder muttered. "Thank the gods, she lives."

Brendon could not convince his feet to move, to jump into action and help the women. His heart twisted with disgust at the realization of it all.

Nika had done this to the women, had betrayed and injured her friends to escape him and Belton.

"Will you fetch a glass of water, Brendon?" Emmett called out, glancing away from Molly.

Brendon gave a sharp nod and forced himself to stride to the refrigeration unit where the water was kept chilled. He filled a glass and hurried back to the bed, where everyone had gathered.

Talia still appeared pale and entirely too still, but the rise and fall of her chest proved her to be alive. Molly reclined against a pillow, her gaze unfocused and diluted with pain.

"Do you know where she went?" Brendon asked, his voice harsher than he'd intended.

Molly gave a small shake of her head and her eyes filled with tears. "I haven't the faintest. I was attacked first."

Gods. Denial and disbelief raged through him. That he could have again been duped by Nika. He almost refused to believe it. It just didn't make sense.

"Talia might have learned more than I," Molly added after a moment. "For I am certain I heard him speak with her before I lost consciousness."

"Him?" Ryder asked sharply.

Brendon blinked, trying to comprehend the shift in the conversation. *Him?*

"There was a man here?" Brendon asked slowly. "You mean that Nika likely had an accomplice?"

"An accomplice? No, whatever do you mean?" Molly pressed her hand to the back of her head and winced, obviously still in a great amount of pain. "Nika was not involved in the attack. He *took* her. I'm quite certain of it. She was his target."

"Who took her?" Emmett and Brendon asked at the same time.

Molly's lips parted in surprise. "I thought you knew. It was the blood drinker. The bounty hunter."

"I wish you would not insist on going alone," Emmett muttered, pacing the room as Brendon packed.

"I'll be fine."

"Why not let me come?"

"Because you are not on this retrieval mission. I am. My superiors have approved me fetching back the thief." Brendon shut his case and ignored the tightening in his stomach.

Emmett shook his head and grunted with displeasure. "It's suicide."

Quite possibly. But he couldn't live with himself if he didn't try and bring her back.

And if he somehow did manage to retrieve her, that alone created another problem. He would need to discover a way to keep Nika from being convicted. But telling his superiors that he had a lead that the thief was on Multron was the only way he could get the time away from the compound.

What he had *not* mentioned to his superiors was that the man who had kidnapped her was a bounty hunter seeking the reward for turning her over.

There was a knock on the door to his chamber and he glanced at Emmett.

"Would you mind seeing who that might be?"

Emmett sighed and walked to the door. A moment later Ryder strode in, his mouth set into a tight line.

"How is she?" Brendon asked, straightening from the bag he knelt over.

"She is awake and well," Ryder replied briskly, "though quite anxious about the fate of Nika."

"Yes. As am I." Brendon pushed aside any disturbing possibilities of just what Nika's fate might be right now.

One puzzling fact was that the bounty hunter had not simply turned her in for the reward. Which only led Brendon to conclude he'd taken her back to his own planet, for what sinister purpose was still unknown—though the potential made him want to retch.

"It would appear that Talia's assistant and his lover did indeed help infiltrate your room." Ryder shook his head and pressed a hand to the back of his head. "That woman will be the death of me, for the amount of trouble she gets herself into."

"Yes. Well, I am none too thrilled with Molly either," Emmett began and grimaced. "She should have known better.

Though when I tell her as much she nearly boxes my ears for daring to treat her as a child."

Brendon grunted in agreement, not about to argue with either of them as he carried his bags to the doorway.

"Brendon, wait. I think now is the time we must intervene." Ryder stepped into his path. "Before you do something foolish."

Brendon's brows drew together in a scowl. "Whatever do you mean?"

"He means that perhaps you should rethink this mission," Emmett said softly, approaching him from the side. "You have no need for guilt any longer. If you let the bounty hunter turn her in, then it would not be on your conscience."

Drawing a slow breath, Brendon tried to control the slow burn of anger that fired in his gut at the other man's suggestion.

"That would only increase my guilt," he finally said after a moment.

"But why?" Ryder's tone sharpened. "What is she to you, besides just another woman you've bedded? Wait, I can answer that. She is a thief. A woman who used her body to seduce you and steal from the military."

Brendon shook his head, fighting the urge to resort to his inner child and cover his ears to stop the onslaught of bitter words.

"She betrayed you in one of the worst ways," Emmett continued. "And still you would try and protect her? To save her?"

"Yes."

Ryder's brows rose and he shook his head, looking genuinely confused. "But why?"

"Because I *love* her!" Brendon roared.

His friends fell back, their mouths gaping with surprise and—thankfully—finally their harsh words silenced.

"Are we all not guilty of some form of transgression in life? Yes, perhaps it would have been better if I had not met Nika while she was in the midst of her offense. But it is only because of what she did that we were brought together," he said firmly, convinced by his words more and more as he went on. "So I ask you, my friends, would you turn your back on the woman you love if the situation were reversed?"

Ryder and Emmett continued to stare at him, though their gazes had grown less shocked and accusing and were now more pensive and reluctant.

"No, I would not," Ryder finally admitted.

Emmett shook his head. "Nor would I."

"Then please do not judge me in what I must now do."

Ryder finally nodded. "If that is your true desire, then go. I would even accompany you if Talia were not so far along with her pregnancy."

"I would not let you even if she were not. Either of you." Brendon gave them both a firm glance. "This is my cause. I will take it on alone."

"Are you quite sure I cannot—"

"No." Brendon cut off Emmett's offer before he could finish. "If I get in over my head I will call for help, but until then farewell, my friends."

"Farewell," Ryder murmured.

Emmett sighed and shook his head. "And gods be with you."

It was so cold. That was the first thing Nika noticed before she opened her eyes. The next was the metallic smell of blood and the heavy sense of death in the air.

Fear slid through her as she lay still, keeping her breathing steady. She could not alert him that she'd awoken. Even if her hands were not tied behind her back, she wouldn't have been able to move. Her entire body felt numb, immobile from whatever he'd used to poison her.

Nika lifted her eyelids just a crack in her first effort to discover where she was—though she was already fairly certain who had taken her.

The room was dark, with a faint glow of light in the corner. Shadows bounced off what looked to be solid rock. Was she in some form of a cave?

"Are you hungry, Donika?"

Her breath locked at his words. She hadn't seen him, but he must be lingering somewhere nearby.

She did not reply, simply waited for him to show himself. It did not take long.

The blood drinker appeared in her line of vision, his pale, pudgy face smiling down at her.

"I myself am famished. You know, I don't think we've been properly introduced. My name is Leo, I am a blood drinker from the planet Multron—which is where we are now, I might add." He laughed. "Anyway, I digress. So happy to see you are awake, my dear."

It was difficult to speak, but she forced herself to respond. "We are on Multron? Where? Your . . . lair?"

His smile widened, but was anything but friendly. "Oh how unoriginal, Donika. I have a lovely apartment several miles from here. But I didn't find it appropriate to bring you there. Besides, this place has a bit of charm about it, don't you think?"

Unease slid through her and she swallowed hard. "I don't understand. Why not just turn me in for the reward money? That is what you wanted, is it not?"

"It was." He stroked a hand down his jaw as he paced in front of her. "Now, I am undecided."

Her blood chilled at his last words. If he did not turn her in, what could that possibly mean? Scenarios floated around in her head that didn't bode well for her fate.

His gaze slid over her in a way that could only be described as hungry. But it was a combination hunger: a hunger of lust and then a hunger to maybe make her his next meal.

Nausea swept through her and her pulse began to pound.

"You know, I so very much wanted to bring your little friend as well. The plump blonde?" He licked his lips and sighed. "But I realized I would have my hands full with just one of you, let alone two. Perhaps I will return for her after I have finished with you."

Finished with you. Not turned her in for a reward, but finished with her. Gods . . . this was not looking good.

"And I cannot help but wonder," Leo went on, "if he will come for you."

"He?"

"Your lover. I would enjoy the opportunity to kill him."

Her heart nearly stopped. Gods, as unappealing as facing her probable death on this dark planet was, having Brendon travel to rescue her was a worse image.

"He will not. I mean nothing to him," she bluffed with a forced calm.

"I am not so certain. He enjoyed bedding you. But then . . . why would he not?" He knelt down beside her and ran a hand over her neck.

Unable to move, she swallowed in disgust against the bile in her throat.

"Who would not enjoy fucking a woman whose sole purpose in life was to give pleasure to men? Whose training ensured she could suck a cock as if her life depended on it." His thumb pressed against the fast-beating pulse in her neck. "But then I suppose it did."

Through clenched teeth, she seethed, "Fuck you."

"Yes, you will. For I have decided that having the pleasure of a priceless Rosabelle at my command—and then ultimately enjoying her blood and death—is worth far more than any monetary reward."

For the first time in her life, Nika felt the sharp stab of stark terror. Yes, she'd been forced to sleep with men in her past. But somehow she knew this would be so much worse. And then the horrific way he intended to kill her . . .

"You're even more beautiful," he murmured, his face moving close to hers, "when you have fear in your eyes."

There was a rhythmic sound in the distance. At first Nika couldn't place it, but then it sounded a bit like heels clicking against the stone floor.

Irritation flickered in Leo's eyes before he released her suddenly, stepping back.

Nika weakened with relief. Her heart thudded so loudly she was certain it must be just as enticing as a dinner bell to him.

"Leo," the low husky voice of a woman rang out. "Did you bring her?"

A woman rounded the corner and stepped into the cold room of the cavern.

Another blood drinker? Nika wondered.

She was rather on the short side, with pale skin and short black hair. Her eyes were rimmed in black and her lipstick a color that was almost purple.

The outfit she wore showed off more skin than it covered. Her breasts were pushed up beneath a tight black corset-type top and her skirt barely covered her buttocks.

Her curious gaze landed on Nika as she crossed the floor to Leo.

"Isn't she pretty," the woman purred, then slipped her arms around Leo's waist. "Hello, my lover."

"Bernadette, my pet." Leo nuzzled her neck while one hand slipped into her bodice to grab a breast. "Mmm, how I have missed this little body."

"It's yours, my darling. To do whatever you wish. As you well know." She ran her tongue over her lips as he fondled her breast. Her gaze never left Nika. "But I want *her* to play with us now."

Disgust raged through Nika and her mouth tightened. Her face was still the only part of her body she could move. Gods. If it weren't so, she would've made an attempt to remove the life from the two. But then . . . how did one kill a blood drinker? Wasn't there some legend that they could not be killed? Indeed, lived forever?

"Unfortunately, Donika is not able to participate in our play. Not just yet anyway," Leo said thoughtfully. "She is still paralyzed from the injection I gave her."

Bernadette pouted, but slid her hand down to grasp Leo's cock through his trousers. "I suppose we are to entertain ourselves for a bit then."

Further repulsed, Nika closed her eyes, not wanting to see what was certain to happen next.

"For the next few hours, yes. Is that a problem, my pet?"

"Mmmm. No problem. But I want her to watch."

"Of course," Leo agreed and then more sharply, "Open your eyes, Donika. Or I will make you wish that you did."

Grinding her teeth together, Nika reluctantly lifted her eyelids. This was not the battle to fight. Especially when it was literally impossible for her to do so.

Leo's expression turned smug at her obedience. She blurred

her vision, not focusing on the hand he now moved beneath Bernadette's skirt.

They began their vulgar foreplay and coupling, but Nika had already disappeared mentally. She'd slipped back into that vacant, happy place in her mind she'd gone to and been so familiar with when she was a Rosabelle.

And right now, it was a welcome reunion.

22

Brendon fastened himself into the pod and dialed in the coordinates for the planet Multron.

The door began to close when a blur of movement caught his eye. He slapped his palm up to catch the descent of the pod door and frowned, watching as Molly rushed toward him.

"Brendon!" she yelled. "Please, one moment!"

Sighing, he sat back against his seat and pushed aside his irritation. It was still a bit difficult to look at Molly and not feel a little anger. After all, she and Talia had been the ones who set out to free Nika, thus leading in her capture by that savage.

Molly arrived at the edge of the pod, out of breath and pushing her blond hair off her face.

Other pods whizzed by around them, some launching into the universe every few minutes.

"Thank you," she said, giving him a wary glance. "Hello, Brendon."

He gave a slight nod. "Molly."

"I don't have much time. Emmett would not be pleased to

know I slipped out from under his thumb . . . again." She swallowed hard and looked away.

He nodded. The question of how she'd managed to get past his friend had crossed his mind.

"Brendon . . . I really must apologize for what I have done." Her eyes flooded with tears. "And what has now happened to Nika because of my foolish interference."

After a moment, he gave a slight nod. "Apology accepted, Molly. Now really, I must leave for Multron—"

"Please, wait. That is not all." Folding her arms across her chest Molly bit her lip, her gaze slipping away. "Perhaps I should not say this—for there is no proof. But . . ."

"What is it?" he prodded, something in his gut warning him the news would be upsetting. Again.

"I feel it is . . . quite possible . . . though Nika swears it is not . . . though *Talia* thinks she could be—"

"Molly," he growled, impatient to be on his way to retrieve Nika.

"We feel Nika may be pregnant."

The noise of the pods around them disappeared, drowned out by the sudden roar in his ears and the pounding of his heart.

Pregnant. Hot and cold washed over him, making his hands clammy and his head spin.

Nika pregnant. Could it even be possible? Nika had sworn it was not . . . but what if it had been just another lie? She had told him her planet sought the specimens to procreate. What if she'd simply bypassed that step and sought to become pregnant through him?

His head moved back and forth in wonder, even as a tiny spark of pleasure lit in his belly at the thought of Nika carrying his child.

The pleasure didn't last long and was quickly snuffed out at the reminder of her circumstances: right now Nika fought for her own life. And maybe, if Molly's suspicions were confirmed, the life of his baby.

He gripped the edge of his seat, drawing in an unsteady breath.

"Brendon . . . Brendon!"

He blinked, the sounds and vision of the city around him swarming back into focus.

"Forgive me," he mumbled and shook his head. "Thank you for the warning, but it's highly unlikely she is with child."

Molly sighed, but did not look convinced. "That is what she said as well."

"I must go now." He had been determined to leave the planet moments ago, and now he was almost frantic.

"You will go after her still?" Molly asked hopefully.

Brendon gave her a hard look of disbelief. "I would have gone after her with or without the possibility of a child. But now . . . I'm quite a bit more enraged."

"With me?" Molly gulped.

"No. With a fat loathsome blood drinker who, if I have my way, will never see another nightfall." He pressed the button to close the door again, calling out a quick, "Return to Emmett with a clear conscience."

Molly stepped away from the pod as it began to lift from the ground. Brendon shifted his attention from her and to the mission ahead.

Gods. It was almost surely suicide. But he now had one thing working in his favor. A rage that was growing by the moment. A thirst for the blood drinker's demise. And he would have it.

* * *

Several hours later, and after a tiresome but rapid galactic travel, Brendon climbed from his pod out onto the dark surface of Multron.

The smell of sulfur lingered in the air and his lungs tightened in protest at the atmosphere of this unfamiliar planet.

Any building was only half standing, with most reduced to nothing more than a pile of rubble. The streets appeared empty, but he could sense himself being watched, could almost feel the curious gazes of hidden eyes following his every move.

Moving his hand to his side, Brendon stroked his palm over the hilt of his electro-mace.

"Show yourselves," he called out in a calm voice, his words echoing down the street. "I seek your help in locating a bounty hunter."

There was no response, but a rock tumbled down from one of the crumbled buildings and into the road. Yes. There were those who hid.

"I mean you no harm, but if you attempt to harm me, you will not live long." He paused. "I offer a reward for any information regarding a bounty hunter by the name of Leo. Come forward and we shall speak."

Nothing. No more falling rocks or sounds of movement.

And then, just as he was about to lose hope, a man stepped out of the shadows.

The feeling slowly returned to Nika's body. It had begun as a slow tingling, warning her the drug had begun to wear off. But she didn't dare move, would do nothing to alert the two that she was regaining her strength.

Even now, still forced to watch their coupling, she could barely keep her lips from curling in disgust. They were tireless.

"Yes!" Bernadette screamed, gripping Leo's head as his mouth moved between her legs. "*Now*. *Please*. Bite me."

His head moved away from her pussy and he hissed. A moment later Bernadette let out a long wail that sounded a mix of pain and pleasure.

When Leo lifted his head a moment later, blood dripped from his fangs and two burgundy spots glistened on the woman's inner thigh.

A shudder of horror ripped through Nika and she started to close her eyes, but knew they would notice all too soon.

"Oh Leo," the woman purred. "When? When will you turn me? I've been so patient."

Turn her? Nika drew in a swift breath at the realization. The woman was not a blood drinker but human?

"Not tonight, my pet," Leo murmured and stood licking his lips. "Although I'm afraid you've only just heightened my hunger to feast."

Bernadette's smile was entirely too smug as she stood and pulled her skirt back down over her hips.

"So feast from your prisoner. Surely a little missing blood will not be noticed when you return her to Belton for the reward?"

Leo did not respond. Instead, he approached Nika where she lay motionless, watching him with a steady gaze. Did he realize she could move now?

"When do you plan to return her?" Bernadette asked. "Or perhaps I should ask how long will we enjoy her before seeking the reward."

Leo kneeled beside Nika and touched her throat, his mouth curving slightly. "Do not trouble yourself with my business."

"Your business?" Bernadette's tone sharpened. "Do you not mean ours?"

Leo did not look at his woman, but his mouth tightened. "No. I mean mine. I no longer seek the reward. I intend to keep her indefinitely."

There was a moment of silence. And then, "Gods! Are you insane? You fool!"

"Watch yourself," Leo warned.

Nika held her breath, all too aware this conversation was in dangerous waters.

"I hardly think I am the one needing watching," Bernadette scoffed, folding her arms across her breasts. "You are fuzzy in the head over a nice pair of legs and untainted blood. She is not worth the money we would receive."

"That is for me to decide."

"Why should you even want her? You have *me*. You have become quite mad, Leo, and I must say I am not pleased with your behavior lately."

Leo's gaze began to glow red. "Perhaps I no longer want you."

"No longer want me?" Bernadette choked out in dismay. "After I have proven myself for years? This is bullshit. How could you say such—"

Leo leapt up with a hiss and grabbed the petite woman, jerking her forward. Her startled gasp ended on a scream of pain as his fangs slid into the side of her neck.

"No," she whispered, her gaze wide with horror as she attempted to push him away. "You promised . . . to turn me."

Nika could not tear her gaze away, no longer paralyzed from the drug but with shock.

Bernadette made feeble attempts to push him away as he drank from her neck, but her eyes grew more glossy by the second. Her cries became a soft gurgling sound.

Leo growled as his jaws opened around her neck, and a moment later he ripped her throat out.

Nika squeezed her eyes shut, but it was too late. Her body shook with horror and bile rose to burn her throat.

The vision she'd just witnessed would leave her scarred for the rest of her life—no matter if that were only a handful of days.

Footsteps sounded and she knew he approached her.

"I apologize if that was upsetting," he murmured, as if it had been nothing more than having it rain during a picnic. "I can become quite volatile when hungry and . . . nagged. Bernadette was quite pleasant when she used her mouth for certain purposes. For speaking, not quite as much."

Nika had no desire to open her eyes, to stare at the *thing* she had no training to fight. The blood drinker who would ultimately destroy her. But not before playing with her long enough that she wished for her own death.

"Please, Donika, stand for me. I know that the drug has lost its effect."

The breath locked in her throat and her heart slammed against her rib cage. He knew. If she ignored him, he would likely grow angry. And after what she'd just witnessed . . .

With her hands still tied behind her back, she scooted to a sitting position and then slid up the wall until she could stand.

Her cheeks flushed with humiliation as his gaze slid over her. Gods, how she wished she wore more than Brendon's shirt. Something that at least covered her past her thighs. And yet having it on her, with the scent of his body surrounding her, gave her some sense of peace.

"You are rather lovely, aren't you?" he murmured and stepped closer to her, fingering one of the buttons on the shirt. "Perhaps it's because I just feasted, but I cannot see myself killing you anytime soon. You will be an excellent pet."

Her stomach churned with dread and it became all too clear. She did not *want* to live for days, perhaps weeks on end as his little sex toy. A death immediately, no matter how painful and violent it may be, could only be preferable.

Which meant provoking him into killing her early was the only way.

Leo's finger slipped beneath her shirt and brushed against the swell of one breast. He sighed, an expression of wonder and desire slipping over his face.

"Such soft skin you have, my dear."

It was time to act. *Now.*

With a growl deep in her chest, Nika threw her weight forward and slammed the crown of her head into his nose.

There was a loud crunch and Leo fell backward with a scream, clutching his nose. Blood seeped through his fingers.

Not giving him time to recover completely, Nika lunged forward and lifted her right leg, driving it into his side.

He stumbled back and hit the stone wall of the cave with a gasp.

"Bitch!" His eyes were wild and blazed red as he pulled himself back to his feet.

Everything inside her shut down. There was no fear. No sense of desolation as he charged her. It was her time. And she knew this. She did not run. And even if she'd had the use of her hands, she would not have tried to defend herself.

Leo wrapped an arm around her neck, winding her hair in his fist and wrenching her head back so her throat was exposed. His mouth opened and the small light in the room gleamed on his deadly fangs as his head descended toward her neck.

"Hey, bounty hunter." A voice rang out in the cave. "How about a fair fight with me instead?"

Brendon's voice finally registered in Nika's head. And it was not just something her imagination was producing. Her mind whirled back to life and her body trembled with immediate horror. Brendon was *here*.

The man she had fallen in love with had come after her, and would likely die with her because of it. Gods. Why did fate have to be so merciless?

Leo blinked in confusion, and the wildness faded from his gaze as realization set in. In a heartbeat, he was once again in control, his expression cunning and pleased.

She let out a small whimper, praying for a miracle as Leo spun them both around so he could face his opponent.

Brendon breathed evenly, keeping his stance relaxed as he stared at the blood drinker who held Nika hostage.

Though he knew he appeared calm, inside rage boiled through his blood, adding to his incentive to slaughter the bastard. He'd almost been too late, had arrived within seconds of witnessing Nika's death.

"You should not have come!" Her gaze sought his. It was bright with fear, but he knew it was not for herself.

His chest tightened with relief and he forced away the vulnerable emotion. He could not afford the distraction of reassuring himself that she still had the breath of life within her. For the moment.

"So you came?" The bounty hunter asked in amusement. "Not like I had ever doubted you would, as the bitch is carrying your child."

Brendon stilled, the air stranding in his lungs. He glanced to Nika who looked equally staggered. How could the blood drinker possibly know?

Leo threw back his head and laughed. "Do not look so surprised. I knew the moment I took her that she was with child. Breeding women have a certain smell about them." He shrugged and then inspected his thumbnail. "No matter, though. She will not have the brat inside her much longer as I can't tolerate my newest pet growing fatter by the day."

Brendon's vision blurred red and he could not stop the primal growl that erupted from his throat.

"And you do realize, soldier," Leo continued conversationally, "that you are on my planet now and that I am held by no laws to not kill humans."

"I am well aware," Brendon snarled.

"Good. I shall enjoy killing you." Leo laughed and jerked Nika's head toward him, forcing a hard kiss to her lips. "And then, soldier, I will enjoy fucking your woman."

Gods, this blood drinker was going to die painfully. And not a moment too soon. "I can't let you do that."

"Ah, but, human, you cannot stop me if you're dead."

"No." Nika pounded a fist into the blood drinker's chest, while her foot connected with his shin.

"Easy, you wild little bitch." Leo's hand tightened around her throat as he moved forward, still holding her in front of him as a shield. He grabbed her breast and squeezed. "We'll have our fun soon enough."

Brendon flexed his jaw, trying to silently convey to Nika to stop fighting. He needed the blood drinker to put her aside before he could take out the bastard. It was too much of a risk with her beside him.

"Leave him be, Leo," Nika begged. "Please, do whatever you want with me, but leave Brendon be."

"I don't need your permission to destroy, Donika," Leo replied with a harsh laugh. "Or your lover's. Let us fight, you pathetic human soldier."

The blood drinker bared his fangs and then shoved Nika from him. She stumbled several feet away before landing on the ground on her hands and knees.

Now! Brendon did not wait another second, but pulled the

gun from beneath his jacket and fired one shot into the blood drinker's chest.

Leo looked down at his chest, mouth parted in surprise. "Whatever happened to our fair fight?"

"I lied."

"You realize I am immortal and bullets don't kill blood drinkers?"

Brendon's mouth curved into a humorless smile. "Potassium chloride bullets do."

And he fired another four rounds into Leo's chest.

Leo's face distorted into a mask of pain as he crumpled to the ground, choking.

Brendon walked over to him and knelt beside him. "Right about now, *bounty hunter*, those bullets are traveling to your bloodstream. Once they hit . . . it's all over."

Leo's mouth flapped as he attempted to speak, but no words came out. Then his gaze glassed over and his body went rigid on the ground as the life left his body.

Brendon stood up and muttered, "Not so immortal now, are you, motherfucker?"

A choking noise came from his right. He turned just as Nika launched herself awkwardly at him, her gaze bright with unshed tears.

"You fool! How easily you could have been killed!"

Brendon caught her forearms, jerked her against him, and closed his mouth over hers. He needed not her fury, but her passion. His tongue teased past her lips to find hers.

She responded with a soft moan and leaned into him, tilting her head and giving him better depths to explore. Her tongue wrapped around his, sucking with an urgency that conveyed the relief they both felt from being alive.

He lifted his head a moment later and sighed.

"I would not have been killed. Have you no faith in me?" he chided softly, sliding his hands down her arms behind her back to unfasten the cord that bound her. "How do you feel?"

"Angry," she said, though less crossly this time as she rubbed her wrists. "You risked your life for me."

"And I would do it again without hesitation. Give me one moment." He reached into his jacket and pulled out his communication mobile, typing in a quick code to Emmett before putting it away again.

Nika shuddered. "I hate blood drinkers. Despise them worse than my former owners on Zortou."

"They are not all bad," Brendon said gently, while pulling her back into his arms. "In truth I met a very agreeable one when I landed. He was the only way I found you."

"Nevertheless, I'd rather not run into another one anytime soon," Nika said fervently and slid her arms around his waist, pressing her cheek against his shoulder.

"Understandable. You've been through quite a bit today."

Gods, he couldn't even begin to imagine how traumatizing the last hour had been for her. He pulled back just enough so he could slide a hand between them and pressed his palm against her belly. "Is it true?"

Her eyes widened before her gaze shifted away. "I do not see how it *could* be possible. I told you of the injection I was given."

"Regardless, we will have a test done when we return to Belton."

Her gaze jerked back. "You intend to return me to your planet?"

"Of course."

He glanced around the room at the two deceased bodies. A

plan had been formulating since his journey over, one that would hopefully free Nika from any guilt in what she'd done.

"I see. Yes, I suppose that is best."

"Have no fear, Nika. All will be well." He kissed her forehead. "I promise."

23

Gods, she really hoped she wasn't going to get sick. Again.

Nika gripped her seat in the tiny pod. Surely they couldn't be much farther from Belton. Her head ached and her stomach churned, combining for a most unpleasant nausea.

"Are you feeling well?" Emmett asked, casting her a sideways glance.

"Well enough." She gave a wan smile.

Outside of the physical ailments, she wouldn't confess to being upset that Brendon had stayed behind to "deal with the cleanup" as he'd put it. He'd given her a quick kiss good-bye, before placing her on the pod with Emmett the moment his friend had arrived. No preliminaries. No explanations.

"How are Molly and Talia?" she asked, after a period of silence.

"They are doing well," he replied curtly.

Nika chewed on her bottom lip, her cheeks flushing with regret. He blamed her for their condition, it was clear.

"I did not encourage them to try and free me," she said huskily. "I would never have put them in danger."

Some of the tension eased from Emmett's shoulders as he steered the pod. His lips quirked.

"I realize that, Nika. Molly and Talia do quite a good job of putting themselves in danger."

"But you are still not happy with me." It wasn't a question.

Emmett was quiet again before he finally said, "I am not sure you deserve him."

Nika made no effort to pretend she didn't know whom he spoke of. Her throat tightened with emotion, because she knew he spoke the truth.

"I know I do not," she managed to say, though the tears burning her throat made it difficult.

"He risks his life and his career for you."

"Yes."

"But he loves you." Emmett shook his head. "So do not hurt him."

A bit too late for that.

Nika closed her eyes for a second and then turned her head to look at the blackness outside the window of the pod.

They arrived back on Belton quite a bit later. Emmett had made several stops on the way, insisting that Brendon needed to arrive on Belton before they did.

Once they finally did arrive back on the planet and went through the decompression chamber, Emmett took her to Molly's lodge. Nika didn't bother to hide her surprise, having been convinced they were to go straight to the base.

"Watch her," Emmett ordered Molly with a pointed look as they stood in the room Nika had stayed in just a few days ago. "I need to go retrieve Brendon."

"Of course." Molly nodded eagerly. "We shall have some lovely girl-bonding time."

Emmett's mouth twisted into a wry smile. "Yes, not much like the last time, I hope. Where you all nearly ended up dead."

"We ended up fine. After a bit of a bump in the road," Molly scoffed and leaned forward to press a kiss to his lips. "Go, my love, and bring Brendon back to Nika soon."

Emmett sighed and gave a nod. "Indeed. Please perform the test we discussed."

"Test?" Nika asked sharply as Emmett left the room. "What kind of test?"

Molly scurried over to her dresser and pulled out a small black case. "Oh just a little test. Shouldn't take a moment."

"Yes, but what is it?" Nika asked, watching the other woman pull a few small objects from the case.

Molly smiled and walked back to her, grabbing Nika's hand. "We're going to check to see if you're pregnant."

"If I'm—ow!" Nika tugged her hand back, scowling at the drop of red blood that now swelled on her finger.

"Yes, it will take just a moment." Molly took the sample of blood and began to mix it in a tiny container in the black case.

Nika wiped the drop of blood on her shirt—or Brendon's—and watched Molly uneasily. It was impossible. She'd been given the injection. The same injection that had kept her from creating a child for years on Zortou. It was simply impossible that she could be—

"Pregnant. You're definitely pregnant." Molly set the black case back down and grinned. "Congratulations, Nika!"

The room spun, and the nausea that she'd successfully kept at bay during the second half of the journey home returned in a rush.

"Brendon will be so thrilled," Molly said with a sigh. "And he will also be a wonderful father."

Nika shook her head and bolted to the bathing chamber and

ran to clutch the sink. Sweat broke out on the back of her neck and her stomach churned like mad.

Pregnant. There was truly a child growing in her. A child who would suffer with her while going through endless questioning by the military. Who would likely be taken from her the moment it was born, for no incarcerated criminal would be allowed to raise a child.

Slipping a hand over her stomach Nika stared at herself in the mirror. Gods.

Molly clearly did not realize the extent of Nika's crime. How could she be excited about this? Fate certainly had a sadistic sense of humor. There was no idealistic future for her or Brendon. And especially their child.

Her head moved back and forth in denial, and before she realized what she was doing she'd left the bathing chamber and was striding toward the door of the room.

"Nika?" Molly stepped forward, concern in her gaze. "What are you doing?"

She didn't answer, just shook her head faster as she pressed the button that would open the door of the room. She had to get out of here.

Molly rushed forward. "Nika! Wait a moment!"

The door hissed open and Nika darted forward, running smack into Brendon as he stepped into the doorway.

"Going somewhere, love?" He raised an eyebrow, amusement on his face.

"Step out of the way, Brendon," she said fiercely. "You cannot stop me."

Brendon sighed, even as a smile played around the edges of his mouth. His gaze lifted behind her to Molly.

"Did you perform the test?"

"Yes. She's pregnant."

"Indeed!" Brendon's smile widened. "Would you give us some time alone, Molly?"

"Of course." Molly stepped forward, giving Nika an encouraging squeeze on the arm and then disappearing from the room.

Brendon didn't remove his gaze from her and pressed the button to shut the door of the room again.

He stared at her for a moment, his gaze still amused but now considering as well. "You were about to run. Weren't you, love?"

How dare he make light of their situation? Nika's chest rose in frustration, her cheeks reddening.

"Would you have me be incarcerated while carrying our child?"

Brendon clucked his tongue and nodded. "I agree, not the ideal choice."

"You jest?" She slapped his chest with an open palm, while inside her heart seemed to be ripping in half.

What had gotten into him? Was he not at all worried about the future of their child? Or—it was silly to even hope, but—worried about *her* fate?

"Not at all. It is no jesting matter," he said solemnly and slid her hand up to cover his heart. "A very skilled thief infiltrated a highly secure lab on the military compound, assaulting several soldiers in the process. Then she stole priceless specimen samples right out from under our noses."

Each word he uttered was just another nail in her sealed coffin of future imprisonment. He had changed his mind, realized there was no other way, and come to take her back to face charges.

Her mouth trembled and tears pricked at the back of her eyes.

He was far too honorable of a soldier not to turn her in. Of course, she had been expecting this. Her stomach clenched and she closed her eyes. She had *not* been expecting the baby.

"That woman should be punished. Should be accountable for her crimes," he went on severely and lifted her hand to brush his lips across her knuckles. "But sadly she never will, because she is dead."

Nika blinked, only vaguely aware of the tremble of pleasure that rocketed through her body at his lips' caress.

"Dead?" she repeated uneasily.

"Yes, quite tragic, really." He turned her hand upside down and placed a kiss on the inside of her palm. "Had her throat ripped out by the blood drinker she was working for."

Nika's jaw fell as his words began to sink in. Was he implying . . . ?

"It was rather convenient," Brendon said lightly, "when we returned her body to Belton and found a few of the specimen vials in a pouch tied about her waist. The military is closing the case as we speak."

She shook her head. "But my DNA . . . you said a sample had been found—"

"You toured the lab, Nika. No one would be surprised to find your DNA in there." He traced her palm with his forefinger. "And besides . . . you have an alibi. You were with me the night the specimens were successfully stolen.

Her heart slowed and then picked right back up again, thudding with excitement.

"What are you saying, Brendon?" she asked on a whisper.

He pulled her against him and lowered his head, his lips almost brushing hers as he murmured, "I'm saying I just saved your ass."

Her knees went weak with relief and amazement. "How . . . why . . . ?"

"Because I love you, Nika." He slipped his hands beneath

her knees and lifted her into his arms, moving to the bed to lay her down. "And I need you like I've never needed anyone."

He undid the first button on her shirt and then the next, finally plucking the shirt off her and tossing it aside. "And I will *not* lose you because you made an incredibly stupid decision to rob my planet."

"Incredibly stupid," she agreed and gasped when his mouth sought her breast, his lips closing over the tight nipple. "Gods, I love you, Brendon."

"You had better," he teased, flicking his tongue over the tip of her breast.

She lost all ability to think as his hand moved between her legs and he slipped his fingers inside.

He suckled her breasts while penetrating her slowly with his fingers, bringing her higher onto that plane of pleasure. When his thumb touched her clit, she arched off the bed and came with a soft cry.

Brendon settled between her legs and then entered her swiftly. He caught her hands in his, intertwining their fingers as he began to move them in their familiar rhythm.

Nika wrapped her legs around his waist, drawing him closer, needing that contact of body to body. To feel his hard strength on top of her and know that everything was going to be okay.

"Love you . . . so much," Brendon murmured as he moved faster inside her. "So damn . . . much."

He groaned, his fingers tightening around hers, and she felt him come inside her.

Her head fell back against the pillow as the pleasure spiraled upward, finally erupting in a release that left her shattered.

Tears rolled down her cheeks as she choked out, "I love you, too. Gods, Brendon, I am lost without you. Never leave me."

"Never," he agreed on a whisper. "Never, Nika."

Epilogue

Ten Months later

"Is she asleep?" Nika asked, sitting up in bed and clutching the blanket beneath her breasts as her husband came back into the room.

"Out to the world." He smiled and climbed onto the mattress beside her. "I think we tired her out after having dinner with everyone tonight."

"It was good to see them all. Molly and Emmett seem so excited about their upcoming nuptials," she murmured. "And Ryder and Talia's little boy is simply adorable—crawling already. I do think he will be a suitable husband for Briana someday."

"Hush. I want to hear nothing about my daughter and marriage," Brendon scoffed and pressed a kiss to her naked shoulder. "Gods, I've missed you."

She smiled and let the blanket slide free of her, almost shy in her nudity. Her body had changed so much after giving birth to their daughter.

"Oh, but you are a sight." Brendon breathed and cupped her fuller breasts. "Are you sure it is not too soon?"

"The physician assured me it is fine." She closed her eyes as pleasure swept through her body at his touch. "Make love to me, Brendon."

Needing no further encouragement, Brendon pressed her back onto the mattress and followed with his body, his lips seeking hers.

An hour later she lay with her head upon his chest, her heart still pounding from their lovemaking.

"I have been thinking about it," Brendon murmured. "Do you think Tresden will attempt to send another mission to Belton some day?"

"No. They will not attempt it again. They assume I was captured or killed here and it would be too risky."

"Pity, it would have been some excitement."

"As if you need it. You're not even guarding the lab anymore," she teased and grazed her teeth against his nipple. "Promoted since last year, might I add."

"Indeed." His tone turned smug.

Nika laughed and laid her head against his chest again. Her amusement faded. "I'm glad they think I am dead. Especially knowing now that Rachel lied about me being given the injection to prevent pregnancy, hoping you would impregnate me."

"Yes, that was a bit of a shock," Brendon agreed. "I think we were both surprised when your physician announced that in your blood test she'd found trace elements of a drug that would actually kill off the Y chromosome in my sperm. It seems Rachel wanted to ensure that if you became pregnant with my child, the baby would be a girl."

"Yes . . . and Rachel must have hoped I'd return to Tresden carrying the female child of a strong, amazing soldier," she murmured and lifted her head, reaching a hand up to stroke his jaw.

"I would have *never* given you up." He caught her finger and nipped at the tip.

Her heart swelled with emotion and she inhaled unsteadily. The love between them was so strong that at times she could barely remember what life had been like without it.

"When I was on Zortou I never even let myself imagine I could have a life like this," she said softly. "That I could be so happy and have wonderful friends. Have a child and a husband, both of whom own more of my heart than I ever thought to give away. You have truly changed my life, Brendon."

He smoothed a hand down her back and kissed her forehead. "And you have done the same for me. Never doubt it, love."

"Oh, I never would." She grinned. "If I remember correctly, before we became involved, you seemed to enjoy climbing into women's beds—"

"That's a bald-faced lie."

"It is not in the least!" She slapped his chest playfully and let out a soft laugh.

"Ah, you are right. I was a bit into the sport of it." He hugged her tighter against him. "But I cannot imagine anyone but you in my bed now, Nika. When you entered my life my vision became focused. There was only you. Always will be only you."

"You promise?" She lifted her head and met his gaze.

"Do you doubt me?"

"Not at all." She smiled, her heart pounding a little faster as such complete happiness slid through her. "You need me as much as I need you, Brendon."

"Truer words were never spoken," he murmured and lowered his lips to hers again.

Missed Talia and Ryder's romance?

Turn the page for a taste of the first Rosabelle's story in *Take Me*, available now from Kensington Publishing.

1

By the gods, she was late. Talia stepped off the walkatron, ignoring the electronic voice that blared a reminder that she was tardy for her next scheduled meeting with the Council. Dragging a towel across her forehead, she headed toward the bathing room.

The physical wellness hour was the one time during her day that she absolutely savored, that she considered her hour. Complete isolation and privacy, taking out her frustrations and wants in the only way she was allowed. Forty-five minutes of running on the walkatron, until her legs were sore and her mind rid of all the dreams that could never be.

She could simply be Talia, a twenty-two-year-old woman blessed—or cursed—to be one of the few dozen women alive and well living on the planet. She was no longer Natalia, the well-pampered and well-used commodity of the Council. A highly educated, groomed plaything for the most powerful men on the planet. In here she could escape the reality of her life as a Rosabelle.

Her mouth tightened and she shook her head.

Stop feeling sorry for yourself. Every woman blessed to be alive on this planet bears the same reality as you. Only most do not have your luxuries.

She was envied by the other Rosabelles, as well she should be. Though every woman alive was groomed and sold to the highest bidder, she was the only woman who now kneeled at the feet of the Governing Council.

Pausing to look in the mirror, she toyed with a strand of red hair that had escaped the severe knot on top of her head. Her lips twisted downward. Such freedom that strand of hair had. A freedom that was never to be. She pulled the hair taut and tucked it back into the expected knot on her head.

"Mistress Natalia, you must begin your bathing ritual." The male voice rang out through the bathroom.

Her stomach dropped as she met the bored obsidian gaze of her male servant who waited in the corner. *And now the return to reality.* She turned around and approached the large basin, already filled with near-scalding water.

"Did you enjoy your run?" Dane asked, taking her arms and urging them above her head.

"It was quite lovely as always, thank you." She waited as he unfastened, then unwound the strip of fabric that bound her breasts.

"You always seem to look forward to that hour." He grimaced. "I don't tolerate exercise, or sweating. The physical wellness hour would be my least favorite time of the day." He dropped to his knees in front of her and untied the fastenings at each side of her hip, plucking the fabric away and leaving her completely naked. "Then again, I see nothing wrong with being surrounded by the most powerful men on the planet who want only for me to please them."

"Yes, now why doesn't that surprise me?" Talia rolled her

eyes as he cupped the mound of her sex and ran a thumb down her slit.

He nodded in approval. "Still smooth. The treatments last summer appear to have killed the hair follicles in this region." Standing again he gestured toward the bath. "Let us begin."

Talia climbed into the basin, wincing as the water stung her legs. Protesting the temperature would only gain her disapproval from her owners. As with every Rosabelle, she was to be cleansed with the hottest of water that would not damage her skin, but would leave it pink and clean.

She sank all the way under, rinsing all the sweat off her body and wetting every square inch of flesh. When she sat back up, Dane held a sponge drizzled with honey and a creamy, moisturizing soap.

"Hands in the air, please," he ordered.

Raising her hands above her head, she laced her fingers and closed her eyes. The first stroke of the sponge moved over her breasts and her nipples tightened. She went through the bathing ritual daily, with a man who would never be aroused by her, yet her body continued to respond to the silky touch of the sponge on her flesh.

"Jeez, Talia, you're so damn responsive. The Council members must love you."

She bit back a sigh. Yes. The Council members did indeed love her. Although, love was probably a poor choice of words. They loved her body and her skills as a Rosabelle. Never had she, nor would she likely, feel the warmth of another's love.

Her gut clenched and the familiar sense of despair and feeling trapped washed over her. The recurring *this can't be my life* moment that threatened to rip apart her soul.

Dane moved the sponge between her legs and heat speared through her body.

"No, love, don't get yourself aroused. That's the Council's job. It will only anger them if you arrive already prepared."

A spark of irritation ran through her. Of course it would. Gods help her if she were to be aroused when she wasn't in the Council's presence.

Every moment of her life revolved around pleasing men, but only the select three men who owned her. Anyone outside the Council and Dane was forbidden from ever touching or even gazing upon her naked flesh.

And never was she allowed to touch herself. A Rosabelle caught touching herself was to be punished in the most severe manner, where she would only begin to wish for death. Though never would she actually be killed, for to do so would mean one less woman on a planet where there were already so few.

Her expression turned bitter. Life on the endangered species list could be a real pain in the ass.

"Close your eyes while I wash your hair."

She obediently closed her eyes and enjoyed the moment where her hair was let free down her back. So rarely was that allowed; only if one of the Council members requested it. Otherwise, she was to wear it in a knot atop her head.

Dane massaged her scalp and worked the cleanser in her hair into a lather.

"Rinsing now. Keep the eyes closed."

Warm water sluiced over her head, down her face, and over her breasts.

"Very nice, love. All done. You can get out now."

Talia stepped out of the tub and into the fluffy soft towel that Dane held. He wrapped it around her, patting her down. Once she was dry he pulled her hair again into the severe knot atop her head, and then began oiling and lotioning her body.

A half hour later her body was dewy and perfumed. Her lips were topped with shiny pink gloss and her lashes curled and inked. She donned a pale blue silk dress with sleeves to the wrists, an empire waist, and a low bodice.

Dane gave her an appreciative glance. "Look at how nicely you've cleaned up."

"Only with your help, as always." She gave a slight smile; the movement felt awkward as the muscles around her mouth stretched. When was the last time she'd smiled?

"Well, I do try. Now, we should go, because I have a lunch date with a certain warrior in training."

They left the bathing chambers and she cast him a sideways glance. "I take it things are well between you and Thomas?"

"Quite well." The slight flush in his cheeks and brightening of his eyes surprised her. Perhaps Dane was developing an attachment to the younger man?

On a planet with so few women, it was not uncommon for men to take other men as lovers.

They moved into a busy corridor, passing a general.

"Good day, mistress." He bowed slightly, his hungry gaze moving over her.

Talia curtsied and lowered her eyes demurely. The general was just one of the many men who would never be allowed to touch her.

"The Council has already begun meeting for the day." Dane cast a nervous glance her way. "They will not be pleased to find you late."

"I'm sure they will not," she agreed mildly and glanced through the window in the corridor down to the city below. Men roamed the streets, their clothes tattered as they begged for handouts. They would not be outside for long, though; the air outside was not safe to breathe for long periods of time.

She bit back a sigh. Even with the dangerous environment, she wished just once to be able to experience life outside the Council's headquarters. Once, as a child, she'd been taken outside, but the memory was so vague she couldn't tell what was real and what was simply made up in her head from watching the teletron.

But that is not your life, it never will be. She lifted her chin, squelching back the bite of loneliness. Turning her gaze back to the corridor, it locked on a pair of dark brown eyes.

She had no idea who he was, yet he watched her rather intimately. Irritation pricked her. The man leaned against the corridor a few feet ahead of them.

He was quite attractive. Tall, dark hair, broad shoulders, and a predatory stillness in him that sent a frisson of alarm through her. Alarm and . . . heat. She felt a warm flush steal into her cheeks. But why? She was no virgin unused to a man's sexual interest.

Dane escorted her closer to him, and the breath in her throat seemed to lock. He did not bow, she realized in shock. With so few women in existence, all Rosabelles were held in the highest regard. It was required that every man bow in the presence of one. Instead his gaze moved over her slow and thorough, to the point where she wondered if he might have the impossible ability to see beneath her dress.

Her pulse, which had already begun to race, throbbed for a different reason now. How dare the man? Had he no respect?

He straightened from the wall as she came abreast of him, but instead of bowing as she assumed he'd do, he gave her a mocking smile and lifted one eyebrow as if to challenge her. She jerked her gaze away from him, her heart thudding like mad.

How foolish he was to stare at her so, to not bow. If she were smart she'd report him. It was no less than he deserved.

Even after she'd passed by him, she could feel his gaze burning into her back. She was accustomed to being stared at, but never had it unsettled her so. Never had something as common as a man's stare created heat that spiraled throughout her body and settled low in her belly.

Her nipples tightened and she groaned in dismay. This was not good. Her arousal was now blatantly apparent, and the Council would note as much the moment she entered the room.

"Come." Dane punched in the code that opened the automatic doors, and they hissed open.

Talia took a deep breath and, unable to resist, glanced back at the man. He continued to watch her, but his eyes were now narrowed and his mouth drawn tight.

He didn't appear pleased with her being led into the Council's chamber. The thought perked her spirits a bit and she raised a mocking eyebrow back at him, before turning to enter the chamber alone.

Ryder watched the doors to the Council's chamber slide shut and clenched his fists. Fuck. She was the target Rosabelle? He shook his head and walked to the window that overlooked the city. Now this was just a complication that he didn't need.

What should have been a simple plan had just become a helluva lot more complicated. The last thing he needed was his dick rock hard when he set the events in motion. *As long as you think with the right head you'll be fine.*

And they would be blindsided if all went well. He rocked back on his heels and envisioned the Rosabelle who'd just passed by. Like all Rosabelles he'd encountered on this planet, she had been beautiful. With lush breasts, a small waist, and slender thighs that he already imagined spread wide for him. But there had been more about that woman. A fire he'd seen within those pale blue eyes, where as in most Rosabelles he had encountered there was simply a flatness, a resignation to their lives.

The blood in his cock stirred and his breathing grew heavier. He would have her. Hot and willing when the time was right, but now . . . now he needed to stick to the plan.

* * *

Talia entered the Council's chamber, pushing aside the familiar despondency and apprehension. She walked with her head held high and her shoulders back, allowing her breasts to thrust against the fabric. *Always present your body's curves in the most provocative manner.* She'd learned the manner of walking from the day she was first groomed to become a Rosabelle.

The room was cold with steel walls, circular in structure with each of the Council members' desks spread throughout. In the middle of the room was the couch that could be altered into a bed. Just looking at it brought a cold trickle of sweat down her spine.

"Natalia, my dear. You're late, but have impeccable timing. We were about to begin our first break of the morning." One of the Council members, Victor, arose from his desk and approached her. His gaze moved over her possessively. "You look absolutely stun—"

He broke off and the sudden silence in the air was wrought with tension. Oh gods. He'd sure noticed quickly enough. She'd hoped he'd not see it, be too preoccupied.

"Take notice, gentlemen," he said and closed the distance between them. Reaching out he cupped her breast through the dress, capturing the tight nipple between his fingers. "It appears our Natalia has found something to be aroused by outside our chamber."

"And I apologize, sirs," she murmured uneasily and lowered her gaze. "It was simply the thought of you three that has put me in such a state."

The lie was reasonable enough, but would they believe it?

"Really?" Victor's tone indicated his doubt. "How aroused have you allowed yourself to become? Shall we check, my dear?"

She kept her gaze lowered and gave a submissive nod. Her pulse quickened with trepidation. She heard the scrape of the other chairs across the hardwood floor and knew that Ramirez and Franklin were approaching her.

The warm air tickled her ankles as one of the men lifted her dress. With her gaze still downcast, she recognized the age spots on the hand that held the fabric. It was Ramirez, the eldest of the men, who was somewhere in his mid-fifties.

The dress was raised past her knees, up her thighs, and then over her hips. Her naked pussy was revealed to the men in the room. Men who knew every inch of her body the way a painter knew every detail in his painting.

Ramirez's fingers slipped between her legs and rubbed over the lips of her cunt. She closed her eyes, knowing her body would respond at this point. Heart and emotions out of the equation, her body knew pleasure.

"She is already wet." His disappointment was evident.

And her body also knew pain. She knew what would come next. She bit her lip and a tremble shook her body.

"I see." Victor sighed.

Her dress was once again lowered. She heard the rasp of a zipper and opened her eyes, lifting her gaze to the men. Franklin had his cock out, and was stroking the thick purple erection as he leered at her.

"Remove your dress, Natalia," Victor commanded.

Without hesitation she undid the single button in the back and let the dress slide off her body and onto the floor.

"Now you will assume the position for punishment." Victor glanced over at Ramirez. "You may participate if you wish."

The older man nodded and went and sat upon his desk, hastily reaching for the fly of his pants.

Talia took a deep calming breath, walked to the desk, and leaned forward, thrusting her ass out toward Victor. She placed her palms on either side of Ramirez, watching as he freed his erection and lifted it eagerly toward her lips.

"Take him within your mouth," Victor commanded. And then the first stinging slap of his hand rained down on her buttock.

She barely flinched and parted her lips, allowing Victor to press his erection into her mouth. The slaps continued, harder as she suckled upon Ramirez's flesh. She went into her zone, the only way in which she got through these moments. Not thinking, only performing.

His fingers clenched in her hair, holding her mouth to his cock as she brought him to orgasm. He spilled his seed into her mouth and she swallowed automatically, trying not to focus on the hot burning of her buttocks.

Ramirez released her just as an arm wrapped around her waist and pulled her upright.

"You are forgiven, my dear." Victor turned her around, his gaze full of lust.

Ramirez slipped off the desk, which allowed Victor to lay her down upon it. The wood was hard upon her spine, but she offered no protest as he stepped between her thighs.

He ran his hands over her body, squeezing her breasts and then moving down between her legs. He thrust two fingers inside her and wiggled them around.

"Wet indeed. A woman's cunt is like the rarest fine wine. So few can afford it. We are entitled, we are blessed." He fell to his knees and buried his face against her pussy.

His tongue moved over her, rough and eager. He found her clit and lapped at it, at her, devouring her like a man deprived.

The warm arousal she'd felt when she'd seen the man in the corridor returned. His image instantly embedded itself behind her closed lids, and suddenly it was not Victor pleasuring her, but him. The dark-eyed man in the hall, sucking and licking her flesh.

The pleasure spiraled until it seemed to spill over in waves. Her body trembled. She blinked. What had just happened?

Victor stood and ran his hands down her thighs. "How interesting. I do believe our Rosabelle just had a small orgasm."

An orgasm? She had not thought it possible. Confusion swept over her. The pleasure had built while she had thought about that man in the hall.

"Do not get a swollen head over it. I am sure it was an accident," Franklin grumbled. "I believe it was decided that I was to have her during the morning break?"

"Yes, that was what we agreed upon this morning." Victor's reply sounded reluctant.

She opened her eyes, watching Victor step away from her and Franklin move between her thighs. Since the day they'd purchased her when she'd turned eighteen, never would they take her one after another, always spreading out the actual act of sex throughout the day.

"Hello there, baby." Franklin grinned, pinched her nipple to the point of pain, and thrust his erect cock hard inside her. "I've missed you."

Victor climbed atop the desk and straddled her chest. He freed his own erection and rubbed it across her lips.

"If you don't mind, my dear?"

She opened her mouth and took him inside. Why did he ask her when they both knew she had no choice? This was her life. Yesterday, today, and tomorrow.

Ramirez leaned over the desk and a moment later his fleshy lips closed over her nipple and he began to suckle.

What if there was some way to have more? If there was an out from her life as a Rosabelle. *Don't be a fool. You know it's impossible.* Yes. Completely impossible. She bit her lip, squelching back any hope, and went back into her zone.

Two hours later Talia was in what she liked to refer to as the midday lull. Where the three men had been pleasured, and her only duty was to sit with them while they discussed business. Or perhaps serve them food or beverage if they so desired.

"Ramirez, what is the course of action we have lined up against the planet of Belton?" Victor asked while she sat on his lap. The hand that rested around her waist slid upward to idly fondle her breast. "Are the troops prepared to be deployed?"

Talia lowered her gaze, all too familiar with this topic. The Council was organizing an unplanned assault on a nearby planet that they had a supposed alliance with. The reasoning behind their plan was to gain resources that were dwindling upon their own planet.

"Indeed they are. The preliminary attack is scheduled for the fifteenth of next month. By all accounts Belton's government has no reason to suspect we have anything but good intentions."

Their discussion might have unsettled her, yet she'd heard enough in previous talks to not be bothered. The planet Belton was nothing but a wasted planet run by violent barbarians. She sighed and pressed a hand to her head. How long until she could leave?

"My dear, are you well?" Victor turned his attention to her fully.

Talia saw her opportunity and jumped on it. The men would be in discussion for at least another hour.

"I fear I am on the verge of a headache." She ran her tongue across her lips. "I would request a few minutes to return to my bedding unit and lie down?"

"Oh. Well, I suppose there's no harm in it." His tone was reluctant as was the arm that left her waist. "So long as you return by the two o'clock hour. And make sure you summon Dane to accompany you."

"Of course." She lowered her gaze and slipped off his lap, stepping into her dress again.

At the door she glanced back into the room and found Franklin's gaze on her. She could sense the lust and cruelty radiating off him from across the room.

For the most part she was treated well and never harmed. Yet Franklin possessed a cruel side that he on occasion let loose on her when they were alone. Fortunately, they were rarely allowed in that situation.

Suppressing a shudder, she turned and exited through the door. She made her way to Dane's chambers, reluctant to interrupt him during his time with Thomas, yet knew there was no choice. A Rosabelle was never allowed to be alone in her bedding unit.

She reached the corridor that led to his chamber; a glass window above looked down upon his room. Spotting Dane and Thomas in bed together, her heart sank. She sighed, hoping he'd forgive her.

Truly there was no privacy in this community. The entire building that housed the Council and its staff was made up of mostly windows.

Sex was nothing to be ashamed of within these walls, therefore was never hidden—with the one exception being with a Rosabelle. The Council's chambers and bedding units were equipped with privacy shields that would slide down to cover the windows. No man, save the three Council members, was allowed to watch her in any sexual act.

She clasped her hands in front of her and glanced down again at Dane and Thomas. It was time; she could avoid the interruption no longer.

Talia stepped toward the stairs to his chamber, but hesitated as the men exchanged a long kiss. Rarely, if at all, had she ever seen two people so completely besotted by each other.

She watched as Dane urged Thomas onto his hands and knees. He kissed the younger man's neck, wrapping his hand around Thomas's cock. The trembling in the other man was visible even from where she stood.

You should not watch this. A hot flush made its way through her body. It was not the first time she had seen two men make love, but she had never seen her assistant. She would almost consider Dane a friend, and to watch this intimate moment felt awkward. But the obvious love they shared held her entranced.

Dane now stroked his fingers between the younger man's buttocks. He picked up a small bottle that sat next to them on the bed and squirted lubricant over his fingers. Talia's breath caught while she watched him press two fingers into Thomas's asshole. He moved them in and out, while continuing to stroke the other man's cock.

"Oh . . ." She bit her lip, cutting off her husky groan.

Dane removed his fingers and lined his cock up with the small hole, then pressed steadily inside the other man. His thrusting started slow and then grew faster, while still he continued to stroke Thomas's cock.

Talia shifted her stance, trying to ease the pressure of the slick cream that gathered heavy in her cunt.

Minutes passed and she continued to watch them make love, transfixed by how both men's passion seemed equal and was not feigned, forced, or even lukewarm, as was the life she was accustomed to.

Dane thrust deep and stayed within the other man. She could swear she heard them both cry out. Then he pulled out of the younger man and kissed his shoulder. Thomas rolled over onto his back, reaching his arms up and drawing Dane down for a deep kiss.

Talia closed her eyes. How was she supposed to walk back into the Council's chambers in such a state of arousal? How would she explain it? They would never believe the same excuse twice in one day.

She stepped back, hitting something hard. Steel-like arms slipped around her waist, wringing a gasp from her and holding her immobile.

"Release me." She struggled, attempting to twist her head to see who held her.

"Interesting. A Rosabelle who not only likes to perform, but enjoys watching as well?"

Though she had never heard him speak and could not yet see him, she knew it was he. The man she'd seen in the corridor earlier. Blood raced through her veins and heat spread throughout her body.

"Do you have a death wish, sir?" She clenched her teeth and attempted to pry his fingers away from her waist. "No one outside the Council is allowed to touch me. To do so is grounds for immediate execution—"

He spun her around, his hands gripping just above her elbows. He backed her up against the wall in the empty corridor, his dark eyes boring into hers.

Her back slammed into the cold metal wall and her eyes widened when his head dipped just inches above hers.

"Well, if I'm going to die, princess, I think I should do so having gotten to know you a little better."

His breath feathered over her cheek, sending shivers of awareness down her spine. So new was the sensation that all protests died on her lips. She met his gaze, her own eyes wide.

No man had touched her outside of the Governing Council.

Now this man, a stranger with eyes that burned like the devil, touched her as if he had every right to.

"What is your name?" he asked, his lips nearly touching hers.

Her knees felt oddly weak and she gripped his solid forearms. "Talia."

His mouth closed over hers, confident and demanding, sending shock waves of pleasure through her body. His tongue pressed past her lips and delved into her mouth, rubbing slowly against hers. The onslaught of sensation and emotion was confusing, yet pleasing.

The Council rarely kissed her and when they did the gesture was hurried and sloppy. It was nothing like what this man was doing to her. Even knowing that if discovered he could be put to death and she would be severely punished, having this one chance at an unusual type of freedom was suddenly worth the risk.

He pressed her harder against the wall, sliding his hand beneath her dress and up her leg. The pleasure of his rough hands upon her was so intense her body shook. He moved one finger between her thighs and honed in on her clitoris.

The first touch sent her onto her tiptoes, pleasure spearing every inch of her body.

He lifted his mouth from hers and whispered, "Do you like me rubbing your hot little clit, princess?"

Yes. Oh gods yes. She gripped his arms to keep her knees from giving out.

"All slick and swollen." He dropped another hard kiss on her mouth, his finger rubbing harder against her clit. "Just waiting to be licked."

She moaned, and his tongue stroked deep into her mouth, taking control of hers as the finger on her cunt worked her harder and faster. The pleasure built, spiraling up higher than ever before. Lights flashed in her head and she cried out sharply into his mouth. Her legs gave out, but his arm around her waist kept her from falling.

The explosion he'd given her was ten times more powerful than the orgasm she'd had earlier just imagining his touch.

"Talia . . ." He lifted his mouth from hers. "You are so sexy when you come."